WAITING FOR THE SKY TO FALL

KENNETH MARTIN was born in Belfast in 1939. He grew up in Bangor, Co. Down, where he was adopted into a poor family. He began work on his first novel, *Aubade*, at the age of sixteen, and when it was accepted for publication by Chapman and Hall with an advance of £100, he moved to London. *Aubade*, published the day after Martin turned eighteen in 1957, was a modest success, selling well enough to run into a second printing in 1958 and was also published in America. Martin followed his debut with two more novels, *Waiting for the Sky to Fall* (1959) and *A Matter of Time* (1960), but the reviews of these novels were disappointing, and Martin turned from fiction to journalism. He moved to the United States in 1970 and earned degrees from Columbia University, the University of Minnesota, and San Francisco State University. In 1977 he became an American citizen. He returned to fiction writing in 1989, publishing *Billy's Brother* with Gay Men's Press, which also reissued *Aubade* as part of its *Gay Modern Classics* series. A fifth novel, *The Tin Islands*, followed in 1996. Kenneth Martin lives and works as a psychotherapist in San Francisco.

By Kenneth Martin

Aubade (1957)

Waiting for the Sky to Fall (1959)

A Matter of Time (1960)

Billy's Brother (1989)

The Tin Islands (1996)

WAITING FOR THE SKY TO FALL

KENNETH MARTIN

WITH A NEW INTRODUCTION BY THE AUTHOR

VALANCOURT BOOKS

Waiting for the Sky to Fall by Kenneth Martin
First published London: Chapman & Hall, 1959
First Valancourt Books edition 2013

Published by Valancourt Books, Kansas City, Missouri
Publisher & Editor: JAMES D. JENKINS
20th Century Series Editor: SIMON STERN, University of Toronto
http://www.valancourtbooks.com

Library of Congress Cataloging-in-Publication Data

Martin, Kenneth, 1939-
 Waiting for the sky to fall / by Kenneth Martin ; with a new
introduction by the author. – First Valancourt Books edition.
    pages cm
 ISBN 978-1-939140-18-0 *(acid free paper)*
 1. Youth – England – London – Fiction. 2. Chelsea (London, England) –
Fiction. I. Title.
 PR6063.A716W35 2013
 823'.914–dc23

                    2013004081

Cover photo © Shutterstock.com
Set in Dante MT 11/13.5

INTRODUCTION

AT AGE 16 I wrote a novel, *Aubade*, about a romance between a teenage boy and an older medical student. When it was published in 1957 in England and 1958 in the U.S. it became one of the first widely read gay novels. If that sounds explosive, it was – a youngster writing about illegal, generally despised, "perverted" behavior – but the explosion was muted in the interviews in the popular press, which focused on my age and mentioned the subject matter only to say that it was "shocking": so shocking that journalists didn't know how to discuss it.

A few months ago I answered a call in my office from an editor in Kansas City. "Is that Kenneth Martin the novelist?" I remembered my old identity in time to say yes. These days if I talk about my writing it's about my years as a journalist; the last time *Aubade* was published was in 1989 by a small press in England.

"I'd like to publish *Waiting for the Sky to Fall*," Jay Jenkins said.

"I'm surprised," I said.

Waiting for the Sky to Fall, my second novel, was going to make a lot of money and propel me into the company of full-time writers. I was summoned to the offices of A.D. Peters, the London agent who represented Evelyn Waugh and Graham Greene. Peters sat on a sofa at the far end of a dark, fire-lit room with Jack McDougall, my editor at Chapman & Hall, the firm that had been Dickens's first publishers. The two old men, their faces in shadow, told me they didn't like *Waiting for the Sky to Fall*.

I'd just turned nineteen and was used to being treated like an extraordinary prodigy. Naively, I defended my book: it was so much longer and had more characters than *Aubade*. "Longer," Peters said, "but not deeper." "You write like an angel," McDougall said. "It's just a question of time and experience." That was as far as they got telling me why *Waiting* wasn't a good book, and that was the way we talked about books in those days. In warning me that it would be a long time before I could make my living as a full-time writer, Peters cited Waugh and Greene, whose later, more commercially successful books he said weren't as "good" as their earlier books, though he didn't say how. In those days the editors and writers I met didn't seem to have a language to critically analyze literature beyond a few stock phrases.

At least McDougall was going to publish *Waiting*. "He's only doing it because it's you," Peters said. But my relationship with McDougall frittered away. That first meeting with Peters was my last. As we ended he suggested that I change the title of *Waiting* to *Someone to Love Me*. "That sounds like a romance novel," I protested. They laughed at me.

The reviews were mixed. Someone called *Waiting* "an astonishing disappointment" (interesting that I remember favorable reviews word for word but not even the source of the worst review), but the *Daily Telegraph* reviewer judged it to be "more genuine" than Saul Bellow's *Henderson the Rain King* and "tremendously capable and intimately revealing of a generation and a class." The *Yorkshire Post* picked it as One of the Ten Novels of the Year. The *Catholic Herald* called me "an exceptionally gifted writer, [who] has the rare gift of arousing compassion," which didn't stop *Waiting* being banned in Ireland. A year after *Waiting* was published, McDougall wrote me that he'd read it again one night drinking wine at his home in Gloucestershire and liked it very much. But by then I'd internalized the view that *Waiting* was a bad book. Freddie Young, the literary editor of *Punch*, told me the book was word-spinning, which didn't stop him giving it a decent review. I learned that people don't necessarily write what they believe, or that you can fool some of the people some of the time, or that just about anything can be viewed as a matter of opinion. It was easy to sink into pessimism and revert to blunt Northern Irish contempt for pretension. "Paper refuses nothing," we used to say.

Into my late twenties I regularly dreamt intense dreams about writing a successful second novel, then woke paralyzed, my body a self-created straitjacket. I'd lie struggling between panic and trying to remember if that successful second novel was real.

I forced myself to read *Waiting* after 50 years as a necessary step to writing this introduction. For a long time I circled it as if it might bite me. When I opened it at random I read the following sentence: "He took the cigarette from her lips and pulled at it, leaning his head against the wall." I groaned. Filler, an attempt to give significance to something that has none. A book full of such sentences is akin to Agatha Christie pounding out the requisite number of words in the service of a devious plot and cunning dénouement. Except that I didn't remember *Waiting* being either devious or cunning.

When I was 18 I typed x number of sentences at night in my room in Goldhurst Terrace after my miserable bread-and-margarine job that barely paid the rent. I ate one good meal a week, on payday. A reviewer rightly guessed that perhaps I was hungry when I wrote the book: the characters in *Waiting* eat frequently and well. They're middle- or upper-class postgraduates who work part time, get allowances from home, live in Chelsea or Kensington, and consume an inexhaustible supply of whisky. They're poseurs, trading sub-Wildean epigrams and paradoxes that seem to me to contain less than meets the eye: "He felt thoughtful, then discovered that he had nothing to think about."

Waiting is a fantasy about the life I wanted to be living. I based the characters on the friends of Julian Jebb, an agent not long down from Cambridge and working in his first job when he discovered me. Julian lived in a basement flat in Edwardes Square in Kensington, to me the epitome of Bohemian glamour, and introduced me to friends whom I met once or twice and had no intimate contact with because they were working on being grown-up and I was really just a child. Some were aspiring artists, actors and writers, and I expect some envied me for being published and getting so much publicity because of my age. I took revenge on a couple of them when I became a journalist, even if they'd been kind to me – maybe especially if they'd been kind to me – because they'd seen me vulnerable, blushing and embarrassed. Julian told me he had reservations about *Waiting* because the characters were similar to his circle of friends but he viewed them differently. I know that one of them became a historian of note, one worked in advertising and wrote a couple of books, several became alcoholics. Julian, the friendliest, cheeriest of men, and a Roman Catholic, killed himself.

The disappointment my few young friends in London expressed about *Waiting* was with my character, the person I'd become. "I expect Debbie Reynolds will star in the picture," someone said cattily. I remember discussing *The End of the Affair* with the young composer Alan Ridout. I wondered why he thought it was so much better than *Waiting*: the Greene book didn't seem much deeper to me. He stumbled trying to explain that its characters were more truly engaged with the deepest human concerns. The adolescent hero of my first novel had been similarly engaged with the world, embarked on a journey in search of life and truth; the characters in *Waiting* betray their ignorance of the world by assuming it has nothing to teach them. I'd imposed upon them my own post-adolescent feelings of emptiness, disappointment, confusion, fear about going nowhere.

Yet the book struck a chord with some in the generation I pretended to be depicting. A Cambridge don told me it created a stir amongst his undergraduates. I was surprised they'd even read it, because I assumed Cambridge students had a level of education and maturity beyond me at that time. (I didn't take a college course until I moved to New York in 1970, but armed with one A-level I'd abandoned fiction and gone on to write journalism for the newspapers most Cambridge graduates aspired to write for.) Some reviewers assigned to *Waiting* an authentic generational significance. The Italian edition – their new title translated as *It Makes No Difference* – was promoted as "London after the angry young men." "Anyone who feels as if there were a curtain between him and the younger generation should read this novel," the *New Statesman* said. I thought older reviewers probably didn't know what they were talking about. Another possibility is that I didn't know what I was writing. Perhaps (probably?) the book had meanings of which I was unaware. But were those meanings valid? And to whom? I was incapable of formulating such questions as a teenager. The best I could have hoped for was that *Waiting* might somehow be alive with collective meaning.

The communist *Daily Worker* called *Waiting* "an astonishing indictment of capitalist society," which was news to me. Inspired by Simone de Beauvoir's *The Mandarins*, I'd thought of having my hero Perkin publish and edit a small political paper, but dismissed the idea because I couldn't come up with topics for him to write about. I lacked the supportive inner structure that comes from a background where ideas – and goals, with strategies to achieve them – are part of the air we breathe. I came from Northern Ireland, that land where much was off limits, including inwardness and history, at least among the Protestants I grew up with. Over the years I started educating myself with the help of London's quality Sunday newspapers, Everyman's Library and the Penguin Classics, and the BBC. When I finally went to Columbia University in my thirties, I recognized that I knew very little about anything, but that only increased my engagement with the world. I'm still working on it.

KENNETH MARTIN
San Francisco

February 19, 2013

WAITING FOR THE SKY TO FALL

. . . waiting at evening on the hill-tops for the sky to fall, that I might catch something, though I never caught much, and that, manna-wise, would dissolve again in the sun.

HENRY DAVID THOREAU, *Walden*

CHAPTER I

Perkin worked in a bookshop in the Charing Cross Road; it was small, quiet and of necessity dark. He typed invoices, statements, and took charge of a small easily-run sideline: the shop sold "art photographs" of naked men and women. Perkin was deliciously shocked when the proprietor, a cheerful little German-Jew, first told him about this aspect of the business. "I would not do this, you understand, if it were not absolutely necessary, in order to pay for the overheads on the rest of my business." He would have preferred to sell the works of Gautier and Baudelaire, but alas! the market was small, although he must admit – grinning from ear to ear – that a translation of *Mademoiselle de Maupin* could do very nicely, thank you, with the right sort of jacket.

The job suited him perfectly. Nine to one, Monday to Friday, and an opportunity to borrow as many books as he wished, although he soon tired of handling the photographs. At first he had been surprised to see how many poses the human body could take. He had known only three: the balanced square – sitting down; the horizontal – bathing or lying in a bed; and the perpendicular – walking or standing at the window of his flat, watching the square below. The young men and women in the photographs were often amazingly contorted, but they looked not at all exciting. Their bodies were most aseptically waxed.

The shop sold *Room at the Top* and *Peyton Place* at half-price if you exchanged them within a fortnight. *Sixteen – what it's really like – told by A Boy* rubbed shoulders with *Anglo-Saxon Attitudes* and *Giovanni's Room*, and Perkin took the job because he met all sorts of odd people who seemed amusing when he told his friends about them afterwards.

The best part of the day was mid-afternoon, when he sprawled on the couch, reading a book and tipping ash on the floor. He surrounded himself with records, magazines and his brother Simon's paintings. He went to the window and watched the gardens in the square. Coloured smoke rose from the charred and sodden leaves, and stark trees and bleak sky were shot with wonder at sunset. He watched in amazement, like an animal that cannot conceive glory.

At night he grew restless and had to get away from the flat; if he had made no arrangements he walked beside the river and in the black water saw reflections of things he had never known. He wandered in the quieter streets of Chelsea, gazing into small restaurants and wondering if that veiled window was another little club or bar he did not know. He watched the faces of the people who passed him, each line on their skin increasing his bewilderment and making him want to stop and stare until he could be sure about them: their lives, their work, each little passion that made them ridiculous, each little ambition that made them petty. He would shrug and repeat quietly to himself for the thousandth time that these things were not serious, they were light and comic. He leaned over the wall and looked down into the river. Cigarette smoke tunnelled into the icy air and the sky swung overhead.

During the day he was possessed by a great weariness, so that he found it almost intolerable to make a meal or wait in a restaurant until it was brought to him. What would one do, sitting alone at a table for fifteen minutes, staring at nothing? He ate cheese and fruit instead. When he watched the trees and behind them the windows of flats with bright curtains and whitewashed ledges, he felt that he was looking at these things for the last time. He thought that one day soon he would be extinguished and belong to a past, a short period of time that would go unremembered. Nothing seemed of consequence. He was incapable of creative work, even if he had wanted to work. He could dispense with people and knew too many. To his friends he remained a shadowy figure, lying almost sleeping on a couch or propped against a wall if there were too many people at the party. It required an effort to observe the convention of talking, and he felt that anything he said justified itself. They said "This book is bad". He answered "It's good" and believed himself to be too clever and too tired to continue. Sometimes he came upon his image in a shop window: it was two-dimensional, without depth of any kind except that it belonged to some kind of darkness and should have been enclosed by mist. His untidy hair and pale smooth skin made him look artistic and he wondered why that adjective should condemn anyone. Perhaps it didn't. He was not certain. He remembered reading in a book that someone was ashamed because she was too good-looking and tried to hide it by refraining from using a cigarette-holder, which drew attention to her face. Perhaps he should stop wearing red socks.

And everything was very lovely. His absence of emotion with regard to people was replaced by a sense of wonder which he realised in the time of year, the bright colours of clothes people wore, the trees in the gardens, the cafés where they had taken in the little tables to shelter them from the rain, the concerts and the books in dusty shops or on the stalls at Farringdon. These things which held the echoes of his life had a liquid meaning and interpreted the fixed unsubtle movements of the days.

This day at the beginning of November was wonderful. Last Sunday he had seen with a shock of sadness that the trees were suddenly bare, and the leaves were a drifting lake around their trunks. He counted the smoking fires on the grass still white with frost and thought: This will go on for ever without changing. If I could do that, if my brother and I and our friends could live without changing except for a certain birth and a certain death each year, we might be happy, and all would be accustomed, ceremonious. For the race this is true, but for each of us, who are small, it is the reason for unhappiness, for we cannot change and repeat ourselves importantly.

The sky today was bright. The air was exultant, shivering with frost, and pieces of leaves swept by the wind from the ground where they had fallen. Mist had taken the place of rain and hung from the trees and in doorways. The streets were calm in expectancy and heartbreak, for it had been like this and would be so for days of unfulfilled waiting and watching.

Perkin went by tube to Sloane Square, and walked the rest of the way home. In people's faces he looked to see the doomed buoyancy which the weather had effected in him and he saw their crystalline skin, wet eyelids and lashes. They conspired to keep these heartbreaking days.

Simon and Perkin had rented a flat above a garage in the King's Road, and Simon paid to have a hole knocked in the roof. Thus they called it their studio, and self-consciously agreed that it was very romantic and slightly silly. It was almost cheap, very large, and the smell of oil from the garage was suitable though not refined enough. They whitewashed the walls, bought an expensive fitted red carpet for the living-room, then covered it with sacking, for that was where Simon painted. He worked at a picture-framer's, and was paid a fixed sum each week, although he sometimes had to work all day for four or five days a week, and sometimes only two or three afternoons a week. The room smelt of gin and various other things. It was the sweet smell which clings to clothes and skin and hair, and it pervaded the rooms of all their friends. Sometimes Perkin thought it was like greasepaint: it belonged in a way of life, a habit that would be hard to break.

He climbed the stairs slowly, wondering if there would be letters or a message. Jonathan was sitting on the floor, his eyes upturned like a very fallen angel's, waiting for nobody. His lashes fell and he rubbed his eyes.

He smiled. "Hello, Perkin."

"Hello." He threw his coat on the couch and went to open a tin of orange juice. The room was warm and filled with smoke. "Were you at a party last night?"

Jonathan blinked nervously. "Well, yes. But it was all rather strange." His voice was oddly emphatic. He seemed to be trying to squeeze the words until they sounded younger and more appealing. "I knew nobody, not even the host, so I sat on the floor. Halfway through someone asked me to recite a poem so I did and left soon afterwards. I wrote a poem about it, actually."

"Writing a poem about reciting a poem," Perkin said automatically. Say anything rather than be silent.

"There was a girl I wanted to talk to, but she was eating from somebody's hand. She ignored me. I don't even know her name."

"I'm sorry." He knew this experience.

Jonathan smiled wearily and rubbed his eyes again. "It doesn't matter. Not a bit. Can I have some coffee?"

"If you make it. With tinned milk?"

He stared towards the kitchen, calculating the distance and got up, still wondering if it was worthwhile. His lethargy was quite genuine, but most people thought him affected. He was smoothly handsome, but his mouth was small and fitful. His eyes were always wet and he seemed to know all about the loss of innocence without having experienced it. He was tall enough and fat enough but only laughed aloud when he wanted to attract someone's attention. His disposition and physique were faulty in such a curious way that Perkin sometimes wondered why no-one loved him deeply. He was accepted because he could be interpreted in so many ways, but he was not popular.

He returned, handed a cup of coffee to Perkin and stared carefully but without interest into his own cup.

"Shall we go somewhere for the weekend?"

"I hadn't thought about it. Where do you want to go?"

He shrugged. "Someplace warm perhaps."

"In England!"

"Oh well." He stirred for a moment in the fat of his lethargy and solitude, but slid back into the warmth and veiled his eyes. "I didn't really want to go away."

Perkin wondered what he had been thinking. It was always impossible to tell. He watched him, then got up and went over to the window. The frosted air had begun to darken, so early, and already lights were shining.

"Isn't it strange, though," Perkin said.

"Stranger and stranger," Jonathan said with delight.

When Simon came home that evening, his younger brother was immediately jealous of his smile, his freshness and his determination. His eyes were always bright, and although often bloodshot always looked appealingly blue. Jonathan and Perkin liked people whose eyes, they imagined, contracted in the daytime. Simon was, and would always be, the boy in the advertisements who despite his faults buys the girl the box of chocolates in the end.

"It's going to be a party," Perkin said. "Anne's coming later."

"Anne? The quiet one who works in the shop with you?"

Perkin nodded. "She's incorruptible, Simon, and terribly sweet."

His brother put on a sweater and sat beside him on the couch. They knew each other so well, and had such a bad opinion of each other and themselves, that they knew they could never hurt each other.

"Sweet, working in a shop like that?"

"Yes. I know it's unbelievable, but she still doesn't know what it's all about."

"No-one could be as innocent as that. By this time she must have served half the perverts in London."

Perkin laughed. "Wait and see. And for heaven's sake be careful what you say."

"I'm going to disillusion her tonight," Simon said firmly. "Anne sounds too good to be true."

His brother made a face. "You know, I'd like to believe that one day your bad wicked life will recoil on you, and you'll spend the rest of your days chasing a nymphomaniac."

The idea appealed to Simon, and he smiled. "Perhaps I am too efficient."

"I'd like to write a poem about you," Jonathan said.

There was a moment's silence while minds were adjusted. His remarks were often so tangential that the mood which had existed was broken.

"But it will be no use until the tables are turned. No one wants to read a poem about the sex life of a rabbit, or rather it would be awfully hard to write."

Simon frowned.

They had been sitting in the dark, the glow of the electric fire making grotesque shadows on their faces. Lights of cars stopping at the garage below played briefly on the walls and ceiling of the room. Jonathan seemed to have gone to sleep, and Perkin felt discontented. It was like one of those evenings when we are meeting someone for the first time, or plans for a party have fallen through and we have four hours to spend in awkward company, not having enough to drink and talking spasmodically. We know that at the end of the evening we must go to bed and we feel cheated. We have wasted so much time. Perkin hated to waste his time dully, although he would have wasted his life for excitement.

Simon had been treating Anne with careful consideration, but had gently made fun of her shyness and lack of sophistication. He got up suddenly and switched on the lights, then sat on the arm of her chair and put his arm on the back.

"Be very careful, Anne," Perkin warned her.

She laughed, looking up at Simon.

"How pretty you are," he said. "How did you meet a fool like my brother?"

She blushed. "Didn't Perkin tell you that we work in the same shop?" Her voice was almost hard, controlled by a great effort to hide her uneasiness. She was wearing a very plain green wool dress, and her pale brown hair was pulled back and coiled in a bun. But she could not make her rather round face look severe. She had brown eyes, a pert little nose and freckles. Perkin wondered why his brother was pretending to be interested in her.

"You work in that pornographic bookshop with Perkin?" Simon asked, overdoing the incredulity.

Her eyes rounded. "What do you mean?"

Simon stared at her. "But such innocence! Don't you read books?"

"Of course I do," Anne said indignantly. "I've read most of the books we sell in the shop. Zola, Joyce, Sartre. What do you mean, pornographic?"

"My brother has a dirty mind," Perkin said quickly. Simon leaned down and kissed the back of her neck. "I think you've made a conquest, Anne darling. If you ever grow tired of me you'll know whom to turn to."

She blushed excruciatingly, too confused to reply.

She loves him already, Perkin thought.

"Anne," he said, "if I were you I'd run while there's still time. I'm almost sorry I asked you to come tonight. Simon's the sort of person who follows little girls down dark lanes."

She raised her eyebrows, wondering if she should laugh.

"You see, he's jealous," Simon said.

She looked at him, her face glowing. He drew back and glanced at Perkin triumphantly.

"My brother is a rabbit," Perkin said.

"He likes to talk that way," Simon said. "He's terribly frustrated."

"Poor Perkin," Anne said inadequately.

"But I know someone for you, Perkin. She saw you with me at an art gallery one day. Her name is Angela, but just call Angel and she'll come running."

Anne laughed loyally.

"Personally I found her rather dull. So terribly, seriously eager." Absent-mindedly, Simon reached down and took Anne's hand.

Jonathan awoke. He drew back his lips as if to bite into the glass he was holding, and looked at Anne.

"Aren't you shocked, Anne?"

"No, of course not," she stammered. "One hears this kind of thing so often these days."

Jonathan tittered, and Simon frowned.

"Shall I find a girl for you as well, Jonathan?"

He blinked, closed his eyes, and did not bother to reply.

"I've often wondered where you spend your nights. Tell us."

"Parties, plays," Jonathan said sleepily. "Sinful little cellars, oh so sinful. Perkin comes too. We must take Anne one evening. To hell and back."

"I'd love to go," she said, fascinated.

"But they're really so dull," Perkin said. "Those places are only good for drunk tired people who can't bear to go to bed alone. They become a habit, you grow used to the empty mood and the grey light, the smoke, the atmosphere is so ridiculously hopeless. Nobody is that hopeless."

The room was growing colder, and Simon switched on another fire.

"I know what you mean." He glanced at Anne, and added hastily, "Of course I don't go to those places very often. But how can you be attracted to emptiness if you don't feel empty to begin with?"

"Oh well." Perkin shrugged. "We were so ambitious when we were children in Ireland. I don't know. That's all over."

Simon smiled. "Children know nothing about work or time."

"When will you be old enough to paint a masterpiece, Simon?"

"I won't live in obscurity all my life. This exhibition is the first step."

"It's like those magazines that took my stories. They'll take anything as long as you're young if they don't have to pay for it, the good and the bad. Some good people start that way I suppose, but how many of the people at your exhibition will ever be heard of again?"

"It's only a beginning for me." It occurred to him that he did not want his brother to be a waster. "You haven't written for so long."

"Writing needs a creative mood, an ability to accept the fact that in a year's time you may still be working on the same book. You may be able to work. I can't. Maybe when I'm older."

Some of his short work had been rather successful about a year ago, and if he had written a dozen more stories they might have been published in book form. But he had pretended to be too lazy to work. The truth was that he desperately wanted to write the stories, but had not been able to get as far as plotting them. He would have a wonderful idea, especially when he was lying in bed. A mood of nostalgia seized him and he wanted to convey it on paper. The truth in the world could, he would think, be told in a little story about an old man and a little boy on a hot summer's day. He would rush to the typewriter, and twenty minutes later push it aside in disgust. He had conveyed the idea beautifully in six lines, and had nothing to fill the remaining pages. He was capable of writing one brilliant short story a year. In the end he used the title of his truth-about-life story for a mystery story that was never published. He called it, *Old Man in a Dry Month*.

Perhaps he is a waster. Simon shrugged. Surely work was something which you had to do, then forgot until next time. You remember the pleasure of achievement.

Anne withdrew her hand, stood up, then sat down again.

"I must go," she said.

"I'll take you home," Simon said quickly.

"That's terribly kind of you."

She got up again, glanced at Jonathan, then looked twinklingly at Perkin.

Good God! She believed Simon. She thinks I'm in love with her or something.

He said, "Don't offer to make my brother any cocoa."

She smiled and glanced over her shoulder daringly as she turned away. Simon helped her with her coat, and gently brushed the back of her neck. She shivered.

Perkin opened the window and leaned into the night. The air was delicious. It would smell of whatever he would have it smell. He chose a summer beach and immediately had a warm sense of suntan lotion. He laughed delightedly at his witty conclusion to the game.

"Why are you laughing?" Jonathan had been calculating the extent of his boredom.

Perkin closed the window and went to pour the last of the gin into two glasses. He could not even guess the reason for his sudden gaiety; he seemed to be glowing with goodwill, hope.

"I was laughing at myself," he said, and buried his nose in the glass, sobbing with laughter. "Us. How foolish we are."

"I've heard you say that more than once before," Jonathan reminded him grimly.

Anne sat nervously in the corner of the taxi, while Simon slumped in the opposite corner, delaying the climax that the girl was awaiting with horror and excitement. She had been kissed by four men, and one of them was her now-dead father. The other kisses had been wet, clumsy and most embarrassing, the duty paid for a dull evening. Glancing sideways she could see the lights of passing cars playing on Simon's skin, and she wished she had his photograph to pin above her head. But he was too adorable and so sophisticated. To kiss him would be as unthinkable and impossible as to kiss her favourite author, Colin Wilson, whose books she had never read.

She had a little basement flat, or room and kitchen, in West

Kensington. When the taxi stopped, Simon said, "I won't compromise you by drinking your cocoa, luv." He paused for just the
right length of time. "I'll see you sometime." He moved to tell the
driver to return.

Anne gasped with disappointment. He had obviously decided
that she was unattractive and too inexperienced. She floundered,
stammered and was lost.

"I'd love to make some cocoa for you," she said tightly.

"How foolish of you."

She blushed. As she led the way down the narrow wooden steps
to her door she missed one and almost sat down. He pretended not
to notice, and screwed up his stomach trying to stop laughing.

She turned on all the lights in the room and took his coat. He
looked terribly big as he sat down. She had hung the coat in the
cupboard before she realised what she was doing. She took it out
and threw it beside his chair as if it were burning her, then stood
uncertain of what to do next. For the first time Simon regarded her
as a girl and not an object for strategics, and felt as much interested
as if he were looking at a sister. But she really would be pretty if
she learned to take more care of her appearance.

"I'll get the cocoa."

Simon felt an odd pang. She had made the room look like a
home. He was used to the flats of transients who tried to hide angu-
larities by depositing letters, books and Italian ashtrays at carefully
irregular intervals around the room. Anne's room was inexpen-
sively and sparsely furnished, but there were no large lonely spaces
between the pieces of furniture. She spoiled the effect by bringing
the cocoa in large red cups, and plates laden with cake, sandwiches
and potato crisps.

He could not prevent himself from smiling.

"You shouldn't have troubled."

Anne smiled more confidently. "Boys living by themselves in
flats never eat enough." She turned away from his amused stare
and her eyes fastened on the bed, rearing hideously in a corner.

"I'm really not hungry, Anne. You must eat a lot to make up for
me."

She nibbled a crisp and it was as formidable as a loaf of bread.

Simon held out a cigarette packet.

She shook her head, staring at the floor. "I don't smoke."

"Ah, you must begin." He leaned back against the couch. "Relax. You needn't be frightened of me. I'm terribly gentle and not at all wicked."

She suddenly wanted to cry.

"I won't do anything to hurt you, Anne."

"Why did Perkin say those awful things about you?" she asked like a little girl.

"He's very disillusioned, you know. He treats all girls casually. I don't believe he's ever loved anyone but himself, and an imaginary past. Nothing is ever easy for him." His words made him feel tender and he held out a hand in sympathy: Anne was so young. He felt that he really ought to teach her to enjoy life as a civilised being.

"Come and sit beside me." His voice was as warm as her memory of her father's voice. How could Perkin say such cruel things about his brother. She sat down beside him and looked into his face adoringly. She wanted to touch his cheek, but he raised his head and pointed to the street and the bit of sky above.

"Look at that single star. Have you ever seen anything so lovely?"

She discovered depths of feeling inside herself that she had not realised existed, and her face looked mature and smooth as he watched from the corner of his eye.

"It reminds me of when I was a little girl. I wish I could go back. Everything is so confused and embarrassing now."

"It needn't be, if you have someone to care for you." He put his arm around her shoulder and after a moment's hesitation she nestled awkwardly against his chest. She discovered that the only place for her free arm was on his waist. For the first time since she had been living alone she felt warm and protected. How could she have been frightened?

Unfortunately Simon's clinical habits reasserted themselves. When he put his arm behind her legs she moved closer, and forgetting that he was dealing with inexperience he automatically moved a step further. Everything was pleasant for a moment, then the sight of her slip suddenly terrified her. She jumped away and screamed, "Leave me alone! Go away, please." She rushed to the kitchen door and hid behind it.

Simon was so astonished that he reached for his coat, and only his surprise saved Anne from looking ridiculous. He went over to her.

"I don't understand. What happened?"

"Go away, please. I never want to see you again."

He stared at her, certain that she would be relieved if he took her in his arms again. Then he shrugged, blew her a kiss and turned on his heel. It was the first time in years that he had been refused by a girl in her flat. He tripped as he was climbing the stairs outside, and almost fell on his face. The cold air reminded him that he was no longer a schoolboy, and recalling her dialogue he wondered how she could have been so corny. Then he felt depressed.

Anne rushed to the bed and lay down on it, expecting to burst into tears. Five minutes later she was still lying there, waiting for something to happen. She discovered that she had chewed a hole in the corner of the sheet, and sat up, rubbing her lips. She realised that people passing in the street could see her, and she drew the curtains savagely. She cursed for the first time in her life. She looked round the room, wondering what to do.

Perkin and Jonathan were sitting on the floor, playing poker. They had been using cigarettes for chips, but now there were only three left. The room smelled like a billiard saloon.

"I have to work in the morning," Perkin said unnecessarily. It was one o'clock, but he had felt tired for so long that he was not sure if he wanted to go to bed. One might exist for ever in a coma, and nothing would be essential; it was a pleasing thought. And he could go to bed next afternoon. If he had nothing to do he often went to bed after lunch and fell asleep immediately. When he felt lonely he embraced the pillow.

They dealt six empty hands, and were too uninterested to bluff. They pushed the cards under a chair and played slow football with an empty bottle, over-emphasising each movement as the bottle rolled backwards and forwards between them. Simon came and they showed no surprise at his early return. He had intended to tell a funny story about Anne, but no one was interested and he decided that it wasn't really funny. He opened a window to let out the smoke.

"Do you want to sleep here, Jonnie?" Perkin asked.

"No. I want to do something. We've done nothing all evening and walking home will be enough."

"I'll call you tomorrow."

He went to his room and lay down on the bed, thoughtless, lifeless, and did not move when Simon came into the room and sat on the end of the bed.

"From tomorrow I'm going to work harder." When desire had been sated or unreciprocated he always turned to his work.

Perkin opened his eyes and looked at him. His brother's blue eyes, the oval shape of his face, the smoothness of the bone underneath the skin, and the clothes he wore made him look always young; but the light behind his head showed his hair to be rough and dry, and his skin was grey and the pores thick.

"I feel old," Simon said slowly. "I feel as if I had lived for a hundred years and done nothing really useful."

"Go to bed," Perkin groaned.

Jonathan's room at Holborn was shabby and small, in a tall black house of bedsitting-rooms mostly occupied by bank clerks and young men who worked in bookshops. He could have afforded to pay the rent of a small flat for six months, but he was trying to make the money he had saved while in the army last as long as possible. He ate in sandwich bars, never bought books and shopped at the market in Rupert Street. He had not decided what he would do when he had to get a job. Journalism perhaps. He enjoyed writing poetry, but could not sell it or even get it published.

When he got home he made some coffee from a tin and sat down in the uncushioned leather armchair. He stared at the ceiling and wondered what would happen to him. Where would he be a year from now? He was not yet accustomed to Perkin's uncaring acceptance of the knowledge that each year he would look back and look forward and everything would be the same.

Something must happen. The job was unimportant. He was

prepared to work at anything. But he had been alone for so long. It was easy for Perkin. He talked about not loving, never caring. Jonathan had never made love, he recoiled from the touch of someone's skin. Each week he loved someone new, thought about her at night, and wondered what it would be like to have her warmth, feel the stretch of her body beside him. Sometimes one of these girls was attracted to him, and he arranged for her to come to his room. He knew that she expected him to make love to her. He made preparations, bought cigarettes, Scotch. At last he had found the human being who would make him come to life. When she came, when he saw her face, his body seemed to turn into a lump of stone, undesiring and unresponsive. He talked nervously, frightened that she would move towards him, expecting to be embraced. And if she did, he kissed her and made the movements which he had hoped would come naturally. In the end she left, puzzled. He felt sick, then hours later he would curse himself and want her, want someone until his skin crawled with hunger. The search began again: on the tube, at a theatre or a party, but he did not change, except that he had learned to simulate desire to a certain point, and the girl's real or assumed reluctance to go further made it easier to get rid of her.

At last he learned not to show very much interest in anyone. Next time he would be certain, he would pretend to be uninterested until he was sure that it would be successful. Meanwhile he walked the streets like a stranger, some indefinite and frightened being from another world.

The year when he was eighteen.

He had already forgotten the years between, the time in the army might never have been; but he had thought about that year so much, analysed it so many times that he felt he could tell each hour of it with truth.

He worked hard during his last year at school. He read a great deal and lived a happy life with his parents. In that environment sex was regarded as something which occurred when he was thirty, and had a secure job and his parents were growing old and he began to think of marrying. He lived in Cambridge, in an old house in a crooked street in the centre of the town. Everything was accustomed, youth and age, large fires and drawn curtains in winter, church on Sunday. His parents were so happy and ordinary and good. His father was a retired army officer who smoked a pipe and cigars at Christmas. His mother had the simplicity of a child and was soft and gentle and loving. She cared deeply about his clothes, his health, his school. His father taught him to shoot, row and drive the car. Their sense of duty to each other was born of understanding, and their responsibilities were not habit-formed but born of regard. Jonathan was in a tennis club, a cricket club and that year his father began to take him to meet friends in a bar on Friday nights. One day, while his father was looking at a gun it exploded in his face. It was as meaninglessly easy as that.

His mother was watching, and she ran to hold the flesh to her body. Something snapped in her mind, and she was unable to register shock, but stared uneasily at the hands which held her husband's head, as if her eyes could not focus properly. Jonathan ran to a neighbour for help, and when he returned hid in a corner. He hated the mess on the floor. It was too horrible to be inflicted on him. His mother went mad, and spent the days preoccupied with her lack of understanding.

In July the aunt who had come to live with them left, and Jonathan was alone with his mother. She tried to cook meals, but she could not grasp the connection between a lighted match and an unlighted gas jet. Food and plates slipped from her hands, and she hardly heard them breaking on the floor. The summer grew hotter and she sat sweating, unaware that she should feel uncomfortable. Jonathan sat opposite her, watching until he was hypnotised by her madness. The sun shone into the house, and the traffic in the street, the sound of footsteps skittering on the ground, filled the house with horror, and it became a trap for all smells of sickness and sounds of nervousness. One day she went into the kitchen to make a cold lunch. Twenty minutes later Jonathan went to find her. She was standing beside the refrigerator, holding an unopened tin. He shook her, and screamed with terror. When he opened his eyes she was smiling, almost laughing. Through the window behind her he saw the blue sky and the yellow sun. The house had turned yellow, the walls fidgeted in the heat. She died three months later in an asylum. Jonathan was called-up. His moodiness was accepted as homesickness, and the army was the only place in the world where men would have taken him as a friend and treated him with kindness.

He undressed, got into bed, and curled into a ball, hugging his knees. Why couldn't he sleep for ever?

CHAPTER II

THE exhibition of young artists' work was being held at the Haymarket Galleries. Simon had three paintings on show: two still-lifes and a self-portrait. They were hung together, well to the fore. As soon as they came into the large room where most of the work was being displayed, Simon left his brother to see if anyone was looking at his paintings. Perkin stared at the people around him, many of whom seemed to be typists on their lunch break. He smiled at the thought and attracted the roving eye of a tall fair girl, who was looking lost in front of a large and bad abstract. She raised her eyebrows, examined him carefully but casually from head to foot, then returned the smile. Perkin opened his mouth and widened his eyes in a gasp of gawky adoration. She raised her eyebrows still further and turned her back.

"Perkin!"

"George!"

"Well, how nice to see you again, luv. I thought I'd find you here."

"Really, George," Perkin said feelingly. "Did you have to wear that pullover?" It was violet coloured with a scarlet neck.

"Violent violet." He giggled. "I do have to dress the part, you know."

"It's absolutely beautiful, but I'm afraid to be seen talking to you."

Perkin liked this elegant young man very much indeed. They met at a party when George told a joke so blue that no-one laughed. Perkin had been listening at the edge of the group and had not for a moment grasped the point. He opened his mouth to cool the whisky he had just sipped, suddenly realised the implication, and whisky spluttered over the necks of half a dozen guests. In those days Perkin used to blush exceedingly. George was much attracted by such innocence, and immediately enlisted him as a friend who would be either shocked or amused by his most banal accounts of everyday happenings in the underworld of London. Perkin loved to hear all about the famous people who were queer, and which suspects were not.

"How are things with you?"

George tried to look evil. "Terribly boring, luv. Nothing new under the sun. But I do think your brother's paintings are pretty."

"But not good?"

"Of course not. But he thinks he's good?"

Perkin nodded. "He may get better. I do hope so."

"I'm sure he'll be a great success and go on thinking he's good. By the time he has a chance to learn the truth he'll be dead." George looked forward to death as some people look forward to Christmas: having made private hell a habit he decided to enjoy it with delicious malice, but his life was poisoned by boredom. He would have liked nothing better than to slip gently away. He awaited his old age, when he could sleep and be alone most of the time.

"Aren't these people terribly stupid?" Perkin said.

"Terribly. A dozen of them know something about painting, but it isn't the artists. Someday I'll show them."

"It would have to be in another world. No-one would dare to display your paintings."

"Then I'll buy a gallery in Bloomsbury."

Their eyes roamed over the faces of people looking at paintings and each other. Fish, thought George. Not one person in the room to whom I could talk without wanting to run away or make an obscene gesture.

Perkin thought: All the nice ones are funny-looking. It would be so easy to think of loving them, but in the end I'd die of boredom. How conceited I am!

Jonathan came up to them.

"Hello. I wasn't going to come but the only alternatives were a picture or another gallery."

George stared at him, trying to calculate the nature and extent of his sex-life, but was confounded.

"Jonathan Moore, this is George Tench."

Jonathan nervously held out his hand, as if touching a not quite dead crab. George shook the thumb vigorously.

"Charmed, I'm sure."

Jonathan gaped.

"Do behave," Perkin sighed. "Look, talk to each other. Simon's beckoning me."

George smiled. Jonathan smiled, terrified.

"Are you an artist?" he asked, gazing with fascination at the pullover.

"In a small way. You might say so. Are you?"

"No." He remembered with an effort that he was Jonathan, frustrated and too preoccupied with his own problems ever to feel embarrassed. He must stand back and watch himself behaving politely but aloofly to this young man.

"Do you like any of these paintings?" asked George.

"Yes. It's like an exhibition of students' work. Some of the colours are lovely." Did I say that? he wondered. George was the kind of boy you stared at in the street. He was reminded of a waiter called Malcolm he had once seen in an Olde Tea Shoppe in Cambridge. But what did one say?

"Do you like students' art?" George asked brightly.

"Yes. No," he stammered. Damn! "Do you earn your living as an artist?" He remembered to seem to look into his eyes, when he was in fact looking behind him.

"Oh no, luv. I own a club." He decided that Jonathan looked disdainful and rather unintelligent. It would be useless to try to shock him.

"A drinking club?"

George grinned ambiguously. "Among other things. You must come and see me sometime. There's no membership fee."

"That would be lovely." He visualised a purple room full of Georges, and shuddered. Violet and pink, and pale blue and fawn, raised eyebrows, titters and tipped cigarettes. Ugh!

George watched him with amusement for a moment, then turned away. Jonathan retreated sullenly to a corner.

"This," Simon said, "is Angela Brunyate."

Angela smiled, dark and cool, and supporting a long ivory cigarette-holder.

"She likes men to call her Angel. But perhaps my brother is too young, darling?"

"Not at all." The remark sounded innocent. "Simon pretends that I'm a femme fatale, which is very nice but rather disconcerting sometimes." She looked at him frankly, wavering on the edge of a laugh.

"Never mind," Perkin said. "You don't look too terrible. I mean, you look nice but not dangerous."

"I'll leave you," Simon said, "to stand beside my paintings and trap people who look as if they might pass by without looking at them."

"My brother has plans for us," Perkin said, laughing to show that he was not ravening.

"I have a boy friend at the moment."

"How nice. I won't try to steal you."

"He's a painter. He's going to take me to the South of France. But that's what they all say." Having established her sophistication and seeing that Perkin was only politely interested, she went on, "It all began when I modelled for him."

"Not at all original."

"In the nude."

"I always think there's something immoral about that."

"We all have bodies."

"Yes, I know you know." She smiled. "But," he went on seriously, "some inhibition I have tells me it's wrong. I'm sure it isn't."

"Perhaps you're right. It encourages promiscuity." She paused. "But I like doing it. They take me to dinner afterwards. That's all they ever give me, they're all so penniless."

He ignored the last remark. "I'd hate to have anyone paint me in the nude."

"No-one is likely to ask you," she said, exasperated. "You're too skinny."

He blushed and looked away. They laughed when their eyes met again.

"I'm sorry."

"It's perfectly true. I'm like a rake."

"Simon tells me that isn't considered unattractive."

He blushed again. How young he is, and innocent, she thought. Perkin was thinking the same about Angel.

"Well, then, what do you do for a living?"

"I model a little. Sometimes I'm paid cash. I sometimes take a temporary job in a shop or an office. My parents send me money too. So I manage."

"Who bought that cigarette-holder?"

She stared at him for a moment. "The man who seduced me when I was sixteen. It used to be too old for me. I've only begun using it." She felt triumphant when she saw his eyes widen. He was not sure if she was trying to shock him or merely being helpfully autobiographical, telling him the story of a life which she thought quite ordinary. In fact she was an unassuming girl, who knew that sex is the one topic, most talked about, most practised, that is a sure way of making interesting conversation.

"He took me to lunch afterwards."

"How romantic. In the morning!" He was so pleased that he no longer cared if the story were true. "In the morning! How did he contrive it?"

"On a couch."

There was a silence while they savoured their different images of the event.

"Sometimes," he said, "I think that sex is the most tiresome thing in the world, yet I can't stop talking about it."

"I know."

There was no conflict between them now, no desire. They were surgeons operating on their bodies, wondering how they could ever know passion. At that moment it seemed more pleasant to be young, clean, cool and dressed in crisp clothes, than to lie sweating and clinging to someone in bed.

"The feeling I like most," he said, "is to be very cool swimming in a river. I hate too much warmth."

She almost understood him, but she had last felt like that a long time ago. There had been no certainty. Parents and school and plans for the future had not been enough. It was better to know that there was someone in the world, however imperfect, to whom you could turn for consolation.

As he watched her, Perkin knew that she would be easy to have, and that one day he would want her. But she was really a very ordinary girl. Already they had expressed most of their views, the opinions that seemed to matter. Sex might be the everlasting topic, but only if you continued to meet new people.

"Where did you spend the summer?" she asked. "You look very pale."

"London. I promised myself that I'd do some writing to deserve a holiday. But I slept most of the time."

She nodded understandingly. "I spent July and August waiting for my boy friend to take me to the South of France, but he never got together enough money. I'll go next year."

"I've stopped caring about work now. Next year I'll go away for a long time and find something to write about. It's enough to hope for. It doesn't matter if I never do." He smiled.

"I'd love a drink," Angel said.

"I'd buy you one but I must find Jonathan. I think we're going to a picture."

Simon came up to them again. "I think I've found someone to buy one of my paintings. Just someone unimportant who wants it for his flat."

"Congratulations. You're a success."

"With that crap? I'd feel better if I'd sold none. I'm going to give a party to celebrate. You'll come, Angel?"

She nodded.

"Not another party," Perkin said. "Can't we buy some new records?"

"We only buy records to play them at parties."

"I don't want a party."

"We're going to have one."

They pretended to fight.

"You can go to the pictures that night," Simon said.

"I couldn't sit still if I thought the party was being fun."

"Then what the hell are you arguing about?"

Perkin and Jonathan walked along Coventry Street into Leicester Square, and stood gazing at the cinemas.

"Let's sit on a bench."

For a while they watched the fountain and a girl in a cold sack who was being photographed for some magazine. Rain dripped on her head from the trees and the photographer told her not to wipe it from her face.

"I love London," Perkin said. "There are some things it hasn't got but they aren't important."

"It's just an ugly city like any other."

"Oh no. It has magic. There's nowhere else where we could live as we do, except that no place stays open late enough. I'd love to be all alone in London."

"How can you love places?"

"They never change. Maybe people change much less, and are very predictable, but I'm always unprepared even when I've been expecting a catastrophe."

Jonathan smiled. "People are very predictable, aren't they?"

"That was a conceited remark of mine. In a love affair two or three things can happen, that's predictable enough, and afterwards you may say, 'This is how I thought it would end', but you can never be certain."

"And it's worth finding out?"

Perkin shrugged, and laughed because a raindrop had just settled on his nose.

"Is there anything else?"

They lit cigarettes, which they had to relight and hold in their mouths, because the weather was so cold. Tiredness returned to them as they sat on the bench, like the dark morning after a bad night.

"Your brother was very pleased when he sold that painting."

"Yes. He really is going to be a success. He'll marry a debutante, and be in William Hickey and be terribly fashionable in a pseudo-bohemian way. And have a lot of marriages and no children."

It was an attractive kind of success and Perkin felt rather jealous. Someday I'll begin to work and be a fine writer. Or is it all a dream? We get what we deserve, or usually a little less than we deserve.

"Tell me about George," Jonathan said.

Perkin glanced at him. "He's a very dear friend."

"Why haven't I met him before?"

"Well, he's usually at his club in the evenings."

"I was terrified."

"I don't think he's sinister. We can go to his place for a drink one night, but we'd better take some women to protect us."

They got up and brushed their coats.

"I'm hungry," Perkin said.

"I know a sandwich bar where you can get coffee, two beef rolls and a piece of chocolate cake for one and tenpence."

"Lead me to it. Shall we go to the musical?"

"There's the new Dassin at the Academy. We should want to see it."

"Everyone will be talking about it. We can take the tube."

Simon triumphantly left the gallery, fired with ambition. This was only the beginning. His triumphal march continued until he reached Piccadilly and then he stopped, wondering where he was going. He had nowhere to go. He went into the White Bear Inn and bought gin. He had nothing to do all evening, and it was only five o'clock. He felt deflated. This was not success.

Anne would soon be getting home from the shop, but there was no excuse for visiting her. It would be very embarrassing. He felt angry. He had not wanted her, there had been no reason for her to make a scene. Perhaps she imagined him heartbroken, crying because she had rejected him. The thought annoyed him. As he had nothing else to do he would visit her, tell her how little upset he was, and try to teach her some sophistication.

It was six o'clock when he arrived at her flat. Her eyes widened when she opened the door and saw who it was, and she stared at him anxiously.

"Hello, Anne," he said easily. "I was passing by and I thought I'd come and see you. I sold a painting at the exhibition."

She seemed indifferent.

"I'm so glad, Simon. Please come in. I was cooking dinner." She took his coat and hung it up in the cupboard without hesitation. "Will you have dinner? It won't be ready for hours."

"I'd love to. Is anyone else coming?"

She shook her head. He looks lovely. How could I have been so stupid.

Simon shrugged.

"Well, let's talk. You're the only one who listens to me intelligently without criticising."

She blushed.

"Shall I teach you to smoke?"

"I don't really want to learn."

"But why not?" He laughed. "Afraid of going to hell?"

"I can't really afford it."

He fell silent.

"You're quite rich, aren't you?" she said quietly.

"Our father gives us an allowance which we spend too quickly. I'm afraid Perkin and I aren't very good at handling money. We spend it too quickly."

"Why do you work?"

"The extra money pays for books, theatre tickets. Besides, Tom our father wouldn't like us to be completely worthless." He gazed at her. "You look so domesticated. Will you marry me?"

"Yes. I mean no!"

"I was teasing. But of course you'll marry me. Wife of famous painter – doesn't it appeal to you?"

"A painter who chases little girls down dark lanes?"

"I'll never forgive my brother for saying that. I only chase girls who want to be chased."

"I didn't."

"But you did. You see, I know you better than you know yourself."

"I didn't."

"All right. Whatever you say." He wondered if she were telling the truth. "What shall we talk about?"

"You talk. I'll listen."

"You don't talk enough. What do you do when you're not working in the shop?"

"Make clothes, go to the pictures."

"Aren't you lonely?"

"I've been used to it since I came to London. When I'm terribly sophisticated and rich I shall have lots of affairs in a penthouse, high above the river."

"And your lovers will throw themselves from the window when you discard them."

"Of course." She smiled at the impossible dream.

"Your penthouse will cost you £20,000, and gigolos don't kill themselves for unrequited love. You'll be the one who wants to kill herself."

"Don't spoil it," Anne said wistfully. "First I shall have a real love affair, and my heart will be broken for good and never get in the way again."

He felt very tender. She really was attractive. He felt sorry for her, genuinely compassionate. He had not had this kind of relationship since he was sixteen.

"I don't want to have an affair yet," Anne said.

"You're very foolish." He pointed a finger at her. "This morality is the cause of all unhappiness. One day, when you're not so young, you'll regret your youth. One day you won't be able to care, and you'll want to care passionately, and wish you had something to remember." He smiled. "I'm getting sentimental over you. From now on I shall look upon you as a sister."

She got up. "Do you like love songs?"

"Oh yes."

She glanced at him as she placed the record on the turntable. He looked very young. Affairs did not seem to have embittered him; but when she moved closer he did look older.

They listened to the music without talking. The song was called "A Perfect Love". Simon gazed down at the floor and his eyelids looked wet. His face was twisted and he seemed to be remembering something. He was thinking that he had nothing to remember. Anne suddenly felt poised, assured. This moment was too precious to last for much longer. Rain was beating the trees outside, and running down the steps from the street. The room was warm. As she watched, she fell in love with him completely. An ideal love. If she ever married him, and she felt sure that he would ridicule her for being so ambitious, she would still be frightened on their wedding night. The poise left her.

"What age are you, Anne?"

"Twenty-two."

"You look younger."

"I feel much younger."

"Why haven't you grown up sooner, darling?"

She shrugged.

"Tell me."

"Well, my parents died, you know, when I was very young. I felt so uncertain. I had to look after myself and you make so many mistakes. I felt different and inferior. It's hard to shake off."

He said, to make her feel less shy, "Perkin and I hide our uncertainty by pretending that everyone in the world is inferior to us. It works and I believe people envy us. But we never have friends, only lovers or enemies."

The relationship was delicately poised on such a relationship: Anne trembled thankfully because Simon had confided in her, but she might hate him if he ever left her through indifference, without having committed himself definitely enough for her to remember him with gratitude. And Simon did not really care. It was peaceful to be with her, and safe, for she would not know the meaning of emotional blackmail; but he tired so easily.

"Relationships are so difficult," Anne said.

"The thing is not to care, to wander, not to think too deeply. Every word we say hurts somebody, no matter how intelligent and tactful we are."

She smiled. He had given her some confidence and she was able to enjoy herself, without being too anxious about the impression she made on him.

"Look at the rain on the window. It's dark already."

He watched and words flashed through his head: chiaroscuro, thought and meaning, interpretation and truth. He sighed. He had vowed never to use such uncomfortable terms again. He thought aloud: "How in the world could I paint this evening? Only words could convey it, or music."

"Neither, I should think. Who would want to convey it?"

He stared at her, astonished by her dejection.

"Have you never realised," she went on, "that very little is great art in itself. We call a book great if the author has managed to convey his inspiration. No technique is fine enough to fulfil the conception."

"To convey the promise is fulfilment."

"No."

He nodded. "You're right, of course. The greatness of a book lies in our memory of it. The sentences may be poor. But how do you convey this mood? Simplicity without emotion, and the painting would be damned as sentimental."

He drew the curtains and switched on the lights.

"It's useless. I'm the only one who can judge the value of my work."

"You're very conceited."

He laughed. "Forgive me."

"I'll forgive you because you're an artist, and I'm sure you're not nearly as conceited as some of them. Are you hungry? Dinner will be in another ten minutes."

"I'll help you."

She shook her head.

"Then I'll wash the dishes afterwards."

They slid into easy conversation, sprawling on cushions, and she trusted him because she wanted to trust him. She had been lying awake at night wondering if she would ever see him again, or if he thought her too clumsy to be worth his attention. He was behaving so kindly that she could not help feeling at ease with him.

"Do you make all your clothes?" he asked seriously.

"Nearly all. Except coats, of course. I love casuals, beach skirts and sweaters."

"You must design some for me."

She laughed. "What about measurements?"

He puffed out his chest. "Fifty inches."

Anne got up to change the record. "I'll knit you a sweater for Christmas, if you'll buy the wool. What would you like me to play?"

"*My Fair Lady.*"

"I have it," she exclaimed proudly.

"Of course you have. Black market?"

"An acquaintance of an acquaintance of an acquaintance who was in America. Are you going to the first night?"

He shook his head. "Too grand for me. You know, these are the years of *My Fair Lady*, Sagan novels and literary prodigies. Politics and rockets are quite unimportant beside these phenomena. That's what this silly age will be remembered for."

"And basement clubs?"

"Well, Perkin would place them high on his list. And never have there been so many young people trying hard to be bad. But with this difference – they pretend that they aren't trying to shock, that it all comes quite naturally. So it does, after a while. And they rather regret missing most of the war, because it would have been rather nice to have a Hemingway love affair."

"And trips to Spain in the summer, and everybody has a typewriter and a tape-recorder."

"And nobody reads a novel that isn't fashionable and everybody reads Proust."

"And where will we all end up?"

"Where all the other generations ended."

"Simon, where will we all be twenty years from now?"

"I don't know, darling, and it's just as well, for we'd never be able to face the future if we knew what was going to happen to us. We're such cowards that the good times wouldn't be good enough to persuade us to endure the bad."

She gazed at him for a moment, then got up and went into the kitchen. He stared at the floor, then began to wander restlessly around the room.

"We'll end at the top or the bottom," he shouted through the open door, "right up or way down, for there's nowhere in between for people like me."

He pulled back a curtain and was startled by the sudden rush of

darkness and dazzling light of rain. Sharp lines of brightness were
skimming down his mind. Watching from the corner of his eye he
saw the red light of a bar across the street, in front of the dark trees
and the smooth walls of a tall block of flats, all lit by the glow of a
cinema half a mile away. He felt thoughtful, then discovered that
he had nothing to think about. It hardly mattered if Anne became
his mistress. Even at the height of passion he often felt that he
was inadequate, cheating desperately to make the girls believe that
he was capable of passion. He said that he wanted to be a fine
painter, but the ambition was not as satisfying as he pretended.
He felt uneasy when he argued with Perkin or Jonathan, for at
least they seemed sincere, they made no claim to have discovered
a solution to any of their problems. He sometimes felt like saying,
"All right, so it doesn't mean as much to me as I pretend, but may
I not deceive myself, for if I didn't have painting I'd be empty, and
I don't want to be empty for the rest of my life."

By the time they were eating the fruit salad he had returned to
the gentle pursuit of Anne.

"I'm sorry about that night," he said carefully.

She stiffened and began to play with the spoon.

"You misunderstood me. You didn't realise how I felt about
you. Whatever people say I don't believe in making love to a girl
if I have no affection for her. Don't you know that I like you very
much?"

She nodded.

"Don't you like me?"

"Oh yes. But I'm just ordinary, I can't . . ." she blushed, "*make
out* with any man who asks me. I want to be in love with somebody, really in love, and when it happens I want it to last for good."

"Of course you do. That's why I respect you." He was almost
embarrassed by his duplicity. "Then you could never feel that way
about me?"

She checked herself. "I think I could, but not yet."

He was amazed by his own cleverness. He felt that he could
draw a chart of the affair, giving approximate dates for the climax
and the day he would grow tired of her. She was almost too good
to be real.

"I'll always be around when you need me, and I'll see you often."

She was almost crying with gratitude and joy.

"This is a delicious dinner. You're a wonderful cook."

They danced when they had rested, and he was careful not to hold her too close. Once, apparently by accident, he brushed against her, to remind her of the feeling of being stretched against his body. Then he washed the dishes and they sat on opposite sides of the fire and read their favourite poetry aloud. Anne grew very sentimental, and he was glad to humour her while laughing at his own tenderness.

CHAPTER III

PERKIN awoke at dawn, and at once his mind was drowned in swimming blackness. He closed his eyes again and drew a sheet around his face. It was not warm enough. He smiled happily and searched the other half of the bed with his hand. It seemed empty. He rolled over, once, twice: there was no-one there. He groaned and lay on his back again. Light slid between his dry red eyelids. Another day. "Please, somebody come," he whispered. "What happened last night?" He turned his head into the pillow. Nobody came to him. He had been with somebody last night, but he had no idea who she was.

Ten minutes later his nervous body had become unbearable, and he carefully opened his eyes again to take in the comfort of the early morning light. He could just see the rooftops and chimneys of the houses in the square through the window above him. The sky was bleak, low and small. Everyone was sleeping, but beneath the window on the opposite side of the room he heard sounds of the garage. The rumble of a truck, some delivery car stopping outside, piercing the morning with staccato sounds that echoed and trembled along the pavements, up the walls and quivered across the ceiling where any movement was translated into patterns on the light reflected from the street. It reminded him of patterns on the sea, sliding rolling heaving, slipping off the edges of the world:

the calm-coloured world of childhood, opaque in its purity. The memory was almost true.

He fumbled and lit a cigarette, and after it another, although his throat was so dry that it hurt to smoke. It gave him little pleasure and he wondered why he was doing it. When he felt too lazy to walk or read he had to smoke or drink.

Tom might be coming to London for Christmas. It would be pleasant to see his father. He was a solid man, almost old now, but Perkin could not remember him changing. He never changed, and could judge his sons with a most unsympathetic understanding, although he never criticised. He must sometimes wonder how they could possibly belong to him.

But perhaps he sees me differently, perhaps I am less puzzling to Tom than to myself. He may have been like me when he was twenty-three. He must be lonely now. He reads, walks, gardens.

The house rose vividly before him, perpetual, solitary, unchanging like a happy past, mellowed by time and the flow of remembrance.

A beautiful house, on a hill overlooking the sea; a beach, which was scarred with black salt weed in winter and spring; the autumn tides washing over the sand and killing the saplings; the passage through the bracken that led to the bottom of the garden; the pond without fish; the house that was the white tower of childhood, lonely and forbidden to strangers. And always, always when he was very young, the wash of sky and sea, where there was a clear horizon only in winter, if there was no fog. Sometimes he would play on the beach with Simon, but more often he was alone. Simon was a busy child, collecting butterflies and leaves, wandering in the woods. Perkin would lie down on the beach in damp clothes and go to sleep, hearing dimly the sand beetles scuttling and humming near his skin. There were anemone pools among the rocks, where sometimes he could find giant dangerous jellyfish. He would try to spear them and the poor dull senseless things would finally be trapped at the side of the pool, where he would cut them into uneven pieces with a penknife. His dog Hugo was a fat labrador bitch whose sex had been discovered when it was too late to change her name. She followed him everywhere and was finally buried by Tom on the sands when the tide was out.

If he lay on the beach and watched the sky he could almost imagine that it would come down and take him, so that he could journey forever in childhood, watching the splendoured world beneath him. On summer nights, when he could see the lights of towns behind the hills, he watched the sky anxiously to see if tomorrow would be a good day. It seemed that he usually discovered the promising streaks of red, sailor's delights. One winter night he saw a shooting star, the only one in his entire life, and like a fool he wished that he could be famous and a cosmopolite, away from this enchanted place.

When Hugo died he too wanted to die. His father came and stood beside him on the grass where he was lying, retching violently.

"Don't cry, boy, don't cry. Hugo is happy. She won't be teased any more."

Perkin laughed and grew warm again at the thought of her happiness.

"I don't want people to die."

"Close your eyes and put out your hand, touch Hugo as if she were here again."

He reached out and at first encountered nothing but a stone. Tom intensely repeated again and again, "She's there, Perkin"; suddenly he felt her thick uneven hair, and smelt her warm sweet flesh. He remembered the way she used to lick him, and felt her tongue again. He saw her brown eyes. Tom stopped talking, it was growing cold. Hugo was dead again.

In those days it was good to play games alone with childhood: watch the sea until he wanted to jump in, believe in cities on ocean beds, princes of the sea, lost treasure and monsters. He would retrieve a piece of driftwood from the rocks and wonder what it had been, where it had travelled. How many miles had it covered? It would be wonderful to lie on a piece of wood and drift endlessly to coloured lands.

He inhaled smoke too quickly and coughed violently. He smiled. One of the things which enabled him to live quite happily was his talent for fantasy, and when he was most miserable he could suddenly be enchanted by the face of the girl who sold him a newspaper, or the wonderfully easy good nature of an American who stopped him in the Strand and asked him whether Poet's Corner was in Westminster Abbey or Madame Tussaud's.

He sighed. Jonathan and Simon and Anne and Angel and George. What were they doing? One day he would write a book about them, but what could he say? There was really nothing. It would only be a question of plotting their lives, drawing them towards an indefinite conclusion, pulling a few strings to contrive an accident perhaps, so that one might be saved. What are they doing?

What am I doing? I think too much but if I stopped I'd have to fill each moment with something else and there would always be the night time. I'd have to sleep with somebody every night, it would be very complicated and they'd force me to think. There is no escape from thinking. Once I believed in love and peace. Where has it all gone? I can't remember the exact date when I awoke to despair and found that I bored myself, but I know why it happened. I was lonely, I indulged myself, and I did anything that seemed interesting. One day I looked in a mirror, but it was too late. I was no different, but something, the way I closed my eyes, opened my mouth, showed that part of me was dead. My mind, which everyone said was good and could be used to achieve almost anything, had replaced my heart and now pumped blood and was too busy for anything else. That is not completely true, but I think of my feelings objectively, my life is uncoloured by emotion. I hope – I *do* hope – that I will change. I am not cold, my heart was overworked, I'm resting. And sometimes I do love them, I love them for a few moments. We pay too dearly for the things we do. We are too stupid to know better, so why must we be punished for our mistakes?

Simon came into the room, carrying a tray.

"I got up early and made you some coffee."

Perkin sat up and gazed at his brother ruefully.

"I feel sodden. Jonathan went home after the film and I wandered about for a while, went to some bar. What time did I get home?"

"I don't know. I was here by twelve and you hadn't come then. I hope you had a good time. All I got was a little peck from Anne."

"You'll make her all right. I think she's in love with you."

"I'm her first crush. At *twenty-two*." He sipped his coffee. "Whom did you meet at the bar?"

"I wish I knew. It could be terribly embarrassing if we ever meet again. I swear I don't even remember the colour of her hair. I wish I was like Anne. Emotionally retarded."

"What a sordid life we lead."

"Oh please, that's what I've been saying to myself since I woke up."

"We'll have plenty to remember when we're old."

"Not if I can't even remember whom I slept with. Anyway maybe I didn't. I don't feel as if I did." He tried not to laugh. "It isn't funny, not at all. Simon, isn't there any way out? Couldn't I change and become decent and respectable and ordinary?"

"Why bother? Why do you always wish you were somebody else? You're yourself. You don't want to be like all those people with plain faces and ugly bodies, dark and crippled. Don't fool yourself, we aren't bad, we just enjoy imagining that we are."

"Oh well, it's nice not to believe in hell."

"I think I do." He quickly drank some coffee and went to the window. His religion was too personal, it seemed to suit him so well that he hesitated to explain it.

"You will help me with this party?"

Perkin nodded. "I couldn't keep away from it. You know that."

His brother sighed. "What a morning. It looks as if the sun will never shine again."

"It was shining for a little while." He got out of bed and went to stand beside his brother. "There it is, hidden behind that rooftop."

The streets were still deserted, sodden with fine mist, or rain.

"We should sleep all winter, and wake up at noon on a summer's day."

Simon smiled. "And blow the dust from the world and start again. And never see rain."

"The streets at night look better when they're shining wet."

Simon turned to him, and giggled. "You look awful."

Perkin stuck out his tongue, and Simon soon stopped laughing.

"Our world is so awfully small. Hampstead Heath is the only piece of country I've seen for months."

"In the spring we'll go away every weekend, have fun. Only four months, one hundred and twenty days."

"And nights. And four thousand cigarettes each. And how many bottles?"

"It will come, and we'll forget the winter. In the summer we might go and stay with Tom. Do you want to go home? It's been so long."

Simon frowned. "Everything would seem so small."

"There's just one thing I want to do. I want to stand on that beach and feel so uncomplicated again."

"Always running away, and no place is any better than the rest. One day you'll grow up and you'll go on living, whatever happens to you."

"I know, I do. I'm frightened."

"Frightened that you haven't got enough talent? So am I."

"I'd love to go to a psychiatrist."

"I don't want you to be different."

"I don't care, you know. At the moment I feel as if I'm watching myself, standing here with you, and I'm thinking 'Crappy little fool' and I'm laughing at myself. But I think I should care. I think I should care passionately, but I don't. It doesn't matter. Does it matter, Simon?"

"Not really. And oh, damn, I always feel as if I'm reciting lines from a novel or a play that you've written. It's just a pretty mess. But everybody I know is an actor reciting lines from a play. We're so self-conscious about our stage technique and entrances and exits. I don't know anybody who ever says what he means. Decide what you want, then get it. What else is there? What else is there? This is the method I'm doing now, you see, art arrayed in disarray."

"Maybe I want to be a writer, maybe I want security. I never say what I mean because I don't know what I mean."

"One day it'll be too late for anything."

"Can I have a cigarette?"

Simon smiled wanly. "That's the dropline. Completely pointless and effective. 'Can I have a cigarette?'"

"You're a fool."

"Here, I'll light it for you. You needn't worry, Perkin, you look as innocent and fresh as you did five years ago when I began to corrupt you. I'm beginning to be old. I must do something soon."

"If you're a terribly successful painter and I'm a tramp, will you support me?"

"You can mix my paints."

"I know now what I want," Perkin said. "I want a car."

CHAPTER IV

ANNE arrived late for the party. She had never managed to come at the right time for a party, and had reconciled herself to being late or early, though sometimes she was so late that everyone had gone to supper. If the room was crowded she could hide behind a door if nobody talked to her, but she never knew what to do if there were only five or six people in the room. She climbed the stairs nervously, wondering if her skirt and sweater would be appropriate. She was hoping to pass for an interesting bookshop assistant from Hampstead, the sort who are always devoted to still-promising young writers. She had scrubbed her face until it shone and bought a packet of Player's Weights.

She leaned against the wall for a moment, before going through the open door. A Kenton record was being played, and it made her shiver with delight and apprehension. She had decided to favour Italian madrigals rather than Elvis Presley, who Simon had told her was too sophisticated.

It was not nearly so bad as she had feared. None of the other guests seemed to have noticed her arrival, and they were busy talking. Angel and Simon were dancing with a string of beads in a corner, and looked extremely bored. Everyone looked bored. Someone had poured a hundred cigarettes on to a table. They now swam in the pools made by the bottoms of glasses. George had already arrived. He was surrounded by a crowd of stupefied young men, all jealously guarded by their angry girl friends.

Perkin came up to her. He was wearing grey corduroy trousers and a black pullover.

"I hardly recognised you. What's the idea?"

Anne lit a Weight before answering, held it high and hid behind it.

"What do you mean?" she drawled.

"You look as if you've just got out of bed."

Her eyes widened. "Do I really? Honestly?"

He grinned. "I didn't mean that. Where's your teddy bear?"

Her face fell. "You look like an existentialist."

"I am, dear. The Bloomsbury kind. Shall we discuss *significance* or *seminality*? But you really do look wonderful." He could think of nothing else to say, so he said, "So charming. Do you want to talk to someone or would you prefer to look enigmatic?"

"I don't know."

"Have some gin. You can talk to me. Drink half of it at once and wait for the result."

She hesitated, then obeyed him. "It's lovely."

"I know."

"Why are you always so nice to me?"

"I'm devoted to you. I told you, when you grow tired of Simon you can come to me."

"Simon's already proposed. I told him I'd think about it."

"Would you like to dance?"

"I couldn't to that music."

"Of course you could. Try to feel sensual." He held her tight and leaned down against her shoulder. She felt nothing, or felt that she was being held by a statue. Perkin had no warmth.

"I'm so drunk, Anne. I'm so bored. I'll take you home tonight, if Simon doesn't."

What does he mean? she wondered. The gin began to take effect and she no longer cared. It was so easy to accept this attitude which was conveyed in everyone's movement and speech.

"You don't bore me," she whispered.

"I couldn't care less. I bore myself."

"How can you? You lead such an interesting and easy life."

He sniggered. "Ho-ho. Don't listen to what I say. Marry some-one respectable and solid, forget all about interesting experiences, forget you ever met people like Simon and me."

"How could I? I'm in love with Simon."

"What do you mean by love?" he asked wearily.

"I adore him. His face, his skin, his clothes. I could listen to his voice for ever. I think about him all night."

"I once felt that way about a girl. Now I wonder how I could ever have been so stupid. She was so ordinary."

"Couldn't you love her nevertheless?"

She felt his mouth twist into a smile. "Of course. But everything about her was wrong. She was a shop assistant. All she wanted was a good time. . . ."

"How much do you know about love?" she whispered. "Tell me how to handle Simon."

"You don't need advice. If you love him you'll give him what he wants and still love him when he leaves you."

She fell silent. It was easy to talk about taking Simon as her lover; everyone seemed to be in some stage of an affair these days. The idea of being seen with him, having other women talk to her on equal terms, appealed to her, and it would be nice to wake up in the morning with him beside her. But the thought of the bed the night before terrified her.

"For heaven's sake put that cigarette out," Perkin said. "You're burning my hair. You know, I can't endure people who won't make up their minds about sex. Don't make a big thing of it. Simon won't lose respect for you, whatever *Woman's Own* says. On the other hand, he may not be very grateful."

"Tell me what to do. Tell me what to do. Tell me and I might do it."

"No. I don't want to feel guilty. Is he still dancing with Angel?"

"I suppose that's Angel. They don't look very happy. But he hasn't looked at me once."

"She won't steal him. Do you want to make him jealous?"

"Of course. But how?"

"Just follow me."

He raised his head and kissed her mouth.

"Stand still and put your arms around my waist, under my pullover."

She obeyed. It was rather pleasant, but no more exciting than kissing her own body. He put his hands in her hair.

"Enjoying yourself, Perkin?"

They drew apart. Simon and Angel had come up to them.

"Do you have to exhibit yourself in the middle of the room with my brother, Anne?"

She looked foolish.

"Want to change partners?" Perkin asked, smiling.

"Yes." He took Anne's arm and led her stiffly into a corner. By the time he spoke to her she had recovered her composure, and realised that he was jealous.

"I'm rather surprised," he said, trying to look whimsical.

"We were only kissing. I like Perkin."

"I'd better take you home. He's given you too much to drink."

"I don't want to go home. I'm enjoying myself. Why did you have to spoil it? You had Angel."

"She's good company, that's all. I don't understand you. I thought I did."

Anne smiled. He looked so unhappy that she wanted to tell the truth. Instead, because she was drunk, she said, "No harm can come to me kissing your brother at a party. It's more dangerous to be alone with you."

"I told you I could be trusted."

"Maybe I don't want to trust you," she said daringly, and regretted it as soon as she saw the light in his eyes. "Would you teach me how to dance properly to this music?"

When he held her she came alive again. Why had she ever wanted to make him jealous?

"Perkin kissed me just to annoy you. I'm sorry."

"I thought that was it. It was sweet of you to care."

"And how is Angel?"

She shrugged. "Still no chance of him taking me to the South of France."

"I'm so very sorry." He grinned. "There's nothing left to live for."

"I know. Will you take me?"

"No."

"I thought not." She shrugged again. "Well, I might become a singer. I might sing for my supper. Who knows, I might meet a millionaire. He might buy me a car and I might crash it. Wouldn't that be fun?"

"Wouldn't it?"

"You're funny."

"Am I? I know. You're funny too. You look bewildered, always, in your fallen little way. Do you care?"

"Not at all."

"That's nice. I could never get to know you, except that I recognised you the first moment I saw you. You'd always pass on to somebody else."

"So would you. I hope I meet you again when I'm an old woman, looking for a home. You'd take me in."

"I'll be looking for a home too. No, I won't. I'm going to change, you know. I'm going to be a banker."

"It's too late."

"It can't be. Are you going to stay behind tonight?"

"If you like."

"I'm so glad. It would be very nice."

"Really? But I'll stay. Would you have asked me if you hadn't been drunk?"

"I never ask when I'm sober, so don't be offended."

"I have a calendar on which I tick off all the . . ."

He put his fingers across her mouth. "Don't spoil it. Don't try to be amusing."

Angel laughed. "I was only going to say that I have a calendar on which I tick off all the days on which I do nothing. Isn't that innocent enough?"

"I only half believe you, but I apologise."

"Thanks. What a party this is!"

"Good or bad?"

"The same as any other party. Nothing new. Nobody famous or likely to be."

"Oh, that isn't true. Henry Enfield is coming. The writer. And I dare say lots of these people will be famous one day. They'll write, I should think. One or two novels. They might be famous for a while. They'll write about being frustrated writers, or how much they want to be famous."

"Not one of these people has any real talent."

"Yes they have. Artists don't give the impression of being terribly intense or brilliant. Do you envy success?"

"It's just one of the things I haven't got and never will have, so I admire it and wish I had it."

"Never mind. You don't care."

"No."

He looked at her face. "You remind me of a games mistress I once knew. She was wonderfully histrionic. You weren't born in London?"

"Near Brighton."

"Why didn't you stay there?"

"I wanted what I've got. I was a fool."

"You could go back."

"Yes, to my parents. Maybe I will one day."

"Then there's nothing to be sorry about."

"I'm never sorry. Sometimes I wish I were."

"I don't think people are ever sorry now. I don't think there's anything left to be sorry for."

"I think I have some kind of conscience. I think everyone wants what they can never have. Is that right?"

"Maybe. But it's a cliché."

"What isn't?"

"To be happy sometimes."

"We're happy sometimes."

George, having sufficiently shocked his audience, gently broke away from them, and retired to a corner, where he found Jonathan.

"You're dreaming, honey," he whispered.

Jonathan awoke, and was too startled to recoil from George's yellow shirt. "Hello."

"Hello. Are you having a nice time?"

"No."

"Well, you're not trying very hard."

Jonathan frowned. "Let's not discuss the psychology of parties. Who's looking after your club?"

"My boy friend. I took the night off just to meet you again."

"That's nice."

"Yes." He was disappointed when his companion showed no surprise. "His name's Derek."

"They're all called something like that, aren't they? Derek, Mark, Tony. Everybody's in love with the name Tony."

"How did you know?"

"I think Perkin told me."

George grinned. "Any more information you want, just come to me."

"Thank you very much."

George went to refill their glasses, and when he returned Jonathan was stretched out on a window seat, gazing out at the sky.

"Here. This is good. Move your feet. I want to sit beside you."

Jonathan curled into a ball. "I shouldn't be seen with you. I'll get a bad reputation."

"I didn't know you could smile. But don't worry. Half the men here are queer."

"I'm not."

"I'm sure you aren't."

"It's much more original these days not to be, don't you think?"

"It's rather late for me to think anything."

"I suppose so." Jonathan smiled again.

"You aren't censorious?"

"Oh no. I think it's all terribly interesting."

"Don't get burned."

Jonathan stared at him curiously. "Who are you to tell me so?"

George shrugged. "It sometimes begins with bored young men who want an interesting experience."

"I'm not really interested. It sounds messy."

George did not reply, and they stared through the window. The year was growing old. Someone took off the jazz record and played quieter music. The dancing stopped, and everyone began to talk about the same things. Although some won't admit it, people only go to parties in the hope of meeting someone with whom they can fall in love. If they attend too many parties they fall in love with too many people, or become so confused that they have to substitute generosity for love. But it is the same thing.

George sang softly,

> *"When I was very young,*
> *The world was younger than I,*
> *As merry as a carousel.*
> *The circus tent was strung*
> *With every star in the sky,*
> *Above the ring I loved so well."*

Jonathan's eyes filled with tears, because he always grew sentimental when he was drunk.

"What's wrong, honey?"

"Don't call me honey," he hissed savagely.

"Sorry."

"Oh, so am I. I like that song."

"So do I. But I love classical music too, don't you?"

"Sometimes. But I prefer anything that belongs to this century."

"Yes. Wake up, Jonnie. Don't you want to talk to me?"

He looked surprised. "Do you really want to talk to me?"

"Of course. I love talking to innocent young men."

"All right. What do you want to talk about?"

"Would you like to hear a dirty joke?"

"No."

"It's very funny. It's about an old woman who worked in a club for . . ."

"No!"

"All right. Then say something."

Jonathan tried not to laugh. "You really are impossible."

"I'm not. I'm very nice when you get to know me."

"Is that an invitation?"

"No. I told you not to play with fire."

Jonathan waved his hands vaguely. "How did you get to be like this? If you didn't wear those preposterous clothes you'd pass for somebody ordinary."

"It's a sin to be ordinary. The only vice for which there is no excuse."

"Every sinner has a vice for which he can find no excuse. It's usually smoking."

"Where *do* you pick up these little scraps of information?"

"From books, I assure you. How did you get to be this way?"

"The vicissitudes of life. It's such a messy life. I look forward to the day I die more than anything else."

"Me too. If we were suddenly extinguished, painlessly."

"I'd like to share a common grave, or at least have someone with me when I die. I hate being lonely."

"But if you dressed plainly and talked sensibly you'd pass for a good-looking young man and nothing more."

"I have to think of my reputation," George said quietly. "But of course you're right, I hope. I was all alone, under age and somebody raped me. After that my rise was meteoric."

Jonathan giggled. "What a cynical way to tell it."

"I'm cynical and rich. And maybe I won't last much longer. At least my life is various, in a rather sordid way. I'm also bad, Jonnie. Remember that, whatever else I tell you."

Jonathan smiled. "No-one is really bad. I envy you, I don't know why. Were you ever in love?"

"Often, quite passionately. But it all ends in nothing. And of course queers are the most boring people on earth: 'Have you had him, dear? *Haven't* you? *I* have.'"

Jonathan laughed. "Have you ever been in love with a girl, or don't you believe in these aberrations?"

"Once. I was just starting up and I didn't like some of the people I met. This innocent little tart came in one night with her boy friend, who was an actor and made her sleep on the floor when he had one of his friends in for the night. I suppose she fell in love with me because I was kind to her. She was very poor and sick, but somewhere she got the money to buy me presents. Even then I had more money than she's ever set eyes on. Anyhow, before I knew what was happening we were having long serious discussions about all the things that mattered to us then. She'd sit with her knee between my legs, pretending that it didn't matter because we were like brother and sister. She stayed behind one night and it was very pleasant, but what was the good of trying to fool myself? There are girls like that. They can't keep away from people like me, and the end is such a mess. She's probably dead now, or if she isn't she'd be better dead."

They fell silent. Jonathan wished that he were asleep in bed, far away from the phantoms and ghosts with which George toyed. Most people were like unhappy caricatures of what real people should be like. What had gone wrong?

"Have you got a cigarette?" he asked quietly. "Perkin's have been soaked in gin."

George lit it for him, and their eyes met over the lighter.

"The trouble with most people," Jonathan said, "is that they're so romantic and sentimental, but so afraid to admit it."

"I'm very romantic. If I'd been ordinary I'd have been content to settle down with someone."

"Can't you do that even now? What about Derek?"

"He's just a promiscuous little boy. I buy his meals and give him a job. It's impossible."

"Why?" Jonathan asked despite himself.

"Queers never do, although they'd like to. They grow tired of each other or something. Naturally they have less restraint. They realise what they want as soon as they meet. A boy meeting a girl for the first time never expects her to jump into bed with him."

"No?"

George smiled. "Look, honey, let's be friends. I won't make a pass at you."

Henry Enfield remained just inside the doorway, gazing elegantly at the party until someone came to greet him. While he waited he lit a cigarette, knowing that if he did not light one people would suspect him of only pretending to be completely at ease. His great fault, both as a person and a novelist, was that he could never recognise simplicity, and because he was so clever, subtle and intricate he was often completely wrong in his estimation of events and other people.

"Mr Enfield, how are you?"

He stiffened. "Hello, Perkin, dear boy. You know, I like you more than most young people because you simply refuse to bandy my Christian name." He thought, It's rather superior of him, and he knows it.

"It was so nice of you to come. You're the only famous person here. I do hope you don't mind."

Henry stared at him for a moment, wondering just what the words were intended to convey. Dislike, sarcasm, arrogance? But he did not stop smiling genially, indeed he could not. He was famous for his good nature, but fame or success makes only superficial changes. Henry could still be angered by ignorance or indifference on the part of someone younger and less talented. He had made this fault of his the subject of a famous short story.

Perkin wondered why he had come, and thought it must be because he needed a scene or a character for a new novel. In fact it was because Henry liked watching young people. Anyone of his own age, which was forty-five, bored him acutely, although he never admitted it, and would later recount the absurdities of this party to his friends, and in a book of course. He recounted everything in a book at some time or other, because it helped him to stop thinking about it.

"I bought your new book," Perkin said. "Oh, it was so wonderful. Will you sign it for me?"

"Of course. How is your first novel coming along?"

"Which one?" Perkin asked innocently.

Henry smiled benevolently, but decided that the business of being a writer was being ridiculed. "You'll never be a writer if you adopt that attitude, although I liked your stories very much indeed."

Perkin enjoyed Henry's company because he disliked the older man intensely, and he disliked so few people.

"Fortunately writing is one of the arts where crudity doesn't seem to matter. How many copies did *Room at the Top* sell?"

Henry winced. His own first novel, which he liked to describe as a surprise success, had sold only ten thousand copies.

"I hate novels about the provinces," he said, then checked himself. He seldom expressed dislike, and always looked regretful when he did.

"Who is that young man wearing the fancy shirt?"

"George. He's an – artist." It was best to be careful. The characters in Henry's work were notoriously recognisable. "I'll introduce him to you, if you like."

George had been talking to Jonathan about Peynet cartoons, and was annoyed when Henry and Perkin came up to him. He immediately mistrusted Henry, who looked too amiable.

"I've been telling Mr Enfield that you're a painter," Perkin said quickly, "and Jonathan is a poet."

"Well, that's very gratifying," Henry said. He had such confidence in his talents as a conversationalist that he had long ago forgiven himself for ever sounding inane. It was better than having nothing to say.

George suddenly felt ashamed of his shirt. While talking to Jonathan he had decided that in future he would wear plain pullovers.

"I'm afraid I haven't read any of your books." He did not add that he considered it unnecessary, for he possessed all the knowledge and knew all the jokes that made them entertaining. "But you're very famous, aren't you?"

"What do you read?" Henry asked, undaunted.

"Usually love stories. Anything sentimental. My favourite novel is *Peyton Place*. I think it's absolutely wonderful. I mean, apart from the sex. You know, the woods in autumn."

"How charming."

Perkin left them, wondering just what Henry was thinking.

"Do you earn your living as an artist?"

"I decorate clubs," George said. Jonathan choked. Henry was not deceived, and made a mental note to use the remark in his next book, in which he intended to contrast the aimlessness of the younger generation, who had no business to be aimless, with the search for stability of their elders, who had.

"I'm terribly interested in this thing young people have for clubs. What is the explanation, I wonder?"

Jonathan said, "I suppose they're convenient for vice, and the rest like to feel vicious."

"And you prefer basements, don't you?" Henry did not usually care to admit that he was growing old.

"Oh, if you must generalise, we turn to France for our ideas. The only alternative is John Osborne."

"I suppose so."

"Perkin likes Murger," George said, "although it costs more these days to be bohemian than respectable. We're the lost generation, trying hard to pretend that we discovered it without Hemingway's help." He smiled, to show that he was joking.

"Isn't that a little passé?"

"Of course," George said contentedly.

"Does neither of you want to be original?"

"I think it's rather difficult," Jonathan said.

"You could be yourself."

"I don't know myself very well. I think I'm honest. I give way to my instincts and copy people."

Henry felt vaguely sympathetic. He had never been like these people. It might be pleasant to be young, aimless and complicated. But they were so outdated. How could they be so unoriginal?

"Well, I don't suppose it matters what people say. If you must be romantic, you must be romantic."

They nodded.

"But for heaven's sake don't become too sad. Not suicidal or anything. It isn't worth it."

They nodded again.

God, he thought, I'm surrounded by sphinxes. Neither of them looks as if he's suffered from passion once in his life. On second thoughts I'm glad I'm no longer young.

The party was growing tired, and only Rodgers & Hart songs were being played. Those who had not already found someone knew that they would go home alone. Fortunately the music was either happy or bitter-sweet. It seemed to provide a comment on their lives, and made them almost gay. Music and songs are generalisations, and unpleasantness is made to seem pleasant.

Anne was happy, for Simon had danced with her most of the evening. Angel was waiting patiently until she could be alone with

Perkin. George and Jonathan had arranged to go to a film one afternoon. Perkin had smoked his sixtieth cigarette and did not feel sick.

Henry was one of the first guests to leave.

"Come to dinner one night next week," he said to Perkin, who was delighted and surprised. He liked listening to Henry's gossip.

Guests awoke from their stupor for a moment to say goodbye, and soon the room was stale and dead. Mass exit made it suddenly cold. Perkin switched on another fire and began collecting glasses. Angel lay down on the couch and sighed.

"Are you glad I stayed?"

He nodded.

"You're very pale," she said.

"I'm very tired."

She raised her eyebrows, and he grinned, but said nothing. He went into the kitchen, and ran hot water into the basin, in which he dropped as many glasses as it would hold. One of them cracked. He stared at himself in the mirror for a moment, and was neither pleased nor displeased at what he saw. He went back to Angel, and sat beside her on the couch. He could hear rain beating on the windows.

"Like me to play another record?"

She shook her head. He sighed. She too was tired, and felt that making love might be more pleasant because of this. But she did not move. Perkin leaned back until his head was a few inches from hers. He looked at her, searching for a sign of individuality in her face. She looked calm and kind and promiscuous, but not passionate. She was very pretty, but she looked uncertain, not of the result of her actions, but of her motives for acting as she did.

Perkin was not excited. Drink had dulled his senses and reflexes. He put his hand behind her neck and kissed her tentatively. Her mouth was long and smooth. She kept her eyes open. He held her for a moment, kissing her neck, then collapsed with a long sigh, waiting until he wanted her. He opened his eyes after a moment, and could see only the loose collar of her blouse. She was warm, and he relaxed, gently rubbing her arms. She smelled of lavender soap. Her hair was thick. He moved to unbutton her blouse. She resisted and he sat up, suddenly awake.

Angel was watching him angrily. He felt irritated and moved to the other end of the couch, and lit a cigarette. The room was too empty. He could still hear the echoes of conversation and wished that he was buried in it again. He no longer preferred the close contact of one person. He despised himself for giving way to custom and embarrassment.

"Want a cigarette?"

She shook her head.

"What do you want?"

She did not reply.

"Why did you stay behind?"

Her eyes filled with tears.

He listened to his own voice, wondering vaguely if he had been unkind.

"Look, darling, you want to or you don't. I'm too tired to play games."

He looked assured, detached and cruel. She wanted to kill him. She tried to slap his face and he caught her hand and pulled her down to him. She was too weak and depressed to resist. This time he kissed her with a little passion and she held him tightly, tears running down her face. He kissed her eyes.

"Don't cry, Angel, I'm not worth it. I don't want to hurt you. You seemed so careless."

"Just care. Just care once, for a minute or two. I'm so tired of it all."

She was not crying sorrowfully. She had merely lost her temper. He tried to make her stop crying and in the end she wiped her eyes and kissed him. Soon he led her into the bedroom.

Simon kept his hand on Anne's shoulder as they walked home. She seemed to enjoy dodging from door to door in the rain. They laughed when two or three times they could not avoid stepping in puddles. When they reached her flat they stood for a moment in each other's arms, searching each other's faces.

"We're terribly wet," she whispered. Then without thinking,

"Would you like to come in and dry your clothes?"

He smiled, shaking his head. "I'd better go home. You mustn't tempt me too much."

She did not want him to leave her.

"I'll see you soon."

She nodded and slowly opened the door. When she saw the bed she thought of its warmth, and realised that she would not sleep. She would lie awake and wish that Simon were beside her. She tried to clear her mind of the vision of his pyjama-clad body, and clenched her fists in self-disgust.

Simon made his way home smiling contentedly. When he reached the flat he tried the door of Perkin's bedroom, but it was locked.

They had wrapped themselves in a blanket and while they were asleep it slipped from their shoulders and onto the floor. Perkin awoke with his face pressed against her neck. He had been dreaming about a forest in which he was wandering, pushing back the branches of the trees. He pushed her hair from his eyes and lay still for a moment, examining the body on which he was lying. The skin was white, smooth and rather sticky. It was an antiseptic, carefully-tended body, from which he derived no comfort. Her face, in the grey light which was just beginning to enter the room, looked calm and innocent. Her mouth twitched gently now and then.

He kissed her tenderly for a moment, as he would have petted any animal, then rolled out of bed. He picked his dressing-gown from the floor and put it on, then straightened the clothes over Angel's body. The curtains had not been drawn, and he stared at the morning sky, bleak and desolate. It was hard to imagine that it would ever be blue again. The rooftops trickled and the trees were hidden by mist. He switched on the electric fire and searched for a cigarette in the pockets of his gown. He found a crumpled Abdulla which someone had given him at a party weeks ago, but when he inhaled the smoke he felt the dryness of his mouth and tongue. His teeth were furred. He sat on a cushion and gazed at the fire, and played with the cigarette. His mind was a complete blank and he searched for something to think about. He knew this contented feeling: it might last for two or three days, and then he would suddenly be smothered in darkness again. But he felt so happy. Everyone he knew belonged to the night. Jonathan was a shadowy creature, hovering for ever on the field of vision, slipping beyond one's comprehension, his weak eyes blinking in fear. George was a night vendor. Any daylight that he ever saw was a brief respite until he returned to his underworld. It must feel strange for him to stand in the sunlight and stare at the sky and know the illusion of freedom. He most of all belonged to the night. He could only come up to draw air. Angel had pleasure only at night. The daytime worried her. And Simon his brother, whom he wanted to be happier than anyone else in the world, dodged something fleeting, edged away from almost everything.

Perkin conjured with their faces in the fire, played with them and felt no distress as he arranged the unhappy fate of his friends. It would be pretentious to pity them or pretend they were tragic people. They were rather beautiful, still young and gifted, but not at all important. Perkin used the night as an image, and did not care very much if he were at last drawn into it from his colourless plane of existence. He imagined a bizarre world of hideous masks and streaked bright colour and artificial light; the movements of the inhabitants belonged to a ballet; there was spite and danger in their faces. Clothes reeked of sweat, cursed daylight shot through the roof and when it came they hid, grovelled in corners, for the light revealed their withered skin and gaping bodies.

Angel's voice awakened him, for he had dozed.

"What time is it, Perkin?"

He fumbled for his watch and shivered. "Six."

She groaned and hid beneath the blanket. "Why did you get up?"

He could not tell her that he was tired of touching her. "The room was so cold. I had to light the fire. And now the fire's so warm that I can't leave it."

She was not deceived. She drew the stained pillow against her face. She was accustomed to indifference and often practised it herself, but sometimes on winter mornings like these her stomach and heart seemed to shrivel; how good it would be to feel continuing warmth, wake up each day to find a familiar body in its usual place, knowing that the arms would reach out to hold her. Of course she could always get married to someone who would be kind, but that seemed an incongruous end to the way of life she had created.

"Are you all right, sweetie?" Perkin asked automatically.

She sat up, holding the blanket around her, and smiled brightly, although they could barely see each other in the dark.

"In two hours I shall have to get ready for work," he said. Every day until lunchtime he lost himself among the books at the shop, and pounded a typewriter. It made that part of the day during which he had to think for himself fairly short.

"I don't know what I'm doing today," Angel said. "I think my boy friend wants to paint me again. Actually I'm thinking of joining R.A.D.A., or maybe something less strenuous."

"If I didn't know you, I'd say you were an actress."

She smiled. "You look like what you are."

"What am I?"

"A writer, of course."

He raised his eyebrows.

She sighed. "It was lovely, Perkin. You're very cool and clean and thoughtful."

He had almost fallen asleep again, and he started. "Is that a reproach?"

"I don't know. But I've never known anyone like you. I'm afraid you look, you always look, as if you wanted to be somewhere else."

He grinned. "You aren't the first to say that. But honestly, if you'd asked me I couldn't have thought of a better place to be."

"Where will you end, I wonder? I may become just a bitch, but of course the ordinary rules of life wouldn't apply to you."

"I've always wanted to be a prince in a tower, by the Rhine, waiting for a princess who died many years ago. You see I'm still a child. My favourite books are fairy tales."

"Are you a changeling? Who was your mother?"

"She worked in a teashop before she married Tom. But I don't remember her. She died when I was born."

"Does Simon remember her?"

"Very faintly. Tom says she was very sweet and pretty and could be wonderfully vulgar, but she was born in London. She was lost when he took her to the country."

"How sad." She watched him for a few moments longer. "I think I'll go now."

"Stay and have breakfast."

She shook her head, and stood up without bothering to put on clothes under the blanket. She knew that he would not be offended.

He stared at the fire while she was dressing. "You'll come to a play or something next week?"

"Oh yes." She combed her hair.

Any desire they had known for each other had gone, and did not seem likely to return.

He held his dressing-gown tightly round him and took her to the door.

"Goodbye, Angel."

"Goodbye." She lifted her face, and he kissed her lightly on the cheek.

"For some reason I'm terribly happy," he said. "I think that's a good sign."

She nodded. He returned to his bedroom and watched her from the window. She walked proudly and independently, staring straight in front of her. He watched until she turned a corner, then covered himself with the blanket and fell asleep.

CHAPTER V

ON SUNDAYS their flat was littered with newspapers, records, cigarette ends and unwashed cups, and there was always the penetrating sweet unfresh smell of paper, paint and a thousand hangovers. Perkin got up early, at noon, and spent the next two hours reading the literary section of *The Sunday Times* and *The Observer*. He never bothered even to glance at the remaining pages of either paper. All they ever contained were articles on mental health and somebody's memoirs. He was just considering writing letters to the editors when Simon wandered into the room, vaguely wiggling a hairbrush and trying to smooth the circles from under his eyes. He tied the girdle of his bathrobe and slumped down on the floor beside his brother, yawning painfully.

Perkin toyed with a packet of cigarettes and finally lit one for him.

"I don't think you'll taste it," he said grimly. "If I may say so, I think you should go immediately into the bathroom, take a bath, clean your teeth, shave, and make sure that you get all the tar stains off your fingers. When I saw you in the doorway I wanted to run and hide."

Simon sniffed. "I think I've got a cold, too."

"Your nose is certainly awfully red," Perkin said happily. "I was in bed at ten o'clock last night, with a huge martini and Henry Enfield's latest book which I said I'd read although I hadn't. I'm having dinner with him tomorrow night so I thought I'd better. He's terribly clever, but his sex doesn't make me feel at all sexy. It's like those films at the Cameo-Poly – no subtlety. Or in his case there's maybe too much subtlety. What do you think?"

"It was ghastly. It started raining at two o'clock, the taxi ditched us in Piccadilly because the driver thought we hadn't enough money to go any further – don't ask me why – and as a matter of fact I had run out of money. Penny tried to prostitute herself, but nobody seemed to want her."

"No-one is ever called Penny. You made a mistake."

"In the end we walked home – in the rain – in opposite directions. And I can't remember her second name and I don't know where she lives." He smiled. "She was pretty."

Perkin shuddered. "Please don't smile again. It makes you look even more repulsive. Can I get you something? Luminal? A prairie oyster?"

Simon nodded his head, and if he had been capable of clear thought would not have been able to decide if the movement were more painful than talking. When he tried to move his tongue it thumped against the sides of his mouth and he sounded as if he had an impediment in his speech. When he first awakened, only to drift back a dozen times into an oppressive thunderous subterranean cavern, he was terrified and thought that his gums had receded in the night, for he could feel only one rough texture at the front of his mouth. He later discovered that his tongue had probably been feeling itself, however timidly. When he nodded his head a pain shot from the bridge of his nose to the base of his neck. It was a difficult problem. Experience had taught him that the first step towards a cure was a hot bath. The other stages came quite easily and were often pleasant. But at this moment, even if the bath had been run and he was magically transported to the bathroom, he had not sufficient energy to take off his slippers and his bathrobe. He would have preferred to get into the bath dressed in them. He wondered how he had managed to get them on. He must have been asleep.

In the kitchen Perkin broke an egg into a tall milk glass and poured on some Worcester sauce. He added a pinch of salt, then realised that there was no red pepper and no sherry. He stared thoughtfully at the glass, then playfully poured some brandy in as a substitute for the sherry. He felt amusing this morning, perhaps because his brother was obviously in pain. He opened a tin of tomato juice and used most of it to top the glass.

"To mix or not to mix?" In its present state the drink looked rather like a melancholy baby. He stirred it with a fork: it would be a pity if Simon got no further than the tomato juice. It turned out an unpleasant colour, but probably all Simon's senses were dulled today.

"If you open your mouth I'll pour it down for you."

Simon reached out and took the glass. "There are times I'd dearly love to hit you with a poker," he murmured uncomfortably.

"I was only trying to be helpful. What shall we do today? Go for a brisk run in Hyde Park?"

"If I feel better we might go to the pictures." He contemplated the glass, then opening his mouth suddenly swallowed half the drink in one gulp.

"Is it getting through all right, dear?" Perkin asked politely.

It was, because Simon was able to glare at him quite painlessly. He reeled for a moment, then drank the remainder. He mopped his forehead.

"I feel as if I shall soon be sick, but at least I'm human again." He took another of his brother's cigarettes and relaxed against the side of the chair. "Thank heavens I'm out of that mess."

Perkin nodded, watching him. "I don't think I've ever seen you quite so bad . . ."

Simon frowned. "I drank more than usual, that's all."

"Obviously. But I thought you knew when to stop. Remember, I'm the crazy one."

Simon inhaled deeply. This feeling of exhilaration – like the brittle day outside – felt delicious when it was combined with a trance-like state of dejection. This was almost the first time in his life that he had experienced it.

"You can't criticise, there are times when you look like a warning to mothers to force their children to attend Sunday school. But I'm sorry if I depressed you."

"I'm not depressed, Simon." He paused, then went on unhappily, "But you never needed to drink so much before. Why now?"

"The same reason why you sometimes drink heavily."

Perkin stood up and leaned against the desk where he usually did his writing. He stared at his hands. He shrugged and watched himself in the mirror on the opposite wall of the room. He looked well: clear and smooth, like a marble bust on which someone had inked a few plastic lines.

"But I don't know why I get drunk. Maybe because I've got nothing else to do." He dismissed himself. "Simon, is it something to do with Anne?"

Simon opened his eyes and stared at him angrily for a moment. "Of course not. How could it be? She's done nothing to upset me."

"You've been seeing a lot of her."

"She's a friend."

"She's in love with you."

"But I regard her as a friend, because I don't love her and she isn't prepared to accept anything less."

"Why don't you love her?"

He gave an exasperated shout and threw his arms in the air. "Why? If I did love her I probably couldn't give you the reason."

"Maybe you don't want to love Anne," Perkin said.

"What do you mean?"

"Maybe she isn't the sort of girl you'd like to love so you refuse to admit that you want her."

Simon hunted in the pockets of his robe and began cleaning his nails with an orange stick. Perkin knew that the guess had been at least partly accurate, for Simon never cleaned his nails until he had washed his hands. He looked bored and irritated.

He said lightly, "Oh, Perkin, these complicated motives of yours. How did this begin? Are you trying to find a wife for me?"

His brother remained silent.

"Look, why pick Anne, from all the girls I know? She's sweet, rather lonely, and I want to be kind to her."

"She isn't like the rest."

"And because she's different you think she should be my great love? Why?"

"I thought I sensed that you loved her."

"I don't," Simon said vehemently, but he was unwilling to close the discussion. "You irritate me, Perkin. Now I won't be able to stop thinking about Anne. In the end I'll believe you."

"That would be good, Simon," he said. He went to sit by the window. "She's the only girl you know who could make you happy. She loves you."

Simon smiled. "I've always wanted to be loved by somebody nice whom I could hurt."

"That's what I meant. You're afraid."

He had no idea what his brother meant. He toyed with the words for a moment. "That makes me an almost tragic person, doesn't it? I mean, when it was too late I'd regret my capricious youth. I'd have ruined my life to appear interesting, I'd have done it all for a pleasant effect."

"We must remember," Perkin said slowly and passionately, "that we aren't writing a play. This is our life we're directing. It's very short and we won't have another."

"Which makes our caprice all the more effective."

"Be serious," he said angrily, "it's one short life. Sometimes I think it's too late to change. I won't change now, but if I met some-one like Anne, that I could care for, I'd start to learn all over again how to care. All we've ever tried to be is amusing and amused. That's the most trivial and unimportant thing. We go on and on looking for sensations, pleasantly exciting little shivers in certain parts of our bodies, masochistically-narcissistically stopping short of what we really want so that we can still feel uneasy, like a hen on an egg. You won't love Anne because you don't want to be happy. It's too plebeian."

"I should be angry with you," Simon said softly, "but I'm not. You see I couldn't care less. I hate serious discussions, don't you?" His eyes flashed briefly, then the lids fell and he smiled lazily. "I'm going to take a bath. Shall we go to the pictures in about two or three hours' time?"

His brother nodded dumbly.

"Is Jonathan coming?"

Perkin shook his head and his face brightened. "He's going for a walk with George."

Simon was interested. "Are they having an affair?"

"I should think they're moving in that direction. That's why I introduced them. I wanted to see what Jonnie would do. It was obvious that George would make a pass at him."

Simon giggled. "If Jonathan becomes queer you'll be to blame."

"Don't be silly. I didn't *encourage* him to talk to George." He laughed wryly. "I am getting to be a matchmaker."

"Perhaps George is only trying to enhance his professional reputation."

His brother shrugged, then tried to look as if he had been stretching, for he suddenly remembered that he had already shrugged at least four times during the conversation.

"It will last about two months then George will grow tired. He always does. I expect the whole business leaves him rather bored by now, although he won't admit it. He's a kind of walking death. If he were a girl I'd write a story about him."

"You're terribly gloomy, Perkin. You used to be more fun."

"I wasn't being subjective," he protested. "George told me that one night when he was drunk."

"That makes it even more depressing. What will Jonathan do when George drops him, as you say he will?"

Perkin began another shrug but remembered in time and instead changed his position to lean against the window.

"I expect he'll want to die."

"We shouldn't laugh. It's really very sad."

"Well, it's one way of spending time, which you insist is something unimportant."

Simon laughed. "You win." He tapped the letter from their father which was lying on the desk. It had arrived the preceding day. "Are you glad Tom's coming for Christmas?"

Perkin nodded. "We should really have gone home to him."

Simon hesitated, then went into the bathroom. Soon he began to whistle a tune from the latest American musical. It flattered him to think that he had almost grown tired of it, although most of the people who liked popular music had not yet heard it.

Perkin lit another cigarette. He decided that he was ridiculous, and almost derived some comfort from the thought.

CHAPTER VI

THE paths were muddy and George shrieked when his pink socks got splashed.

"We'll be covered in mud," he gasped, jumping on to a thick clump of grass. "Do you think we ought to have come?"

"The grass will rub off the mud. Are you sorry we came?"

"No."

Jonathan smiled. "The sooner those socks are finished the better. I thought you were going to wear plainer colours."

"These were all I could find. I used to think they were very daring. Are you ashamed to be seen with me?" He shrieked again as his foot slid into a puddle, and Jonathan laughed helplessly.

George was quite happy. He would go to any lengths to look foolish and make someone laugh at him.

They came to the top of a hill, and stood under a tree, gazing back. The sun on the opposite hill shone across the Heath, glancing off the pond, which sparkled with thin ice. The horizon was a house, the hospital and two spires, red against the sky. Most of the sky was grey and matt, but underneath the sun clouds moved gently, fields of light. They were silent for a moment, breathing heavily after the climb.

"How convenient that there should be a few clouds near the sun," Jonathan said, "to be turned to gold."

"Those ones just happen to be lucky."

Jonathan turned to him. He was grinning happily and with amusement, for he often laughed at Jonathan's solemnity.

"Why are you smiling?" he asked suspiciously.

George shrugged. "Maybe I'm happy."

Jonathan took off his gloves and searched for cigarettes to hide his awkwardness. It had become their habit to bend over the lighter together. They turned in against the tree for shelter from the wind that was rising. Their warmth together and the warmth of the cigarettes made them content, and Jonathan did not know what was happening.

George said, "I've been having a little trouble. I own the house where I have my club, you know, and I converted it into three flats, one for myself and two which I usually rent to friends. Derek has one of them at the moment, but I'd rented the other to a journalist. If John Gordon only knew! But this one wasn't queer. That was the trouble. He had a girl friend who sometimes came to visit him at night. About a week ago she came to visit him and when she found that he hadn't arrived yet she thought she'd have a drink. So *naturally* she came down to my club, because he'd told her there was a bar in the basement. It was Friday night, and the place was full. There was only one woman in the whole place and she wasn't the sort to make anyone less suspicious. I was at the bar at the time and realised what had happened as soon as this stupid little bitch came in through the door, but before I could do anything some old pansy rushed up to her, kissed her on the mouth, and shouted a dirty word. He thought he'd met a friend. She screamed and of course everyone who'd been watching started laughing. But it wasn't funny. She was almost hysterical. She pushed him away and rushed into the street screaming her head off. I'm such a lucky boy, everything nice happens to me – she ran straight into a policeman. Apparently she gabbled something about being attacked by a pervert, and pushed the policeman down into my club."

Jonathan was listening breathlessly, wondering if George was going to be summonsed, or something even more catastrophic. George smiled when he saw the expression on his face, and almost wished that the incident had been more disastrous.

"Now this was an awfully *innocent* policeman, and obviously Daddy hadn't warned him. In fact I'm not even sure if he knew exactly why he felt suspicious. But everybody tried to look as if they'd come in for a game of darts, and made sure that a space was cleared round the woman, my friend Jane, such as she was, so that she'd be conspicuous. We could have done even better if we'd had time. I ducked round the bar and shouted 'What will it be, Constable?' and everyone laughed heartily.

"He looked awkward.

"'I've had a complaint from a young lady who says that she was assaulted in here.'

"I honestly don't know how he had the nerve to say it, but he did.

"I said, 'Oh yes, I think I know what you mean, Constable. You could hardly call it an assault, although I suppose it must have been unnerving. One of my clients who was a little drunk brushed against her, and I expect he gave her a bit of a shock in the half-light. She certainly screamed, and rushed out again, before the man could get a chance to apologise.'

"'Where is he now?' God, but he looked relieved.

"'I told him to go out and get some fresh air, Constable.'

"He stared at me for a few moments longer, trying to look ferocious, but not succeeding very well. Then he gave me a little lecture about something, I don't quite know what, I was too relieved, and left after gaping at our one and only female customer. She was awfully popular afterwards. He took my name of course, but I have a licence and it's all legal up to a point, so that was only routine."

"I'll bet everyone was very angry with the old pansy," Jonathan said inadequately.

"At first, but he shed a few tears, and everybody told him to cheer up and be a good girl in future."

Jonathan shuddered. He could be entertained by this kind of talk up to a certain point, for it was one of the most common topics these days, but then he would suddenly feel disgusted. He had seen George many times in the past few days, but he could not prevent himself from shuddering.

"Why must you say these things?" he pleaded.

George laughed and did not reply.

"You make fun of yourself when you laugh at these people. You'll be like them yourself one day."

His expression did not change. "I'm like them now."

"You aren't. You're like anybody else, you're like Perkin, you pretend to be affected to annoy me."

"Honey, have you ever wondered why I don't disgust you the way you say the others disgust you?"

Jonathan looked frightened. "I'm beginning to feel cold. Let's walk again."

They strolled to where a game of football was being played, and watched it for a moment. A red-nosed little boy had walked to the edge of the field, and was kicking the grass stubbornly. His parents watched him, the father good-humouredly, the mother with exasperation.

"John, *do* cheer up," she called in a perfect house-in-Keats-Close accent. "(Isn't he *glum!*)"

The little boy glared at her, rubbed his nose defiantly, and growled.

"JOHN!"

The two young men smiled, and continued their walk.

"I hope he beats her with a stick when he comes of age," George said maliciously.

Jonathan was glad to laugh again. "Look, there's ice on that puddle."

"It's cellophane paper. There can't be much ice, except what's left on the pond. It rained during the night."

They came to a bridge and leaned over the wall, looking down into the mud. George smiled.

"There are even life-belts. As if anyone would want to commit suicide in that swamp."

"They might, if they wanted to make a good job of it. If you jump into a pond you can always swim if you change your mind and decide that you don't want to die. You'd never get out of that stuff alive."

"I think the only elegant reason for committing suicide is the wish to join your Dear Dead Love. Otherwise it's a very shabby affair."

"Most people are shabby."

"You *are* miserable," George said.

"Well. Can I have a cigarette?"

He stopped to light it at a little stone hut with a cone-shaped roof. The door was locked, but as they passed the small, high window, they heard a man's voice saying, "But you see, the problem is . . ."

"I wonder who it is?" Jonathan whispered.

"I could make a guess," George said, "but you wouldn't like it."

"Oh, shut up. You really are a bore. You have only one subject for conversation."

"It was Colin Wilson revisiting his old home," George said quickly, and giggled.

Jonathan stared at him, then roared with laughter. "You're impossible. That isn't what you were going to say."

"I know, but I'm ready for anything."

They were at the top of a tree-lined avenue. Jonathan opened his mouth to apologise, then changed his mind. The trees in the avenue were tall, almost without branches, like crazy black scaffolding.

"Last time I was here it was summer," George said.

"Whom were you with?"

"A friend," George lied. "I was very happy."

Jonathan looked at him enviously, but said nothing.

The trees were not completely empty. They had been so engrossed in themselves that they had not listened to hear the birdsong that now echoed through the sharp air. Summer has gone, but it will come again. Winter will pass away, and when the warm long days come you'll remember this time and you'll remember it as a happy time. Wait until April. Wait and see.

"I'll race you to the top of the avenue," Jonathan said, feeling buoyant and beginning to run. They called to each other, laughing, slithering in the mud which seemed to be dragging them back. Soon they were mingling with the groups of people chatting beside the pond at the edge of the Heath, wrapped against the cold in Raglans and duffle-coats.

"What a pity there isn't more ice," Jonathan panted. "Can you skate?"

"A little. It's very exciting, isn't it?"

"Oh yes."

"Shall we have coffee somewhere? I've two hours before I have to get back to the club."

They climbed the hill that led to Heath Street, stopping to look in the windows of estate agents, as most young people in Chelsea and Hampstead stop to look, even if they already have flats. They passed a bookshop where Henry Enfield's latest novel was on prominent display.

"He was rather frightening, wasn't he?" George said. "He made me feel like a piece of machinery which he was taking apart in order to describe it accurately."

"I almost liked him. Nobody can pretend to be kind for very long if he isn't sincere in some way."

"Why does Perkin like him?"

"I'm not sure that he does. But then you never know. Sometimes he's completely dumb, but sometimes I think he's a genius. Perhaps he thinks Henry will help him, publishers and agents and things, if he ever begins to write seriously. One day he's going to write a book about us and show us as we really are. God help us."

"He doesn't know us as we really are."

They were just in time to take the last table in the café, which was always crowded at this time of day. They glanced round the room, at the paintings hung hopefully by local artists, and the people. The women were almost indistinguishable. They all seemed to have long hair brushed upwards and backwards, dark eyes blacked with one lavish stroke of an eye pencil, and long narrow pale pink mouths. Their clothes looked home-made: check smocks, plain sweaters, striped jersey shirts, jeans or long straight skirts, casual shoes that were down-at-heel.

"They're awfully pretty," George said when he had ordered coffee. "They look about ready to jump on the next boat to Paris only they haven't the fares and it's forty years too late."

"They're so unaware. Completely dependent on their boy friends, looking enigmatic because they haven't the brains to work out what it's all about."

"I must say," George said critically, "I like them better than their boy friends. Such terribly *serious* young men, and I bet they don't wash very often. Always remember, Jonathan, that the most important thing to look for in a lover is cleanliness."

Jonathan speared a piece of chocolate cake. "If you're trying to be genuinely helpful, George, thanks but I don't want any more advice. But you're wasting your time if you're trying to shock me. I'm used to you now."

"I'm only trying to smooth the way, honey."

Jonathan looked at him pleadingly. "Please, George, when you start this business you make me sick with nerves, as if you're going to creep up when I'm not looking or something."

He smiled his most appealing smile. "I'm wicked, you see. And I know more about you now."

Jonathan flushed, and forced himself not to light a cigarette.

"I can't tell you how much you'd like it. You're as queer as hell and you don't know it."

"Please." He began to tremble. One step, a few hours, what difference could they make? He liked George too much, although he was aware of his many faults. In fact he always suspected the worst, so that when he revealed a new and pleasant aspect of his nature, Jonathan was surprised and more grateful than if the virtue had been immediately apparent. For the first time in his life he genuinely wanted to know someone. It seemed that self-interest had gone. He wished he knew what to do.

He turned back from the window. "Do you know, in a few weeks it will be Christmas."

"I know," George said gravely. "The time of year when I hide my head in shame and close my brothel for a day. At a great loss, too.

You've no idea how many lonely people there are in the world."

"Where do you go?" Jonathan asked quietly.

"Bed. Alone. Until about noon. Then I get up and give a little party for my helpers, who never have anywhere else to go at Christmastime. Then I do a little tour of my houses and make sure everything is in good running order." He giggled.

Jonathan shook his head. "Why do you joke about these things?"

"I'm not joking, honey." He looked tired for a moment.

There was a long silence. Jonathan stared at his fingernails. "Well, I suppose you prepared me for this."

"I think you'd be more shocked if you knew more about it." He had been waiting for the right moment to tell him about this side of his business which had only recently begun to be properly organised and remunerative.

"I thought you'd shout that you never wanted to see me again, pull a horrified face and rush away."

He shrugged. "What's the use?" He smiled slightly. "You're right, of course. I haven't realised yet quite what you mean. Presumably it means a lot of ruined lives?"

"Possibly. I think I use people who would do it anyway, but for less money and with more risk of being exploited." He paused, then, "It's a business like any other. If I didn't do it, someone less conscientious would."

"Less *conscientious*? That's hardly the right word. And these – boys, is it? – where do they come from?"

"Mostly from abroad."

"Alone they might have changed, reformed, realised there could be no future for them. But when the whole thing is organised like a biscuit factory . . ." His voice was completely flat, giving the impression that he did not much care.

"You put it so elegantly. All right, I can't argue with you. It's just something you'll have to accept, if you accept me."

"Are you thinking of putting a price on me?"

George frowned. "I don't know how much you're – maybe I'd better not say that, but don't get cynical."

"I don't really care, you know. I like you as you are, therefore

I must accept the bad things about you." He shook his head help-lessly. "But I should care. You've spoiled everything, made it more terrible. Or exciting perhaps. It's like a new world, with a different religion. I don't know. Don't let's talk about it any more."

They fell silent. Jonathan returned to staring through the window, thoughtlessly and listlessly. George felt a moment's regret, but accepted the situation and the events which might spring from it as he accepted everything else, patiently and with vast indiffer-ence. He ordered two more coffees and leaned across to put a ciga-rette in Jonathan's mouth.

"What are you doing at Christmas?" he asked gently. Those little boys, what did they matter?

"I don't know. I spent last Christmas alone, on leave from the army."

George hesitated. "I want to give you a present, in advance if you like. I'd be very pleased if you'd accept it. The empty flat in my house. The one the journalist used to have."

Jonathan stared at him. "But it's too much. I couldn't possibly take it without paying."

"I'd like you to have it."

"I'll take it if you let me pay for it."

"No, I want to give it to you. You know I'm rich – and if you don't mind living on immoral earnings."

Jonathan said without thinking, "How do I earn the present? Allow you to make love to me?" He immediately regretted the words.

George stared at him angrily, and said, "Don't be so middle-class, honey. The word is f—"

"I'm a fool, I'm sorry, George."

George said unconvincingly, "You're too good for me, Jonathan. You want life to be beautiful mornings and romantic friendships and elegant farewells. It isn't like that."

"It is for some people. Do you really think I care what you do, how you earn your money? It makes no difference to me. I should be grateful for your little prostitutes. If you didn't have them you'd be different in some way, and I like you as you are. I was just think-ing how much I'd changed, that's all."

George said, "Sometimes I think of the horror with which people who read newspapers, go to the pictures, the local twice a week, must look upon someone like me. I'm a monster to them, a Dorian Gray, except that I sin less self-consciously. But good God, what does it mean? I'm the same as everyone else. I'm kind up to a point, I try to make the most of life, have fun, appreciate it, I'm never deliberately cruel unless I've got no choice. But it's hard to believe that because of two things – that I once prostituted myself (Jonnie, you've no idea how petty, how small it is), and because I own a business that would otherwise be run by someone less scrupulous – I'm a great sinner, degenerate, perverted, all the nasty words that Sunday newspapers use. I did what I could do, I used all I had to use, I had no choice."

Jonathan reached out and pulled at the gold chain which hung around George's neck. He held the little gold cross in his fingers for a moment.

"Why this, George?"

He took the cross from Jonathan and tucked it back inside his shirt.

"People like me don't believe in God, but we'd like to, because we'd like to feel sorry that we'd betrayed Him. I'm awfully sentimental. It's what I have to make up for everything else that's missing."

"What exactly do you mean?" Jonathan asked, suddenly embarrassed.

"Never mind." He sighed. "I must go. It's nearly opening time. Will you come and see the flat I'm giving you?"

They watched each other for a moment.

"Yes. I'd like that. I've got nothing else to do anyway."

He had never been to the house in Chelsea where George lived and had his club. If I sin, he thought, I'll be like Dorian Gray, self-conscious as hell.

CHAPTER VII

THE house where George had his club was in a tall shabby street in Chelsea. Some of the houses in the street had been converted into expensive blocks of flats where journalists, barristers and old young men from the plush pastures of medium-sized advertising agencies lived. It was impossible to guess who lived in the unconverted houses. Sons of industrial peers of the realm paying alimony to their ex-wives? Retired actresses or old ladies who took paying-guests? The ground-floor windows were high above the heads of passers-by, and the basement windows were heavily barred and dusty. The houses were made of massive stone, impossible to modify.

On two or three nights a week the street would be filled with cars. Someone was giving a party. The sound of music but no chink of light escaped from behind thick curtains. To the uninitiated the street seemed merely dull; to the half-initiated it was degenerate and compelled dread and excitement; to the initiated the street was dull, and existed only as a grey background to their complicated lives of which they were hardly aware, except that it was pleasant to escape for the week-end.

The flat which George had given Jonathan was on the third floor, looking out over an unnecessary heap of rubble to the back yards of another row of houses and the car park of a cinema. The flat itself was self-contained and very comfortable: a bathroom, kitchen, large living-room and tiny bedroom. The furniture was plain and unobtrusive, and the fitted carpets were new. Most pleasing of all, the living-room had an open fireplace. Jonathan almost shouted with joy when he saw it. He had spent last winter alternately freezing and blowing away the fumes of the gas fire in his furnished room.

George smiled when he saw the look of pleasure on his face.

"You can spend the evenings getting drunk downstairs. Won't it be a lovely life?"

He nodded. "I'm very grateful, but I still don't understand why you're giving it to me for nothing."

George watched him for a moment. "This way your money will last longer. I'd hate to see you doing work you didn't want to do. I hate to see anybody working when they should be enjoying themselves."

"Why should I have an easier life than other people?"

"You deserve it, in some way you're better than most people, it's just a fact."

"I'm no better, I'm simply more pretentious."

George stared at the floor, considering. He smiled faintly, and said, "Remember, honey, my father was a tailor. He was stupid, brutish, and angry, and shouted and bullied my mother until he killed her, and he'd have tried to beat me into submission if he hadn't died himself. The night he collapsed on the floor I wanted to kick him in the stomach, I wanted to see him trapped by pain and agony and watch him cowering before me. He used to catch me by the ear and drag me across the room, waiting for me to cry out. He once stole all my clothes and left me one of my mother's dresses and told me that as I was a girl I should dress like one." George shook his head and tried to relax against the back of the sofa. His hands were trembling and he lit a cigarette to steady himself. "But you see, I've risen above all that."

But how, Jonathan thought, sickened.

"And I have what I have because I worked for it, I was more intelligent than the people I grew up with. I could have gone on the streets or fallen in love with somebody and finished up broken and ugly by the time I was nineteen. But I didn't."

He saw the expression of nausea on Jonathan's face and smiled bitterly. He put out his hand and touched the other boy's mouth. "You're an escapist, honey, you can't face reality."

Jonathan shook his head fiercely.

"You are, honey. Reality disgusts you, you run away from it." He paused. "When I was twelve my father tried to—attack me." He smiled. "I mean attack is your word for it. There are others."

Jonathan hid his face in his hands and cried out with horror.

George watched, and could not stop smiling. "Why should that disturb you?" he asked at last. "Why should you worry? It didn't make any difference to me, except that I wanted to get away more than ever."

"It must have made a difference to you," Jonathan cried. "I told you what happened to my mother. That summer changed my whole life, it made me what I am."

"Someone stronger would have remained unchanged. If your

parents hadn't died like that you'd have found another excuse for being what you are." He stood up and went over to a cupboard. "I brought up some whisky this morning. I thought we'd be celebrating when you came."

Jonathan wiped his eyes and picked up the half-smoked cigarette which George had placed on the ashtray. George handed him a tumbler half-filled with whisky.

"You can finish it before you go to bed, if you don't want it now. When will you move in?"

"I have," Jonathan said quickly.

"I'll light the fire, and when I close we can come up here and you can tell me what you think of my club. The bed's made up. You can sleep here."

Jonathan nodded. He was grateful, and still upset; the whisky had begun to make him feel sleepy and absurdly he felt that he could trust George, or rather, that whatever George did would be right. He felt warm and tired, but it was only seven o'clock. Somehow he would have to get through the rest of the evening.

When the fire began to blaze they went downstairs to the ground floor, then down the dimly lit stairs into the basement. It was a low-ceilinged room, hidden from the street by Venetian blinds. The bar was at one end, and the remaining floor space was taken up by small tables with large ashtrays. Long seats were built into three of the walls. Jonathan stopped dead as soon as he entered the doorway. The room was dead, velvet air smothering conversation and smoke. There were only six men in the room, three couples, two sitting in opposite corners and one standing at the bar. They were talking quietly, but as soon as the two young men entered they looked up, scrutinising them with bland eyes. They nodded, smiled or waved to George; as soon as he was in the room he assumed new solidity, self-possession. The men stared at Jonathan for a split second, then resumed talking. He suddenly came upon his reflection in a large mirror opposite the door. He looked younger and slightly tanned. No doubt the lighting effect had been contrived by George for the benefit of his clients. He led Jonathan to the bar, and beckoned to the young man standing by the cash drawer.

"This is Derek," he said easily.

Derek nodded and smiled uncertainly, showing rearranged and very white teeth. One large gap at the side had fortunately been impossible to fill.

Jonathan greeted him with the superficial, hard-won assurance that he could command with anyone he did not know well.

"George told me about you," Derek said with a doubtful accent, a cross between an Irish drawl and a Cambridge squeak. He came from Willesden.

He was a small young man, with weak shoulders held severely in an upright position and a tiny mouth and large tearful dark eyes. His brown hair was cut short, for he had sensibly decided that long troublesome hair would make his face no less ordinary. He knew from the start that his accent would be impossible to disguise, but felt that the end-product would be rather charming, indicating a desire to please. The difference between Derek and George was that Derek had a small overworked brain and a placid outlook, so that he tried to be nice to people, whereas George had once been capable of passion, no longer cared, and felt that people who would not accept him were not worth the trouble anyhow.

"Give Jonnie whatever he wants to drink. I'll be back in a moment," George murmured, and went to talk to some people who had just come in.

"I'd like some lemonade," Jonathan said.

Derek felt as surprised as he would ever feel, but from the look on George's face knew that he had better be pleasant. He had always found that sarcasm required too much effort and time, so that his few bitchy remarks fell flat, delivered long after they would have been effective.

He stood a tall glass on end in the ice bucket.

"It's better than putting ice in the drink. It turns to water and the lemonade loses its fizz."

Jonathan looked appropriately grateful. The room was beginning to fill, and Derek went to serve some new customers, but he returned almost immediately.

"George says that you're a poet."

"Officially yes, but I don't write very much poetry."

"I do wish I had a talent," Derek said without regret, "but I'm no good at anything really."

Jonathan opened his mouth to make a dirty remark, but changed his mind. He had not yet discovered how important Derek was to George, and he decided to be careful.

"Is this a part-time job or do you make a living this way?"

"It's enough. George usually pays for my food." He stood back to calculate the reaction on Jonathan's face, and was disappointed.

"How did you live before you got this job?"

Derek shrugged, wiped the frosted glass and filled it with lemonade. "I worked as a barman in a très gay pub and last year I had a job as secretary to an artist I met there one night. I've never really had a regular job. I know where to eat cheaply and I only smoke when people give me cigarettes."

"I'm sorry. Would you like a cigarette?"

Derek stared at him blankly for a moment, then almost smiled.

"I mean have you no definite plans for the future?" Jonathan said, explaining what he had been thinking.

Derek shook his head. "There's no point in making plans. Who knows what will happen." He hesitated, but experience had taught him that almost childlike candour could be touching and disarming. "I'll stay here as long as George wants me. I'm very attached to him."

George had already grown tired of him, and he knew it. In the abstract the situation would have seemed harsh and unfair to him, but in reality he felt no self-pity and accepted it without thought or conscious regret.

Jonathan sipped his lemonade. It was really a much pleasanter drink than whisky, and incomparably better than beer. No-one liked the actual breathless taste of scotch, although sometimes they felt better afterwards.

"May I have a whisky?" he asked.

Derek smiled. It would be fun, in an uncomfortable sort of way, to see George frustrated and impotently angry for once in his life. It would be a sweet revenge.

"Soda?"

Jonathan shook his head and poured the scotch into the remainder of the lemonade.

"This is my favourite drink," he lied, and drank it as if it were only lemonade.

Derek shuddered.

When George came to find him twenty minutes later, he was staring straight in front of him, frozen, apparently oblivious of the people who were now crowding the bar.

"You aren't drunk, Jonnie?"

He did not move.

"Honey! Wake up!"

He blinked. "Hello, George. You're back at last."

"You aren't drunk?"

"Of course not. I've been drinking lemonade."

"Then come and meet some of my friends," George said doubtfully.

He led him to a corner, and introduced him to four blurred figures. They all had dark hair and nice teeth. He collapsed into a corner and closed his eyes, intending to listen to the conversation; but it was a very stupid conversation. Everyone was not talking about sex, trying to look normal and behave as if they were interested in something else. He yawned, opened his eyes, and saw a painting on the wall above him. It portrayed two urchins, and was grossly sentimental and idealised. The dark soulful little boys were clothed only in their vests, and looked revolting.

"That's one of my paintings," George said brightly.

"Is it?"

"Do you like it?" someone in a dark suit asked despairingly.

"Very much." His nostrils curled. The smell. There was no smell, as if the men and their clothes had been cleaned and hung in an airing cupboard. The smell was not objectionable, it didn't exist, and he felt disgusted by its absence and the still suffocating atmosphere. He wished they would all go home to bed.

He got up and swayed past their feet. "I'm going upstairs. I feel sleepy."

George looked bored. "I'll see you later, honey."

"It was lovely meeting you." He beamed round the group.

As soon as he passed through the doorway he felt well again, but wished that he could have another glass of lemonade. He climbed the stairs quite steadily and went into his living-room. He could hardly believe that it belonged to him. He sat down on a stool beside the roaring fire. It would be a pleasant winter with George, but why did he lead such an unpleasant life, have such undesirable friends? His head rolled and he fell asleep.

When he awoke he thought that only a few minutes had passed, for the fire was still blazing. Then he saw George brushing away small pieces of coal which had dropped from the tongs.

"What time is it?"

"Half-eleven," George said quietly, putting down the tongs and leaning back to finish his cigarette. "You're lucky you didn't roll off into the hearth and get burned."

"Have all your friends gone?"

"Yes. You didn't like them?"

"I was too sleepy to pay any attention. I don't believe I even saw their faces clearly."

"They all wondered what I saw in you."

Jonathan was now fully awake, and he smiled. "I suppose they feel that I should swoon in your arms as soon as you want me." He was nervous and trying to hide it.

"Yes, something like that." He was exasperated. "So you didn't like my club."

"I didn't like your painting. I like Derek, I think he's sweet. I like the room, but there was something about the atmosphere, I don't know what. It was – thick, but not just with smoke. I've never tasted air like that before. It clings to you."

George put a record on the gramophone. "This doesn't go with the flat, but you can have it on permanent loan. Have you got any records?"

"A few," Jonathan said abstractedly.

Some dreamy voice began to sing:

> *"You are there, in the night;*
> *You are there, at morning light."*

"What an awful song."

"It's a lovely song," George said. "If I had my way I'd play the most important scenes of my life to a background of music like that." He laid his hand thoughtfully on the back of Jonathan's neck.

"You look as if you're going to cry, honey. What's wrong?"

Jonathan blinked and shook his head. "Nothing." He watched his hand being lifted and placed between George's hands, and allowed his finger to go to George's mouth, the nail playing over his teeth. He closed his eyes.

The fire was almost dead. Every minute or two a small flame licked at the last remaining living lump of coal and the light was reflected on the ceiling, which was already growing pale around the edges. It was almost first light.

George lay on his back staring upwards. Jonathan was asleep, sprawled across the bed. George was trying to remember something he had once had, but he was unable to pin the memory down to any incident or person. He did not love Jonathan. Nowadays his life was cool; the mood of which he was thinking required or engendered a state of non-feeling – lucid, moist, opaque, thoughtless, still, quietly circling beyond joy or passion or indifference. He had it just now, for a moment. It was a form of the highest, most pleasant indifference and detachment, and would depart as soon as Jonathan mumbled something in his sleep, or the curtains were pulled back in the morning. It was like a mood induced by the most precious liqueur, and would be followed by depression.

CHAPTER VIII

HENRY ENFIELD lived in a dark crumbling house in an avenue off Havistock Hill. It was cool and comfortable for writing in summer, and for winter he had installed central heating. Those were his only requirements. After his three sad hours of labour, on fine mornings he took his deck chair into the front garden and read the latest novels to see what he had to beat, or formal pre-twentieth-century French writers to discipline himself, and incidentally to find interesting material or viewpoints which he could use in his own work. He hated parasites, yet as he grew older he was more prepared to be entertained by young men who worked in advertising agencies and had nothing to recommend them but an eviscerated intelligence and a ceaseless flow of conversation. Henry's life was tedious. He had mastered his trade and knew that any too startling innovations in his work would be financially disastrous. He spent the evenings at parties where he automatically and effortlessly gathered raw material, the least demanding part of writing. The reward for the hard work that followed came in the eight weeks following publication, the rosy glow, the lingering glances of strangers and the heightened attention paid to him by his friends, most of whom were extremely successful in their own field. Henry was famous for his superficially brilliant, peculiarly objective portraits of extraordinary people. In fact he knew nobody who was at all extraordinary, and regretted it. Sometimes it occurred to him that his ambitions, on which he had based his whole life because he had nothing else, were really quite ridiculous. But he would smile contentedly, accepting the truth yet remaining quite happy. He knew that almost everyone does get what he wants, but behaved as if he were quite unique and blessed. He was a rather jealous man, but not vindictive, so that when, on seeing a young person smile as if he alone possessed the key to the bright potentialities of life, he felt a momentary pang of envy, he would be more pleasant to that person, and slightly patronising, for he knew all about the adjustments and disillusion that lay in wait.

He smiled indulgently as he helped Julian De-la-Noy to yet another drink. There was something charming about youth going to ruin, and as a connoisseur of literary and theatrical effect he was able to accept as art those things in life which many people find unpleasant or even repulsive, and watch with an artist's eye the swift sure steps of his acquaintances towards the fitting end of a rather sentimental writer's creation.

As always, Julian was smiling generously, and he raised his glass as Henry sat down again.

"To you," he spluttered, pretending to have difficulty in keeping his eyes open. "May all your books be as successful as –" (there was an awkward silence while he stood with the glass held above shoulder level and tried to remember the title of Henry's latest book, but he soon decided that it was not worth the effort) " – as successful as your last." He giggled. "I mean your latest, of course, not your last."

Henry waved his hand. "Do sit down, dear boy. You look rather unsteady."

Julian sat down, then looked offended. "Henry, you aren't suggesting that I'm *drunk*?"

Henry laughed gaily. "Of course not. But you're the sort of person who always looks drunk. In fact I envy you your capacity. How many drinks have you had since you arrived?"

Julian sucked his thumb for a moment. "Three," he said with a note of finality.

"Three? Are you quite sure? I mean, you may drink everything in the house, but three?"

Julian stared at him solemnly, then his face twitched and his shoulders began to shake. He lay back in the chair, laughing violently and with concentrated mirth, as if this were the last laugh he would ever have. When he recovered he sat up and wiped his mouth with a finger which he then pointed at Henry.

"Of course it's three," he shouted, his face beginning to quiver again. "It's *always* three."

This time Henry laughed only moderately. There was no point in carrying the joke too far, and after all the sordidness behind the laughter was only too apparent, and became more apparent each time he saw Julian. When he saw that his glee was only mildly echoed, Julian calmed down, and returned to acting his usual engaging drunken self.

"When is Perkin due?" he asked, sipping his gin precisely. He was trying to do two things at once: appear to be interested in the conversation, and make up a round:

> *"Hear the bird of day*
> *Sing merrily,*
> *Merrily, merrily."*

His chin sank down to his chest as he mentally sang the last merrily.

"In ten minutes. He's usually on time. Meg will be late. She had an extra lesson today."

"I love Meg," Julian said, giving up the attempt at composition. "She's so sweet and silent. I love quiet people, don't you? Talkers intimi –" (he belched expertly, as if he were coughing discreetly) " – intimidate me."

"The thing about Meg," Henry said enthusiastically, "is that she prefers to be quiet. When she wants to she can be quite brilliantly witty. And of course she isn't at all shy." He liked to talk about Meg, and all his other acquisitions. He still retained, or unconsciously assumed, a childlike enthusiasm for something precious. In Meg's case there was very little to possess: her body, and a certain air of never being fully awake, which made him want to conquer her and discover her secret.

"And I love Perkin too," Julian continued happily. "He's so grave and thoughtful. He seems to be writing his life as he goes along, refusing to bring anything to a definite conclusion so that he'll have plenty of material left over for an entertaining sequel." Julian had a weakness for making interesting remarks on which it was impossible to comment. They were only accepted or discarded.

Henry noted the words, to consider before he went to sleep that night. "Ye-es," he said.

"He can also be rather gay," Julian said, trying to keep up the conversation. He liked silences, but it was unusual for Henry to reply in a monosyllable. He had not realised that Henry was only at his best with three or more people. He was inclined to languish when he had only one companion, who would always begin to seem less important, and not worth squandering his humour on.

Julian loved to talk about life because he felt that he needed to justify his own way of living, but he always pretended to be rather self-conscious, in order to show his awareness that he might be considered ingenuous: in this he sometimes overestimated the intelligence of his audience.

"He does the things that most of us would only like to do, jumping in front of a fast car, hoping against hope that it will stop, although I've never actually seen him do it. But he can pretend to live for the moment. I think that's wonderful."

Henry smiled rather cynically.

"I think it's wonderful to burn up the days, burn up your life as if you were going to die tomorrow."

"It must be frustrating to keep waking up to find that you're still alive," Henry said dryly.

Julian was not listening. He had in fact been talking about himself, and not Perkin, whom he had met only once. Apart from that meeting, which would have been embarrassing if it had not been so uncomfortable, he had heard only a few scraps of gossip, laughs behind glasses. Julian was the perfect example of the type of person he had been talking about. Calamity was his goal, and he was so intent on achieving it that he could no longer stand back to see that there was no need to try any harder, it was only a question of time now. At one stage he had tried taking one more drink each day, but after ten days he was violently ill, and realised that he would have to go more slowly if he was to be awake to enjoy his final degradation. He regarded it rather as a perfect consummation.

He smiled blissfully. "I want to seek the most painful pleasures, play, go on playing and beating the drum until you're too tired to sleep. Drinking, dancing, wilfully using up everything that's in the world to use, destroying everything there is to destroy, because if you don't die you have to go on living, and if you live there must be more to experience. If you went on long enough you'd be bound to learn more than any scholar or philosopher or saint." He paused and quickly checked the last phrase for blasphemy, because he was very religious. Reassured, he went on, "I wish I could go on drinking until I came out sober at the other end, but if I have two more drinks after I'm really drunk I pass out or feel sick. But that's the kind of thing I mean."

Henry yawned, and said, as if he were speaking to a child, "Julian, dear boy, I can't believe that there is any virtue in dissipation. I can't think why you gave up your music. If you have this absurd wish to beat everyone else and experience more, then the obvious way is to study music and work until you know more about it than any of your contemporaries."

Julian waved aside the remark. "Playing the piano is interpretative work, the exposition of someone's creation."

"And what is living?" Henry interrupted.

He sighed, and went on, "Writing music is solely a matter of laying down directions which others must follow, which one is incapable of following oneself after a certain point has been reached. But in living you have to go alone, you can never learn from anyone else. Besides, my way is more colourful and exciting."

"And pointless. When you die you'll go out like a flame. A few years from now no-one will know you ever existed."

"That's what I want, Henry."

The doorbell rang just as Henry was going to make a reply. He went out to answer it.

Julian stretched, and emptied his glass because he had nothing else to do. Then he relaxed, staring round the comfortably shabby room, which was decorated mostly with books and paintings by Henry's friends. He heard Perkin's voice in the hall, and closed his eyes for a moment, before having to go on with the exhausting work of fairly polite social intercourse. He was twenty-three years old, and looked younger, although his skin was beginning to sag and he had a double chin. Anyone meeting him for the first time was favourably impressed. He looked clean and healthy. His fair hair was long and expensively cut, his skin was clear and his teeth were good. His rather small head was perhaps inclined to droop, but his thin mouth was firm and his nose small and straight, although the flesh at the sides was beginning to puff outwards. He wanted to keep his appearance as long as possible. He pampered his body with massage, lotions and beautifully cut clothes. He spent at least two hours around noon each day bathing, brushing his hair and shaping his nails. He ate good food in moderation, never ate potatoes or sweets, and drank almost as much water as anything else.

His eyes betrayed him. They were quite clear and during the daytime he remembered to keep them wide open, but after seven in the evening they narrowed into slits, and his skin grew slightly yellow. It usually looked as if it were due to an effect of lighting, but all his work would in the end be quite useless. He could already congratulate himself on his appearance, rather than accept it merely as a gift of youth and birth.

No-one knew very much about Julian De-la-Noy. It was said that he came from a good family and that his parents were now dead. At the age of fifteen he had suddenly appeared on the concert platforms of the world, and before he was seventeen he had made two successful tours. He had good, if patronising, notices, and the public loved the slight, very solemn boy with the shy air, who seemed to have already dedicated his life to music. It was doubtful, talented as he was, if he could have achieved any success without influential backing. His managers remained in the background, and publicity was kept to a minimum. At the age of eighteen Julian suddenly decided to retire, and disappeared for three years. He then returned to artistic-literary society, and made many friends in a short time. He was not a brilliant talker, but he was good-looking, amiable, amusing and mysterious. He still had the air of a prodigy: he expected people to talk about him, rather than to him, and he saw no reason to appear less interested in himself than he really was. He gave people a good excuse to moralise or condone his behaviour and that of people like him. He seemed to be rich. Each year he traded in his car for a new one, and he lived in a luxury block of flats in Knightsbridge. He avoided the subject of money, and would not say if he had inherited or earned his money, or how much he possessed.

His accent did not betray his origin. It was a compromise. Often he deliberately chose the trite word, or one that was common but inaccurate or inadequate. Although he had not played the piano for years he occasionally wrote slight but charming lyrics, kept a journal, and was inspired by *Huis Clos* to begin a play for the Arts Theatre. The theme, he said, precluded completion. In the afternoons he took exercise for an hour or so by playing tennis or visiting bookshops in the Charing Cross Road. During these periods his mind was a complete blank. It was enough to feel his body moving, apparently divorced from his brain, and anyhow he had little to think about.

Perkin preceded Henry into the room, wearing his most immaculate suit, and a well-washed smile. That afternoon he had been to see a new musical film and felt wonderfully happy through identifying himself with the hero, who was an optimistically rich young man who got Kim Novak in the end. He was a film-addict, capable of enjoying the worst and glossiest films if they were expensively made with nice music and a sad ending.

He beamed at Julian and Julian beamed back.

"Julian! It's lovely to see you again. I didn't get your address at that party or I'd have rung you."

Julian patted the empty part of the sofa on which he was now sitting. "I know. By the time we were introduced I couldn't remember my address."

Perkin guessed immediately that he would be pleased if he referred to the incident after which the other boy had altogether faded out of the party.

"The last glimpse I got was when you were sitting on the lavatory floor in what looked like a *most* advanced state of the D.T.s."

They doubled up with laughter. Henry's mouth curled with distaste.

"What will you have to drink, Perkin? Our friend seems to have finished the gin but I can get another bottle."

"Anything at all, Henry. I've become very abstemious. I've simply lost the desire to drink."

"Perkin! Why?" Julian said, frowning and slurring the words to show his disapproval.

"I don't know," he replied, taking the martini which Henry handed to him. "Of course I don't mind getting drunk if you really want me to."

"I do," Julian said vehemently, leaning across until his face was a few inches from Perkin's. "Do you know, there's hardly anyone left to get drunk *with*. Everyone's got a job or a boy friend or is getting married. It's disgusting."

Perkin grinned. "I know exactly what you mean. People have grown so serious. I know it's something to do with the increased circulation of *The Times*. Those advertisements are even affecting me. I have to fight with myself not to buy the damned paper. But I simply refuse to be well informed about politics or the bank rate, or the great naval battle that was fought just sixteen years ago today. It wouldn't be so bad if they weren't so smug about it, but the *Mirror* often expresses exactly the same sentiments but with illustrations and in a more readable form. And I wouldn't miss my horoscope or Donald Zee for the world."

Julian nodded vigorously but rather unsteadily and for the moment could think of nothing to say.

"Have a cigarette."

Henry had been waiting for an opportunity to speak, and now attacked his guests in a tone which he would never have used to his contemporaries. "I don't understand," he began angrily, although still managing to smile. "You discard, without consideration, the things which are beginning to raise the level of existence in the world today. Young people with less talent and intelligence are doing their best to read and understand and help. These things mean that a writer's market will be widened —"

"Not on your nelly, chum," Perkin interrupted; he could be very vulgar. "They'll borrow your books from the public library and buy Van Gogh reproductions to hang on the walls of their bed-sitting-rooms in Tooting Bec just like they've done for the last twenty years."

" – a writer's market will be widened," Henry repeated ominously, "music and painting will begin to be appreciated as they should be – even if it is only Van Gogh – and if they do live in Tooting Bec because they can't afford anywhere better, at least they'll deplore the climate."

Julian looked faintly puzzled.

"Oh really, Henry," Perkin protested. "Do you think it's a good thing that people who should be dancing somewhere stay in their rooms instead to read *The New Statesman* and gape at *The Yellow Chair*? They don't know what it's all about and they never will. God, how I hate dishonesty. Why shouldn't they do what their parents did, laugh hysterically when they see an Epstein in Brighton and hardly ever be dissatisfied because they don't know what they're missing."

He wiped his face and sat back exhausted, then changed his mind and began again.

"No doubt you think I'm very conceited and superior, but at least I do understand my own limitations. I was born lazy and I'm obtuse, but I do respect work, even though I hate it. The trouble with our generation, of which Julian and I are supposed to be the worst examples, is that it's cocksure but ignorant all the same. It knows a little, a very very little, and begins to criticise, or worse still, a kind of inverted snobbery, refuses to criticise. It won't read your books seriously, although it will know all about you if you had two divorces, and it'll go to the Royal Court if William Hickey says the play is shocking. I want to be vulgar or truly serious but something in between is ridiculous and absurd."

There was a moment's silence while he waited nervously and rather aggressively for dissension. Julian nodded in agreement and Henry smiled.

"At last," he said mildly, "you've awakened from your heavy sleep. I thought it would never happen. You're right, of course. Ninety-five per cent of the human race is too stupid or oppressed to understand, and maybe four-fifths of the remainder is committed to something else, but if one reader in a hundred sees a review in *The Observer* and wants to know more, it'll be worthwhile."

"But people don't have a revelation like that. That kind of awakening only comes to philistines. They're attracted by the idea and the prestige. Artists and the people who will appreciate their work are born, and although they have a lot to learn they recognise the quality of difference in themselves almost as soon as they're born."

"I think the two most despicable characteristics are self-pity and lack of enthusiasm."

"There's nothing to be enthusiastic about," Julian muttered, and lay back with closed eyes.

"Lots of people have good reasons for self-pity," Perkin said, "and that's one good reason for lack of enthusiasm. Nothing changes. There's a balance and that's the way it will always be."

"Why do you always look for the worst instead of hoping for the best?" Henry asked irritably. "Why this debility?" The interrogation was an indication of his sincere interest. Usually he preferred to know as little as possible about his friends' motives, for he found it easier to invent the greater part of a character. When he knew a good deal about someone, their instincts and attitudes, he discovered that he really knew very little, and was confounded.

Julian made some vague gestures. His vocabulary was inade-

quate to express the subtle difference which he believed existed
between a passion for disaster and merely suicidal tendencies. He
took the refilled glass gratefully and raised it to his lips. This action
was an affirmation of his belief. He leaned towards Perkin.

"Come on then, tell Henry why you're débile."

Perkin shrugged.

Julian's eyes filled with sentimental tears. "I know a little rhyme.
Do you want to hear it, Henry?"

He nodded coldly, and Julian stood up and advanced to the
middle of the floor and raised his glass to the light. He tipped it
slightly and spilled a little of the martini. It ran down the sides
of the glass and hung on to the bottom. Julian recited, in ringing
tones, lines he had been taught when he was a child, incapable of
grasping their meaning.

> *"My candle burns at both its ends,*
> *It will not last the night,*
> *But ah! my foes, And oh! my friends,*
> *It gives a lovely light."*

There was an uncomfortable silence. Henry turned away in
embarrassment, which had overcome his clinical detachment, and
Perkin went on staring grimly at the floor. His mind was working
furiously, darting backwards and forwards: he wondered how he
appeared to Henry, and if he were wholly in sympathy with Julian,
and at the same time felt disdainful, and at the same time wondered what his thoughts really were. It was impossible to decide.

He heard a small tinkle of glass collapsing, followed by a low
moaning sound and a gasp. He looked up. Julian was swaying
towards the floor, holding his stomach with both hands. His drink
lay in a pool at his feet. His teeth were bared, clamped tightly over
his tongue. Huge tears were rolling down his cheeks. He gasped
for breath, as if it had all been squeezed from his body. Before
Henry or Perkin could move to hold him his knees crumpled and
he fell to the ground. He cried as if he were grieving bitterly or
enduring heavy pain. Henry rushed over and knelt beside him.

"What is it, Julian?"

He shook his head desperately. "I just want to lie alone." He buried his face in the carpet and his shoulders heaved with each deep sob. Henry waved his hands uselessly, unable to act. Perkin stared in horror, and still watching reached out and fumbled for a cigarette. He recognised Julian's behaviour at the party, but he had been too drunk to realise its nature, and watched as if it were just another irregular but unremarkable incident during the entertainment.

At last the crying ceased, and as Perkin lit the cigarette with shaking fingers, Julian turned over on his back and lay motionless. Henry bent over him, his face twisted in pity. Julian wiped the water from his eyes and reached out for the cigarette which Perkin was smoking. He hesitated, then leaned down and placed it between his lips. For a moment he watched the faint drag at the paper around the end, which crumbled and fell away in ash as the smoke began to rise. Julian's face was now calm. His wet eyelids were closed, and he seemed to be concentrating only on the cigarette. He lay flat, as if he had been placed on a stretcher. Perkin stood up again, and he glanced into the large mirror which hung above one of the bookcases, then looked quickly back. A girl was standing by the door, her eyes meeting his in the mirror.

In the moment before he turned round and faced her with a friendly but completely polite questioning look, he thought he recognised her, although he had never met her and she was not the sort of person whom one can visualise clearly when absent. She was an entity, carrying everything she possessed with her, and giving nothing of her aura of experience, character or feelings to the people she met. She was wearing a grey sweater, a narrow check skirt, rather heavy stockings and flat shoes. The thin gold band on her arm was a watch with the face turned inwards to the wrist. She was holding a tipped American cigarette on which ash was gathering perilously. Her small face was almost insignificant in its plainness, for although each feature was fine, it was almost too perfect for photogenic beauty. The total effect was one of flatness, and her pale hair, long and brushed slightly forward, framed her face and seemed to push it into the background. She looked completely at ease, perfectly mobile and too lithe for feminine grace in movement. Her body was small and thin, so that as soon as Perkin saw her he felt large and clumsy. But surely she could teach him tenderness. The sense of fragility was dissipated almost immediately. The way she carried herself, watched with her long eyes, without ever moving her lips, suggested not indifference but great competence in dealing with life, so that it must inevitably seem to her to be without colour. She looked as if she had a secret, something small, of no importance, but sufficient for confidence in herself and calm in any situation. There was nothing enigmatic about her, she was too complete. He felt that he could ask her a thousand questions and still know little about her. She had a past which was either too intense to recall without distress or too trivial to concern her now. She looked as if she committed herself to each moment, and awareness gave depth to her eyes and face, yet these things also made her formidable, for she must cast off every- thing as soon as it was past, or she could not go on being as deeply involved in the present.

Perkin turned and she smiled, then glanced down at Julian and across at Henry, her expression never wavering. Julian raised him- self on his elbows, shook his head and laughed.

"Henry," he said clearly but uncomfortably, "I promise never to get drunk in your house again. This sort of thing amuses me at three o'clock in the morning but I know it's rather unappetising before dinner."

Henry smiled and helped him to his feet, and Perkin led him to the sofa.

"I feel perfectly sober," Julian protested. He looked less drunk than earlier in the evening, except for slightly flushed cheeks. He pushed his glass away and beamed.

The girl kissed him lightly on the forehead. "You're very naughty, Julian. I don't know why I'm so devoted to you." She con- tinued to lean over him, as if waiting for someone else to move. Perkin watched uneasily; he felt rather shocked by the words, which did not seem to suit her. She might have been reciting some- one else's dialogue.

"I'm so sorry," Henry said. "Perkin, this is Meg Santry, my fiancée."

Perkin was hardly listening, but he held out his hand and smiled. Meg looked more assured than ever.

"Henry gave me your stories to read. I liked them very much."

Perkin frowned, then his face cleared. His senses had been dulled, he had not realised what Henry was saying. So she was engaged to him.

"At first I was puzzled by your accent. You're American, aren't you?"

She nodded, and sat down beside Julian, so that he was forced to sit with Henry on the other side of the room.

"It's clever of you to guess so quickly," she went on calmly. "Henry says my accent is getting stranger and stranger, because I'm picking up all his mannerisms and words, but keeping my own drawl."

Henry said, "Yesterday Meg went into a coffee bar and ordered lemonade. The waitress brought her ham-and-eggs." He laughed loudly, to cover the too apparent silence caused by Julian's fixed smile and Perkin's annoyance at the older man's interruption.

"Which part of America do you come from?" he asked.

"I was born in Denver."

"Texas?"

"Colorado." She only laughed when he began to laugh. "Before I came to London I spent most of my life in New York," she explained, as if it were very important that he should know the truth about her. "I'm training to be a concert pianist."

"How wonderful. Did you think you'd have better teachers in London?"

She nodded, crushed out her cigarette and put another in her mouth, lighting it before anyone could move to do it for her. "I'm studying with a private teacher. He was a friend of my professor at college."

"I've never met anyone who worked as hard as Meg," Julian said. "Her ambition is quite frightening."

She closed her eyes for a moment, dismissing him. "I guess – I suppose it's just a habit like any other."

"She works five, sometimes six or seven hours a day – every day, including Sundays. The rest of the time she studies theory or listens to records. I never used to practise more than four hours a day."

"Do you know very much about music?" she asked Perkin.

"Very little. I go to a concert occasionally, that's all."

"Well, most pianists know absolutely nothing about composition. They never get any further than popular biographies of their favourite composer. I just don't want to study half a subject."

Perkin sighed, as he always sighed when he met someone who seemed to have all the qualities necessary for social success, yet was possessed by an idea. He envied her and knew too well that the discipline and solitary experience gave her the character which he found so attractive. It is impossible to love the whole person as soon as we meet them. We fall in love with some gesture or attitude, and afterwards our love makes us accept the rest.

"Have you always worked so hard?"

"No, I only began four years ago, although I'd taken the usual lessons when I was a child. I studied in New York for three years, then came to London."

"What made you begin again?"

No shadow crossed her clear face. She replied immediately, "My parents dismissed the idea when I suggested it, and when I left college I didn't have this interest that I have now. I was married, you see. My husband was an architect and I began practising again during the day when he was working. I worked harder and harder, almost without realising it, and finally I was so excited and restless that I had to begin serious study." She spoke as if she were relating the story of a past discarded so completely that she had been forced to re-learn it in order to oblige her audience. Perkin was not disturbed by the casual reference to a husband, whom he supposed she had divorced. Her whole past concerned him deeply, but only because it must have affected her in some way, made her what she was. The instruments which had shaped her were unimportant. He realised that he had fallen in love with her, and almost laughed aloud. Meg was still talking, but as long as he was certain of her presence he could happily wonder. He had always believed that love was the most desirable thing in the world, but he had been too aware of Freudian motivations and too analytical in examining the reasons why people loved – because they complemented each other in a way which neither would admit, and often because they were impatiently lonely. Clinical experiments, erotic wayward-ness and the company of women as empty as himself had brought contempt and the habit of sneering at any display of emotional honesty; afterwards he would feel acute remorse and misery, but tell himself that it didn't matter as long as only a few people knew about him. How was he to fall in love when he could give an accu-rate reason for every feeling which it encompassed, and could predict from the beginning the way the affair would end?

But Meg was here, Meg was real and of course this was infatu-ation. How could it be love? Yet he loved her, wondered how she would look when she was tired or discouraged. He would love her even more if she needed him. He shook aside these thoughts for the first time in years, and succumbed to the delicious pleasure of watching her and listening to her talk. For all her clarity she had warmth, although possibly it was only reflected from himself.

"My husband was killed soon afterwards, and of course I turned to music even more." Although she suggested appropriate distress, it seemed that it had now passed, and she was living in the present. "That's why I came to England, to begin again."

Henry reached out and pressed her hand gently. "We are the most fortunate couple," he said, turning to Julian and Perkin. "We both have work to do in the daytime, so that neither of us is frustrated because we can't be together. One of the reasons why I never married before was that I thought my wife would wander in and out of my study all day long, trying to make herself useful and driving me mad."

Meg laughed. "What will you do when I'm launched and have lots of world tours?"

"By that time," Henry smiled, "I'll have made enough money to give up writing and go with you."

Perkin began to twirl his glass, suddenly dejected. He felt shut out, barred from knowing the intimacy which must exist between Meg and Henry. There was no reason to suppose that they were not happy together. They were engaged to be married, presumably they were in love. He glanced at her, and she was smiling at Henry.

For once in my life I will act, he thought. I want Meg, and I'll do anything to get her. I'm tired of being cold, I'm not dead or empty, I'll prove it, I'm in love. If I don't try now I'll never try again.

The thought of Meg and Henry together revolted him. It was impossible. How could she possibly consider marrying him? For once Perkin could not find an answer. But he was young, he had something which Henry would never have again. It is futile to say that each age has its compensations. When we are young we can if we wish look forward to old age, but when we are old everything is finished. The simple magic of being young had always worked for him: it had been his excuse, and all the enchantment he had ever known stemmed from it. It must work now.

What has Henry Enfield that Julian and I haven't got? Meg Santry, echoed Henry's mocking voice.

He held the glass more tightly. I won't be ineffectual or apathetic any longer. I'll fight for Meg in every way I can. He looked up to see Henry smiling at him.

"You've been dreaming, Perkin. I just said that if you'd finished your drink we'd go to dinner."

"Of course. I'm sorry." He did his best to look amiable, and catching sight of himself in the mirror as he stood up, saw that he had succeeded almost too well.

"We're going to one of those little restaurants that Hampstead does less well than Chelsea. The food is just as good, but the place is terrible." He took Perkin's arm as they left the house, Meg and Julian following. The rain that had never ceased that day now dripped from the lime tree in the garden on to their heads. A drop settled on Julian's nose and he looked up and stopped for a moment. Meg shivered and moved close to him. He put his arms around her, still looking up at the sky. The moon was floating between two cloudbanks, half-hidden between branches and returning mist. He had now regained all his composure and felt oddly peaceful. He looked down at Meg's face, pale and damp in the moonlight. He ran his finger up and down her back.

"It's just as well we understand each other, and that Henry understands us both so well. Anyone else would think this rather unusual."

"Oh, Julian," she said quietly, "why must you destroy yourself? You're the only friend I have apart from Henry. Isn't it a pity that you aren't my brother?"

"Brothers and sisters don't cling together for a little comfort and consolation."

"Does Perkin like me?"

"I don't know. I know hardly anything about him. I'll ask him if you want me to."

"Don't be silly. I'm tired, Julian. I hate and envy you for not working. I sincerely hope that you regret it one day."

He kissed her hair. "So do I, darling. Regret would be the supreme achievement of my life. I find it impossible."

"You're impossible, Julian. Come and see me tomorrow, and listen to me play. At least it will keep you away from the bottles in your flat. You must find some older woman who understands and will beat you if you don't behave. It isn't too late to reform."

"It is, you know. You see things in black and white: grief, anger, love, hate. What's wrong with me is a little more subtle, and more common these days. I don't know any word for it. I suppose it's a kind of violent melancholy."

Her eyes filled with tears.

"Please don't cry, darling. You'll always be happy, won't you? Promise."

She tried to blink away the tears but in the end had to wipe her eyes. She turned away, so that he could not see her face.

"I promise, Julian," she said. "I'll always be happy."

The words were enough to make him feel content for a while.

"Come along," Henry called from the car. "It's beginning to rain again; and besides, we want to know what you've been doing."

The rain began to fall in large, icy drops. They shouted and raced for the car. Perkin was holding the door open. They fell over each other getting in.

Henry watched them in the mirror as he started up.

"I'm jealous, Meg. I want a full explanation or I won't marry you."

She laid an icy hand on his neck, and in a moment leaned forward and began to kiss him furiously. The car swerved.

"Stop it at once," he shouted. "We'll be arrested."

"I don't care," she cried. "I'm not driving. You'll be charged with being drunk and disorderly and we shall all swear that you drank two bottles of gin this evening. Won't we, Perkin?"

He nodded without turning. He had been thinking that he was a brat. This was not a discovery. He had known it for at least ten years. While they were waiting in the car Henry had talked to him, easily and sincerely, of the future he had planned with Meg. It would add an extra dimension to his life, he said. She was certain to be successful. Another two years and she would be ready for her debut, and when the time came he would be able to help her with backers and contacts, for he knew quite a number of musicians and composers who would advise him. He didn't mean it when he said that he would stop writing, but at least he would get away from his bitchy existence. He no longer needed people, in fact there were times when he hated them. But Meg was a darling, didn't he agree? Perkin had nodded.

"I'm very lucky," Henry went on, "I sometimes forget that. The trouble is, there's the constant pushing forward, month by month. There's very little time to think of anything else. But now that I'm established, I can begin to live like I've never lived before." He lit a cigarette. "If you ever begin to write seriously, you must be serious, avoid all the publicity that's so dangerous these days. There's a lot to be said for ivory towers."

Perkin had stirred uncomfortably. He hated advice and also felt guilty. He wished Meg and Julian would hurry. Besides, what were they doing? Henry's display of warm-hearted kindness annoyed him and only made him more obstinately determined to get what he wanted, what he must have. He knew that Henry would have shown no compunction had positions been reversed.

He decided that it was really quite fair. These kind of manoeuvres took place every day, the only thing was that other people did not deliberately set out to take someone else's place, or rather, refused to admit it. He was puzzled. He couldn't help wondering why they loved each other. It was obvious why Henry was attracted to her. She was pretty, talented and intelligent. But he was one of those people who reach only a certain degree of intimacy in their relationships. It is easier for them to find a lover and convince themselves that they are in love. It is also easier for them to discard their lover when circumstances grow uncomfortable. He was sure that Henry could be just as happy with another girl.

What did Henry give Meg that made her want to marry him? It could be no great passion. Comfort perhaps, and a stable position in a certain section of society. Nothing is more pleasing to an artist who is inclined to shut himself away and work exceedingly hard than to know that he is dedicating his time by choice rather than because he has nothing else to do. Meg would always be certain of entertainment when she needed it. Domesticity and the supposed maturity of an older person on whom she could rely, coupled with the knowledge that soon, as he grew older, he would come to depend on her more and more. She must want peace, but in youth that is only a compensation, not an ideal way of life.

He turned to offer her a cigarette, and she leaned over the lighter with an air of complicity, because she felt gay and had succeeded in teasing Henry. A long strand of her hair fell away and brushed against his hand. Her skin was unpowdered and fine. The quick light revealed the pulled, sallow skin around her eyes. She was not entirely free of the past, then. He wanted to lean forward and kiss her gently, to show that he could give her all his tenderness and affection. She looked into his eyes for a moment, and smiled as if she wanted to know what he was thinking: I could love you in the sweetest way, the way of first love, warmth without spiritual decay. Even as the words occurred to him he knew that they were a lie. He would never be able to stop questioning himself, but this was the nearest he would ever get to happiness. Meg seemed to beckon him, then shied away. Anyone watching them might have said that they were lovers, but he knew that the slight contact could mean nothing. They were young, intelligent and unusually self-conscious: between such people moments of intimacy are bound to occur, for they are honest enough to admit that they will not always want to be faithful to one person.

Julian watched them uneasily and then exultantly. He felt triumphant whenever he sensed that something was about to change, whenever there was a chance of movement. Perkin faced round again, and at the same moment heavier rain began to slash the quiet roads and burst against the windscreen. Henry pulled out of a side road and into the street. The lights, beaten into streaks, showed mass movement. Lights flashed on and off, men and women scurried across the street, hesitated in front of cars and fell back or dashed into doorways. The street was empty again and the rain seemed to beat more steadily.

Henry pulled up outside the restaurant and they ran into the doorway. He entered first, with Meg beside him, and glanced quickly round the room. People were watching him eagerly. He smiled contentedly and told Perkin to sit opposite Meg.

"But in Greenwich Village rents really are cheap, some of them."

Perkin nodded. "You have to pay a hell of a price to be Bohemian in London. You need space, and that's the most expensive commodity."

They were quiet, lost for anything more to say, but very much wanting to talk.

" . . . *sentimental*, Julian, dear boy. Stark dialogue helps to disguise it, but in films . . ."

"Who took responsibility for calling you Perkin?" Meg asked.

"My father, the most wonderful man I know. He's completely ineffectual, I've never listened to anything he told me, but the knowledge that he's there is a consolation. I think he wanted me to be unusual, but he gave me a choice all the same. I was called Peter when I was a child at school, and when I was sixteen I decided to revert to my real name. Tom was delighted."

Meg smiled. "It's hard to believe that you're Irish."

"Do you expect a brass neck and lots of charming solecisms? A good deal of Ireland is hideously affected and most of the remainder is more primitive than you could ever realise without knowing the people well, but as far as I remember it isn't as bad as Barry Fitzgerald would have you believe. I *hate* that man."

"Did you try hard to lose your accent?"

"I was born beside a bog but not in it." He pushed aside the coffee cup and casually held out the cigarette packet, as if they had been smoking from the same packet for years. She shook her head. "I won't smoke any more. I always stop when I really begin to want them."

"How clever of you. Temperance is something I've always avoided. Self-discipline must be very dull."

She raised her eyebrows, and he wondered if he had been impertinent.

"It's hard work," she said and smiled. "I used to live in excess of all kinds. Incidentally, too much self-discipline is an excess. But it was – peaceful to stop wanting so badly so much that was worthless."

Now she will tell me *why*.

He said, "You like to have a pattern in your life, some meaning? For me all the charm lies in unreason, because I do too much reasoning, or think reasonably then act deviously."

"I try to be sensible, for many reasons."

Again Henry's voice cut through the silence. " . . . try to be interesting – either drunkenness, which is merely boring, or a vacuous I'm-in-pain stare, which is supposed to be intellectual, and only . . ." Julian was flipping his lighter.

"You don't have something to hide and therefore do your best to look enigmatic?"

She smiled. "No, Perkin, I don't believe I ever act, unless my whole life is an act."

"You're right not to tell me any more. I liked you because I couldn't understand you. I still can't."

She looked annoyed. "The truth is that there's probably nothing more than you see." Her eyes searched his face anxiously.

"It hardly matters. People are often so disappointing. It's like the forty-nine basic plots in fiction, though there are rather fewer types of people."

She brushed aside the remark as if she had not been listening. "Isn't it strange that we should be talking this way? What are we talking about?"

"We're very quiet," Perkin said. Some relationship had certainly been established during the last hour, but he could not say what it was.

Abruptly, Meg said, "I will have another cigarette. I hope Henry hasn't been counting, he wanted me to stop smoking." She made the remark defiantly, to challenge the mood he had created, for she had not wanted to talk instinctively. She angrily reckoned the pain it would cost her tomorrow, and smiled twistedly. Poor Perkin! He doesn't know what he's got.

"I think we were talking about not caring," he said quickly and anxiously.

"Yes, it's important not to care." Now she sounded bored.

He ran his tongue over his lips. "That only seems a good principle. In fact it leads to more unhappiness than complete commitment to emotion. So I've found, anyway."

"You live it up, don't you?" She wondered about his life and habits.

"Oh yes. For the past five years it's always been a search, for a person of course, not an idea. I gave that up when I was sixteen."

She stirred.

"Ideas are always a compensation." He stared at the ceiling and lisped, "Sex, dearie. That nasty, messy, wough thing." He laughed, suddenly gay. "And kicks, pleasant or cruel." All at once he wanted to ask her about Henry, but he was afraid.

She was laughing. "Go on, Perkin. I'm a game girl. I won't try to contradict you."

And Henry gives her kicks? It might easily be true. Meg, I could give you more. We'd have some wonderful fun, always laughing at ourselves, caring so much while pretending not to care. And it's just a little late. We must be quick.

But he was tongue-tied. The few words which would be enough to tell her would not come. With anyone else it would have been easy, but this was important. He felt that if he could say those words everything would change. He could not even look at her or move his hands or his feet under the table. The sudden silence was dangerous, for Henry and Julian now felt that they must intrude, through politeness, of all things. It was too late. Meg turned away and he felt cold as soon as he was deprived of her. The door of the restaurant opened and damp wind blew into the room and he could hear the winter rain in the streets, smoothing the lives of everyone inside and tearing to shreds the last leaves. It was the first week in December. Time was dead and meaningless until he could walk in the sun again. Other winters had passed quickly but this would never pass if she went away now and he did not see her again. They had not talked about plays or concerts. There had been no excuse to ask to see her alone. He wondered what was going to happen, and Henry glanced at his watch.

Julian said, "Perkin, will you come home with me for a night-cap? Henry has just been telling me that he's driving up to Scotland in the morning, so I expect he wants to go home early tonight."

Henry waved his hands politely, but conveyed that the evening was now at an end so far as he was concerned. They began to put packets and lighters in their pockets, and fumble towards coats. Meg and Perkin did not look at each other. He mumbled something about the food and was silent again.

"At least let me drive you home," Henry said.

"We'll get a taxi," Julian said. Meg was apparently going home with Henry.

They stood in the doorway, waiting for a taxi to come, and hesitating over invitations. Perkin suddenly awoke, to make a last desperate effort.

"I'm staying for a few days with some relatives, because I won't be seeing them at Christmas," Henry was saying.

"Then you must come and see me soon," Perkin said hastily, then remembered that he had better sound respectful. "This was very kind of you, and I'd like to see you soon" – *and bring Meg with you.*

Henry bowed. The taxi came.

Meg kissed Julian on the forehead. "I'll see you tomorrow. Be good, and don't give Perkin too much to drink."

He felt happier as soon as she mentioned his name. She turned to him, and could think of nothing to say. She held out her hand.

"Goodbye." Their eyes met.

"Goodbye." What else was there to say? – It's been lovely meet-ing you – I hope we meet again soon – We didn't say it but we know it, or is it only me?

The little group of four began to split up, Julian running to the taxi and bundling himself inside. Perkin dropped her hand, but watched until she looked away.

"Goodbye, Meg."

Suddenly Henry frowned. Perkin turned up his collar and ran into the street. He was afraid to look back. He smiled at Julian, who gave him a cigarette. The taxi tumbled down the bumpy street. When he looked back Meg and Henry had not yet gone to their car. Perhaps she wasn't going home with him after all. He remembered that he had not asked her where she lived.

CHAPTER IX

H E TURNED to Julian. "Where does Meg live?"
    Julian smiled. He was beginning to feel drunk again. "She has a room in Finchley Road. Baker Street end. Isn't she a lovely girl?"

Perkin nodded.

"I've never met anyone like her," Julian went on. "Henry doesn't know how lucky he is. I'd do anything for her. I'd even marry her but she doesn't care for me that way." Otherwise he would not have said it. He watched Perkin for a moment. "Are you drunk or sad or something? You look gloomy."

"I was thinking."

"Oh. I wish I'd brought my car. We could have driven along the river in the storm."

"I like taxis," Perkin said, "specially for arriving at places, but I wish I had a car too. Tom might give us one, I think. We never asked him. He's given us so much already. I'd like to be really rich without having to depend on him. You're lucky."

"I'm not rich. For all I know my money's run out. I never have anything to do with it."

The taxi passed Hyde Park, and Perkin closed his eyes. He remembered it in summer and only wanted to see it in the sun as he remembered it. Julian took out an emery board and began to file his nails.

"What are you doing at Christmas? Would you like to come to Switzerland?"

Perkin smiled. "Just like that? I've never been abroad at Christmas."

"I'll take you. Can you ski?"

"A little. I can't go. Tom's coming to stay. Aren't you going to see your family or something?"

"I have no family." Julian shrugged. "I hate Christmas. I hate everything it stands for, the insincerity and the embarrassment. When I was fifteen I gave my managers champagne on Christmas Day, then got drunk all by myself. I'm not feeling sorry for myself. It was fun."

Perkin wondered if he were speaking the truth and felt embarrassed.

They ascended by automatic lift to Julian's flat, which was on the top floor of a large building, overlooking a manufactured mews and some quiet streets of Georgian houses which had the usual brightly painted window-boxes and new front doors. Perkin's senses were dulled with too much wine and the tiredness which followed the elation of being with Meg, but he gasped when he saw Julian's living-room.

Julian switched on all the lights for a moment so that he could see the room, then turned them out again except for the light by the bar and beside the large windows.

The decoration scheme was based on black and white: white walls, a black fitted carpet with white rugs, and a pale grey ceiling. The furniture was mahogany, except for the light wood of a low bookcase which stretched along the wall opposite the windows. The curtains were burgundy-coloured velvet. The lampshades and the glass were red.

"Good heavens." Perkin sank on to the couch. "It's fabulous. How on earth did you make it look lived in?"

"Junk," he said, pointing to several piles of old magazines and a battered typewriter. "That kind of thing. That old teddy bear, which is new actually. I bought it in Harrods six weeks ago and rolled it on the street. It all makes the room less angular."

"It could have been ugly, Julian, but it's perfect." He stared at a

huge collage above the bookcase, then pointed to a canvas on the
wall behind the bar. "I've never seen anything like it in my life. It
isn't a painting?"

"I did it myself. It's really only a chart showing how grey can be
made to seem dark or light according to the colour background. I
sponged-on the colour." He handed Perkin a brandy and went over
to the gramophone. Perkin immediately felt happy. His ability to
be made happy by sudden colour or a commonplace tune was an
indication of his precarious emotions. He wanted Meg again, but
felt happy although he did not have her, and there was nothing in
the song to remind him that she existed for him beyond a chance
meeting one night at dinner:

> *"You don't know that I felt good,*
> *When we up and parted.*
> *You don't know that I felt good,*
> *Gladly broken-hearted.*
> *Worrying is through, I sleep at night,*
> *Appetite and health restored.*
> *You don't know how much I'm bored."*

They laughed a little and when they looked out of the window
the rain had stopped. Julian switched on a fire, then opened the
window to let in the cool air. They watched the street lights, and
the bright mist of the West End far over the rooftops.

"Delicious," Julian murmured. "Look up. The sky is invisible.
How I despise people who like the country! What could be more
beautiful than the ugliest London street on a damp winter's night?"

"It all depends," Perkin said, and yawned. "What time is it?"

"Midnight."

"I think I'll go home."

"No!" Julian exclaimed sharply. "Let's go to some club. Would
you like that?"

"I just want to go to sleep. Aren't you tired?"

"I'm never tired. Sleeping pills are no use any more."

Perkin closed his eyes. This was the part of Julian's life that
no-one should ever see. The glitter and the fun were attractive,
but at some point desperation became sickeningly shabby.

"To begin with," he said quietly, "don't have anything more to drink. Relax. You mustn't live on your nerves. Have you ever taken a rest cure?"

"Rest from what? Drinking? Dancing and lying in bed – that's all I ever do. How could I be tired? Will you please just stay here? Talk or listen to music, whatever you like. If I'm left alone I shall tear the house down."

Perkin nodded, and felt cold. He got up and switched on another fire, then closed the window. The night was pretty but he felt chilled. The room looked like a mausoleum. He went over to the bookcase and played at examining the contents. The usual Editions de Minuit, *Intimacy* and Sartre plays, Beckett, wonderful Gollancz first novels by writers who never produced anything else. For just how many people did life end at twenty-five? Afterwards, the fight against oblivion and the constant thinking; the need for love, and the denial of love if it came, because you no longer had any self-confidence. Why bother to fight? Hopeless.

"Can't you ask some girl round tonight, or go out and find someone?"

His voice echoed in the stillness, and Julian's reply came smothered by the darkness and fell dying against Perkin's inability to be surprised: "I've never wanted that kind of thing. I've never been interested in any kind of sex."

Anne lay with her head buried in Simon's neck, and listened to his quiet breathing. She wanted to cry.

"You're very foolish," he whispered, his voice weakened by a certain tenderness which he had not experienced before.

"I love you, Simon, and you love me."

He stroked her hair. "Baby. You want too much." He struggled with his own desire and the need to disillusion her. But he knew that he would win, even after telling her the truth. "I can't love you. I wouldn't be telling you this if I didn't like you very much, but there are two kinds of people, the faithful and those who need something more than the devotion which you say you'll give me. I can give you nothing but a little comfort."

She raised her head and kissed his mouth.

"How warm you are," he murmured. He tried to open her lips but she fell away and laid her head against his cheek.

"You see? You don't want fun, you want peace. Oh, Anne, I'd give it to you if I had it to give. Darling."

"Go on calling me darling, Simon. I feel so lost. I'm not asking for very much."

"Ah, but you've come to the wrong sort of person, that's all. I'll destroy what you have and make you bitter. There's nothing in the world you can do if you love someone who doesn't love you. I can't make myself love you. In the end I'll want to hurt you."

She still did not believe him. "All I want is to love someone who loves me."

"And I happened to come along. You'll meet someone else and it will be better. You mustn't try too hard. You must be patient."

"It's you I want. I love everything about you, your face and hair and clothes."

"I'm not very handsome."

"Your skin is rough and your hair smells of cigarette smoke but it doesn't matter. I love all of you."

He sighed and drew her closer. "It's impossible to make you see that I don't deserve it. I've been no kinder to you than I'd be to anyone else. In the end I'll have to show you the truth, it's no use talking about it, and then you'll be very unhappy."

"It doesn't matter, Simon. Just kiss me. You see, I know you love me."

"How can you know it when it isn't true?"

"Intuition," she whispered.

"You've changed so much. You're still funny and sweet, but this new assurance. Is it because of me? Look at me."

They watched each other, their faces glowing in the firelight. It was the hardest test he could ask her to face. Other girls had looked defiant or turned away, discouraged by indifference or lies, but Anne gazed at him without embarrassment.

"I'm only assured when I'm alone with you. I changed for you, Simon. I suppose you're right when you say you're bad for me. It doesn't matter. I want you."

Hopelessly, he took her in his arms and she cried softly when he began to hurt her mouth.

"There won't be any others, Simon? I'd die if there were."

"You wouldn't die. No girl kills herself for love these days. You'd be sorry, but I can't help it. I want you to know the truth."

"You won't take responsibility for me, that's what you mean. You won't make any effort to stop hurting me."

"I can't, Anne. But you're here now with me. That's the important thing. Don't think about the future."

"I must."

He placed his finger on her lips. "Hush. I've changed you already and I'm sorry. You're very thin."

"Not too thin."

"Hush. Don't fight me."

She screamed when he entered her. He quickly covered her mouth with his lips and tongue, grunting meaningless words formed with his teeth: "All the others – I didn't – you'll never—" He did not know what he was saying. He held her as she squirmed away, but pain exhausted her. She sobbed in terror, trapped, then lay still and let him move her body. Certain of her he was able to relax a little.

"Anne, can you hear me, are you listening?" The words crumbled away in his mouth. She caught her breath, he kissed her and then at last she stretched up to him in passion.

In a dying fall, "Simon – Simon – Simon."

He wiped her face and body with a towel and went over to the bed to turn back the sheets. She was suddenly cold, deprived of him, and she cried with pleasure when he returned. He carried her to the bed and they lay together for a moment. Anne smiled.

"Talk to me, Simon."

He hesitated, then turned away from her. She lay shocked, and put her hand timidly on his stomach. He shivered, and a few moments later was asleep. She fell asleep soon afterwards, and it was fortunate that she did. There would be many nights when she lay awake, until she learned to accept selfishness, take what was given her and be grateful for it.

Julian grinned. "I'm not impotent or anything. I've been analysed, examined, purged. You see, something holds me back, I can't
give, yet I'm certainly not narcissistic, I hate myself. I like to touch
people and lie beside them. I mean I've taken women to bed but
I simply wasn't interested. There was a doctor who said that one
day it might come all right. I know all the reasons why, or I once
knew them and have forgotten. Precocity results in extraordinary
sexual activity – at that age you're not enough aware to counteract
it – or else too much energy is expended and sex means nothing.
One warm day I saw a boy and a girl lying on the grass kissing, and
because I don't like to be without anything I wondered why there
was a large blank in my life. I was once told that I was masochistic.
I want to hurt myself. There's something hard and tight inside me
that squirms every time I'm left alone or humiliated. Happiness
would be a release. I wouldn't know what to do any more."

"In fact, all it amounts to is a feeling of, say, detachment on your
part?" Perkin got up from the floor to put some soda in his drink.
"I suppose there are worse ways of living. There must be so many
people who want so much love and can't have it because they're
afraid."

Julian wanted sympathy. His mouth twitched and he looked out
of the window, opening his eyes wider so that they would not fill
with water. "That's the way it is," he said bitterly.

Perkin sat down beside him. "It isn't as if you were impotent or
something."

"To all intents and purposes I am, or might as well be. I'm
embarrassing you. I shouldn't have told you." His voice was hos-
tile. He felt like blaming Perkin, in whom he had confided.

Perkin smiled bleakly. "I'm not embarrassed. One fine day,
when you're thinking about something else, it will suddenly go
away. How many people have you told?"

"Not many." He lied; he always told anybody who could out-
drink him. "You can go home now, if you wish. I'll be all right."

"You're very very drunk, Julian. If I don't go we'll begin to
fight."

Julian did not reply.

"Goodbye. Go to bed and you'll feel better in the morning. I'll call you soon." He watched Julian's back for a moment, then left quietly. He put on his coat as he went down in the lift. Winter's only consolation was that he could wear nice coats. He felt good as soon as he stepped out into the cold air, and decided to walk at least part of the way along Sloane Street. He watched eagerly for signs of life behind drawn curtains, and amused himself by imagining what might be going on in the houses. He giggled when it occurred to him that his imagination was probably not extravagant enough to be accurate.

Simon was not at home, and the place felt empty without him. He must have gone out early: the ashtrays were empty and all the glasses had been washed and stacked. He was lucky to live with someone. He could never have made a room reflect his personality, for he was as uncertain as quicksilver. He undressed, knew that he should brush his teeth and hair and put his clothes away neatly, but he got into the cold bed and lay waiting until he could see patterns of light on the ceiling.

Meg was going to bed now in her room in Finchley Road. She would be thinking of him, there was no reason to doubt it. As the bed grew warmer he was able to take more comfort from the thought of Meg, her nearness this evening, the love that he was going to give her. He smiled sentimentally. Sentimentality was the only permanent factor in his whole life.

Simon must be with Anne; Angel was with her boy friend; Jonathan would be with George (Perkin frowned here – he did not know if he was sorry or glad); Julian would change, there was no doubt about it; Henry would make a great deal of money from his novels, and find a new girl friend; and he would have Meg. And even if it didn't last he would have fun, something to remember. Everything would be all right! This optimism was something new. He fell asleep laughing to himself.

"Simon is my lover."

She savoured the words when she awoke. Her body and face were warm with his warmth. Other mornings in the past she had buried herself under the blankets, now she eased them from her shoulders. This had been the big step, the incident which had terrified her, but now it seemed unimportant in itself, and wonderful because it gave these small things: warmth, dependence, comfort. She felt vaguely puzzled and worried because in a few hours, with comparative ease, she had shed her virginity and it had meant a great deal to her. She had been taught the Protestant conception of sin, and since no-one had told her of the existence of passion she had believed that intercourse was an abnormality. But her body told her not to think.

Simon's face was very pale when she leaned over him. His open lips were dry and cracked and he was snoring jerkily. The soiled towel was beside his head on the pillow. She pushed it on to the floor without distaste, then suddenly, frantically, put her hands to her face. She wondered if she should get up and comb her hair and put on some lipstick, but felt too content to move away from him. She touched and watched his body shamelessly, and hoped that he would wake up. He looked too self-sufficient when he was asleep. She would never have believed that lovers do not always sleep in each other's arms. She stretched beside him and began to kiss his rather thin shoulder. He stopped snoring, sighed, and lay on his back.

"Anne?"

She kissed his uncomfortable mouth, and he opened his eyes. She wriggled on to his body, and he looked at her with amusement.

"I love my girl to kiss me first thing in the morning. How did you sleep?"

She rubbed her eyes, then began to rub Simon's. She gazed at his face with fascination.

"Why are you smiling? Do I look dreadful? I was going to get up and put on some make-up but it was too warm here."

He burst into laughter. "Nothing could be more disconcerting than to wake up and see a fresh face staring at me. You'd have frightened me away from you for ever. Anyhow, you look sweet."

"So do you."

"I do not. I'm twenty-seven, and look an old thirty, or would if I didn't dress so young. Soon I shall even be able to do without sex."

She kissed him again. "Not while I'm around."

"You flatter yourself." But he held her tight against him. "This is what you wanted, darling."

Anne nodded. "I didn't know."

"But I knew, although I didn't know how much."

She muttered something indistinguishable, then threw her head back, smothered by his kisses.

"I like it better in the morning, Simon. I thought you'd forgotten me last night."

"I'll always hate you for half an hour after I've made love to you. I'm selfish." He was staring at the ceiling, and thinking of other ceilings, other windows, some curtained, some with blinds raised to let in the morning light, fires, dying cinders, electric fires that had been switched off, gas fires that had run out. Some mornings were good, and in a limited way a few simple things could vary pleasantly through a whole lifetime.

"What shall I do with you, Anne?"

"Love me and stop laughing."

"Well, what does that mean? Be kind, tolerant, and understanding. I shall always be selfish. Unselfishness is a bad thing. It leads to discomfort, boredom, weariness. Don't expect me to be unselfish."

"Love means more than that."

"You couldn't say how much more."

"Oh yes. It would mean being unable to do without me."

He drew away coldly. "You don't know what you're saying. I could get up now, and although I might want to take you to bed again, I could do without you. That isn't something which will come to me again. And you're the same. Tonight you could lie in bed with someone else and enjoy it just as much."

"I couldn't," she protested. "I'm not some little tramp."

He stroked her face. "You must forget this morality. What's the difference?"

"Love."

He shook his head. "What is love?"

"I don't know. Do I have to define it?"

"If there were a difference you'd be able to."

"No!" she shouted.

He felt weary now, and wanted to be alone. "I'm bad for you, darling. Keep your illusions, I'd love you to stay innocent. I envy you. I envy you your ability to be hurt, your morality, and all your inhibitions."

She smiled. "I wish I could be like you. I'd have a new lover each week, drive men mad by not caring."

"Don't envy me." He hesitated. "What I'm saying to you now is nearer the truth than anything I say in the daytime. Once you begin to look inward you can't change. You should be grateful that you're still whole. Perkin and I, and people like us, are cripples. You know why I'm selfish? You only think I'm good because you have no experience. Anne, love, I make love to myself and always will."

"But you're what I want," she said desperately. "I don't want you to tell me all this."

"I must. Only cynics or virgins are untruthful in bed. Taking a girl to bed is the best way to find out the truth about oneself."

She nodded. "Apparently." She slipped her hands behind his thighs. "But I enjoy being with you when you make love to yourself."

"Sexy little bitch," he whispered affectionately.

"Simon!"

"It's true." He slipped away from her and pressed his hand against her mouth before she could protest. "Now go and make your man some breakfast. We both have to go to work."

"No, please, Simon, just a little longer."

He frowned irritably. "I warn you, Anne, I'm unbearable in the morning. I'll begin to hit you or something." He tried to brush aside his anger as soon as he saw the hurt on her face. "Besides, I have a headache."

She immediately looked worried. "Oh, I'm sorry, Simon, I didn't know. Can I get you something?" She looked ridiculously childish, sitting naked on the bed.

"No, I'd just like some coffee."

She began to wrap a blanket round her body, then blushed and scuttled across the room to the chair where her dressing-gown was lying. She turned away from him to put it on.

He smiled to himself, and turned over to get a few more minutes' sleep. She must think that because she can't see me I can't see her. He wondered vaguely how long it would last, and if it would end in tears and recriminations. But he must lose this habit of thinking of the end of an affair when it had hardly begun.

Despite everything, he felt happy.

CHAPTER X

THIS was one of the days when she could not work. They came about once a fortnight – lately more frequently – and she would keep her resolution to practise until the very moment she was sitting down and her hands were placed over the keyboard, ready to begin preliminary exercises. Suddenly it was impossible to play even a single note, and she loathed the disciplinary system she had built up and nourished over the years. Beginning had always been the worst part, although it was not so easy to continue, when each day you were pushing outwards, driving yourself to greater effort, to the state where you became too impatient to try something which you knew you could play well.

It was ten o'clock on a windy morning. The gas fire was just big enough to warm the little room, but nevertheless Meg shivered when she passed beyond the circle of its warmth and went to stand by the closed window. At the far end of the street she could see the cafés and fruiterers' and butchers' shops. Opposite was a dancing academy, deserted this morning because term had ended. In the basement of this house there was a rehearsal room for some actors' group. She believed that it was little more than a meeting place for half-hearted beginners. She shivered again as she watched the sky driven by the wind behind the rooftops. She had deliberately chosen this most dismal street because she imagined it would be easier to work here. It certainly offered few distractions. Nor had she bothered to furnish the room. The grey paper was peeling from the walls, the electric-light bulb was naked, and the room contained just two wooden chairs, a table, a camp bed, an old wardrobe and a sink. The new baby grand, standing compact and shiny in the middle of the linoleum-covered floor, looked strange. It would soon lose its shine: it had already begun to gather dust from the pile of music which she had dumped on top.

She lit a cigarette, and went to the gas ring to make some coffee. Julian was not coming until two o'clock, but she supposed the time would pass quickly enough. She pulled the gramophone from under the bed and fitted an adaptor into the electric-light socket. It was the only plug in the room. She fingered the stack of records. The choice was surprisingly narrow, although she always seemed to be buying records; if she liked, say, Beethoven's sixth symphony, she felt obliged to buy the other eight in case she was missing something. In the end she closed her eyes and happened to pick the Chopin Prelude No. 15 in D flat. She carried the coffee over to the bed and sat down with her back against the pillow. The repeated note linking the two parts of the piece made her want to go to sleep and she switched off, and listened with pleasure as the music droned slowly to a stop.

Last night had been oppressive. For some reason Henry began to list the faults of Julian De-la-Noy and Perkin Young as soon as they got home. Something had upset him. "All right," she said at last, "what does it matter? At least they're young. Perhaps they'll learn as they grow older." She had not expected to see such pain on his face as he turned away. She ran to him and cried that she was sorry, that was not what she had intended to say. In the end he fell on her with such desire that she was almost disgusted. She would not be able to endure him if he behaved like that very often. He was jealous, of course, but he rarely seemed to consider her feelings. He loved her in his introverted way, but it was not enough. He only displayed affection when he was showing her to his friends, or when he wanted to make love to her. Tony had not been like that, and she began to cry as she had known she would. She curled up on the bed and hid her face, hoping that she could imagine his body beside her, but it was impossible. It had not been possible since he died. She soon stopped crying. It was useless.

Suddenly restless, Meg got up and went to the window again. A young man in the street, wearing a light black and white checked coat, his fair hair blown by the wind, had stopped to light a cigarette. He seemed preoccupied, not with worry but with himself. That was best, that total unselfconscious sufficiency. He hunched his shoulders and bent over the lighter. For a second his face looked artificially smooth and calm. The smoke tunnelled from his mouth and he passed on, walking easily and with complete disregard for his surroundings. Who was he? Where was he going? She was reminded of Tony's walk, because she wanted to be reminded. Perhaps they had little in common, those two young men, except youth, but Tony might have worn a similar checked coat.

The whole day darkened for a moment as a huge cloud extinguished whatever source of light there might be in the dark street. The scene appeared to waver slightly as the cloud moved smoothly on, and the wet pavements glittered with a smooth surface light again. Tony will not see this light again, never feel the wind on his face, never pray with all his heart that the sun will shine, to take away the cold inside. Meg smiled elegiacally, and with the serene contentment of those who do not hope for anything more, and therefore know that they are prepared to deal competently with whatever may come. The catastrophe is past, and will inform the remainder of their lives.

Tony darling, do you see this cigarette, this early grey December morning in the city? Watch me as I open the window and lean out to breathe in the air. I'm trying to live it for you, for you will not see it again, although you may not care. Have you watched the way I smile when they call each other darling, because you never said love, and turned away at night, laughing at me; you never cared if I was unhappy, for together we had something too rare to allow little things to be important. Do you laugh at my behaviour now, and pity me for still being foolish enough to love you, knowing this?

I can hardly remember you, unless by a series of adjectives which could easily be applied to a hundred young men I used to know. I see your face before me and it really is so unexceptional. Oh, you were handsome, clean, smooth, you drank too much, you knew absolutely nothing about music. It bored you, and I could have killed you for your smug self-satisfaction. You were so ordinary. You actually enjoyed your work, you had *principles*, and four college degrees. You liked dancing, parties, steaks and ice-cream sodas, musicals, ice-skating, the beach, Ella Fitzgerald, your convertible and Californian houses. You hated nineteenth-century writers and you despised musicians. You were so patronising. Life was so easy for you, and you wanted it to be easy for your wife. You liked fun too much to have children, and you converted me to your selfish way of life until I had nothing that did not belong to you. That was what I wanted. There wasn't a single reason why I should love you and I loved you because I needed you, and thought you very stupid. You were fabulous. It was the kind of marriage that Americans do well. We would have gone on being happy and secure, you would have put on weight, I should have bought glasses with interchangeable frames and we would have settled down to alcoholic domesticity. When we were forty-five we'd have spent a summer in England, you'd have owned your own business by then. And I'd have forgotten my music, or kept it for my children if we ever had any.

The end was unreal, meaningless, an artistically bad ending. We had one of our arguments, which were always fun in a way. It was Saturday morning, one fall. We were going on a picnic, and I felt too lazy to make sandwiches just yet. I was playing the piano. You shouted at me and I shouted back. "Oh, hell, it doesn't matter, we've got the whole weekend and you flip because I wasted half an hour. Wasted? What am I talking about? You see what you've done to me?" "Well, honey, I never made provision for marrying an egghead, and I'm not going to adapt myself to your little ways now." "You're so damned smug," I shouted. "Haven't you got any sense of humour." I wanted to make you angry. "Sometimes you're ridiculous. Do you remember our wedding night? The mattress slipped"—I couldn't stop jeering at you, you looked so shocked when I mentioned it—"and we almost tumbled on the floor. Anyone else would have laughed, but not Tony Santry. He was so embarrassed that he was no good for twenty minutes afterwards." You flushed, and looked so violently angry that I had to go on mocking you. "Well, where's your sense of humour, Tony. Laugh at that." You turned white then, and threw a coffee cup on the floor. You cursed me and I thought you'd slap me, but instead you seemed about to cry, and you kicked aside a chair and stalked out of the house. I heard the car starting, and then I began to make the sandwiches and slice a cake. The fight meant nothing. It was part of our living together, I wanted nothing changed. But ridiculously, your car mounted the sidewalk and crashed into the high iron fence of a children's park. When I saw it the car was crumpled like an empty cigarette packet. You were thrown past the windscreen against the bars.

At the time I didn't believe it was real, of course. You might die of sickness but a car crash was just too queer. I mean that's the way people like us are *supposed* to die. After a while, though, it seemed only too real, and what had gone before seemed unbelievable. Two people aren't allowed to be as happy as that, they don't deserve it. That sort of thing always ends with a bang. We paid for our pride, our ignorance and our happiness. We were perfect, and other people – those common ugly unhappy little people we ignored – envied us so much that they had to be revenged. They looked so hard for a flaw in our happiness, we must have seemed so unconvincing. We were cleverer than they: we gave each other everything we had, we needed love so badly. We had to be taught a lesson, but now I've learned it absolutely. I've nothing more to learn but it goes on and on. I will go on loving and remembering, loving and remembering, loving and remembering, and I don't know when it will end. You won't come again, not in time or when I die. I see your face before me. I can't guess what you'd have me do. I suppose you're bewildered too. You weren't made to deal with anything big. *Why?*

Meg shouted the word aloud. She could think of many reasons but ultimately they were untrue and meaningless. She was committed to him whatever he did. She was left suspended, in this room or wherever she might be.

But the only things essential for pleasant living are an ability to speak when one is spoken to and an engaging smile. Meg had these and many other assets, so she found life easy. She could switch off all thought and lose herself in a pleasant tune or a rapid flow of trivial conversation. She only felt sad when she started wondering if she was happy. By the time Julian arrived that afternoon she had prepared a cold lunch: the little gas ring was useless for cooking. Julian looked flushed and shiny from his walk in the cold.

He sat down on the bed. "You have rings under your eyes. Have you been working hard?"

Meg shook her head and sat beside him. "You can have orange juice and cold ham."

"I was going to take you to a delicious little restaurant where artists go."

"Never mind," she said solemnly. "I'm not hungry."

"That's hardly the point, sweetie. What did you do this morning, if you weren't working?"

"Nothing."

"At all?"

"I stood by the window and watched a young man in a black and white coat. I wanted to shout to him to come up but I was too shy."

"And he'd have come, too. I wonder why we're afraid of people we haven't met. If you'd been introduced to him at a party you wouldn't have been at all frightened of asking him to come and see you."

"I know," she said without interest.

She handed him a glass of orange juice, and they drank with the air of two people who for some reason must talk, although they are quite at ease together without conversation.

"What did you do this morning?" Meg asked politely.

"I had a bath, then went and had a turkish bath and a massage." He pulled at his lower eyelid. "See? Pink and clear."

She giggled nervously. "You only think so because you're never in a fit state to see properly anyhow."

Julian looked offended, but blew her an indulgent kiss. "I might just pass for thirty. I'm content."

"Have some ham and salad."

They each lifted a plate to rest on their knee, trying to look as if they might possibly eat some of the food.

"I'm not hungry either," Julian said at last.

"Of course not. Oh darling, one of these days you'll be really sick."

He gobbled two or three mouthfuls and put the plate aside. "Guess what I'm going to do now?"

Meg stared at the ceiling. "You couldn't possibly – let me see. . . . Surely you're not going to light a cigarette?"

He clutched his heart. "How did you guess?"

They burst out laughing, and stopped quite suddenly.

"You're a fool, Julian."

He grasped her hands tightly. "But Meg loves me just the same?"

"I suppose she does," Meg replied wistfully and regretfully.

"How much does Meg love me?" he asked carefully.

"A lot." She shook her head.

"Why?"

She turned his hands and gazed at the palms. "I love Julian De-la-Noy first of all because he has such a funny name. I don't know where he got it and it doesn't suit him," she recited in a child's voice. She turned back one of his fingers. "The second reason why I love Julian De-la-Noy is that it's a cold winter's day and everyone should be loved on a cold winter's day." She turned back another finger. "The third reason I love him is that he really is a very handsome young man. He smells terribly sweet, and I'm so young and innocent that I don't recognise the sweet smell as the sweet smell of gin-and-it. And he really is so handsome." She turned back a third finger and rested her hand comfortably on his knee. She hesitated and closed her eyes for a moment.

"Go on," Julian said quietly.

She smiled. "The next reason I love Julian is that he's so very tender. It's so very pleasant to be with him. He makes me feel warm in winter and cool in summer. When I touch him I feel safe. He's the safest and dearest person in the world. He wants what I want, although we don't know what it is."

He leaned forward and kissed her gently on the forehead, pressing her hand against his stomach. The mood was broken for a moment, but returned. She did not look up, and he was the first to move away. She gently straightened his hand, then bent four fingers to their former position. She took a handkerchief and wiped away the sweat that had begun to form in the hollow of his palm. She took hold of his thumb. "The fifth reason I love Julian De-la-

Noy is that he is so extremely lovable." She shrugged then, and squeezed his hand into a fist. "And now I seem to have run out of fingers and reasons as well." She raised her hand and gazed boldly into his eyes, with faint hostility. He felt as if some source of warmth had been turned off.

"Those are a good many reasons, Meg, enough for me." His voice wavered and he dropped his eyes.

Her mouth quivered. "As I am very young and innocent, only nine years old, Julian De-la-Noy is the boy whose wife I would be pleased to be."

He clicked his fingers. "But you're not really nine years old." The spell was broken, and he picked up the cigarette. "Oh Meg!"

"I'll light it for you," she whispered quickly. The cigarette and the flame trembled. He was just like Tony and the young man in the street.

The cigarette was an excuse for biting his lip, and his face hardened.

"Isn't it pretty that we both have a talent for whimsy?"

Meg inclined her head. "Isn't it?"

He stood up. "I must go. Would you like to come to a film? We could hold hands in the back row."

"No. I must do some work to make up for this morning," she lied.

"Well, I'll see you." He turned to go, then paused. "What do you want for Christmas?"

She laughed. "Anything you like to give me," she said shyly.

He nodded. "We'll see. You'll get your present early. I shall be in Switzerland at Christmas. But I'll see you in the new year." He waved his hand, dropped it quickly, and backed out of the room.

Meg stared at the plates of uneaten food. She poured the jug of cream on a plate of fruit salad, and began to eat it.

CHAPTER XI

PERKIN flung his arms around Tom when he saw him again; Simon hung back, wondering happily why he felt embarrassed. He had always believed himself to be the less favoured son: he did not know that it only seemed so because Tom preferred Perkin's name.

Tom Young still had the same air of restrained, huge vitality. He was an old, tall man, diffident and so polite that no-one had ever decided where affection ended and love began with him. He could inspire love, but perhaps he never returned it. Perhaps he regarded the world with an aesthetic disdain. He disliked vulgarity, but was prepared to be amused when he detected it in his children. He did not seem to be demanding, yet in fact he gave only when he received. The father and his children exchanged gifts quite regularly, but never wrote letters. The allowance was paid through Lloyds.

Perkin and Simon had never been completely happy with Tom, for he constantly withdrew from them in fear of intruding in their lives. If he had been more demonstrative or stern they would have resented it, but they would have felt more secure. He gave them tolerant understanding, advice which he never hoped would be accepted, and money; he did not give them an example or a pattern of life. When they were uncertain he gave them no solution which they could accept or reject. He gave them a choice. He had gone to Cambridge, travelled, gone into business for some years, then married and retired. He read moderately, liked pictures but knew nothing about music. He was quite wealthy, but saw no reason why his sons should have a large sum of money to spend before he died. Sometimes they wondered if he ever thought about them very much, but they realised that he gave them what they deserved. Since the age of sixteen Simon and Perkin had hesitated their lives away, Perkin probably following his brother's example. Tom had no intention of trying to make up their minds for them. At the core of the relationship was this conflict, which was never realised in any verbal argument.

On the evening of his arrival, the day before Christmas Eve, they took him to dine at a little Chelsea restaurant with travel poster décor and waiters in butchers' aprons. He was amused, and wondered idly if they thought the place decadent. They did, but would never have admitted it. He sat opposite them and watched in silence until they flushed and bent their heads, in the awkward moment between sitting down and ordering a meal. He laughed and shook his head. All the lines on his face had smoothed away. They frowned. It was too bad that everything seemed to amuse him.

"You're both looking very well." He was not going to provide brilliant conversation as a substitute for the questions which he intended to ask them. He knew that if he did not talk they would soon give themselves away.

"The restaurant is very bohemian," he said, his eyes twinkling. "The waiters are very handsome. Perhaps I'll be mistaken for a pederast taking his two beautiful boys to dinner." He chuckled into a spoonful of soup.

Simon and Perkin gaped at him.

"I thought perhaps I'd adapt myself to the – eh, artistic life." His eyes widened innocently.

Tom was one of the few people with whom they disliked to talk sex.

Simon smiled uneasily. "You've got the wrong idea, Tom." The words tasted uncomfortable.

"Well," Tom said, wiping his lips heartily, "tell me about your friends. Where do you spend your evenings?"

"At the pictures. We often sit at home and read," Simon said. He had not seen his father for two years and suddenly he felt very young. It was obvious that Tom still thought of him as a child.

"We really don't go to many parties," Perkin said eagerly, then wiped the grin from his face and tried to look sophisticated. "We just feel as if we do. Sometimes I look at my diary after a busy week and find that I've only been to one party, maybe, a play and a few drinks at some friend's house."

Tom looked pleased. "In that case you must save a lot of money."

There was an awkward silence, of which he did not seem to be aware.

"In fact I'm not quite sure what we do do," Perkin went on desperately.

"Well, neither of you is suddenly going to get married, anyhow?"

"Oh, not for years," Perkin assured him.

"I don't want to settle down," Simon said grimly. "I'm like you. I'll get married when I'm fifty. Actually I know just the right girl, if she'll wait that long, but domesticated women irritate me." He laughed artificially. "God, how I hate babies! In fact I think children should be kept in a sealed room until they're over sixteen." He felt that his maturity was now firmly established, and heartily disliked Tom for forcing him to take such pains to do it. Perkin nodded agreement.

"Well, you've got plenty of time yet." Tom seemed fascinated by the waiter who was placing their steaks on the table.

"Besides," Simon continued relentlessly, "I grow tired of people so easily. You can be bored by someone you still like. I'd hate to hurt someone who thought she was in love with me." He almost blushed, then realised that his words were true. He hated to make anyone unhappy, although he pretended to be heartless.

"Ah." Tom sipped his burgundy with moderate satisfaction. His sons had been saving part of their allowance since the beginning of the month in order to entertain him properly when he arrived. It looked as if they would have no money left by Boxing Day, and they prayed that he would give them a cheque for Christmas. They were ready to pawn all the jewellery they possessed rather than admit that they had run out of money.

"You know, you must never be afraid of hurting people," Tom said benevolently. "You'll hurt them in the end, so why not make a clean break of it? You only worry because you're young."

"It isn't as simple as that," Simon said coldly. He had hoped to impress him by implying that he had a conscience. "You can't help worrying when you know the girl's probably crying her eyes out."

"You flatter yourself," Perkin interrupted, smiling brightly. Simon ignored him.

"I know I'm selfish, but I also know what it's like to be dropped by someone. I'd hate to leave someone else in the same state." He anticipated with relish the tear-stained farewell scene with Anne, which he believed would soon take place, and almost cried for her when he thought how unhappy she would be. It hardly occurred to him that he was being hypocritical. Everyone enjoys exciting emotion in others, for it makes them feel attractive and desirable.

Tom smiled, grateful that he was no longer young. His memories of youth were impersonal. He could not recall the exact day
when he knew that he had grown old. The expected time had
never come when he thought he would wake up to find that morning had changed colour and topography had been upset and he
had a time to recall with nostalgia and thankfulness that he was
no longer part of it. Perhaps he had spread experience too evenly
over the years. How uncomfortable they must feel! They seemed
to have little enthusiasm for anything except the outward show
of having a good time, although non-commitment is a form of
caring. Heartache – inadequacy – fear – variety – colour – danger
– uncertainty – squalor – joy. Words beat in his ears for a moment
until he retreated and bowed his head. After all, he had been right
not to tell them how to grow up. The money he left them when he
died would last if they were sensible. For the rest, well, it was like a
screen on which they wandered for a while and the first cold wind
that blew would smear the paint and they would be finished like
everyone else. And like everyone else they would have compensations. He could not understand why they should not be happy. He
had never understood unhappiness.

"You mustn't think it's admirable to have a conscience," he said
abruptly. "It doesn't matter a damn. Don't be harsh, but tie yourself to someone through pity and you'll regret it for the rest of
your life. I don't know anyone over fifty-five who has a conscience.
It's a malignant growth peculiar to the young, newspapers and
ministers of religion." He chuckled. "That's enough of that. Give
me one of your spurious American cigarettes, Perkin. I don't want
any sweet. The sight of ice-cream and chocolate sauce makes me
feel sick. What did you buy me for Christmas?"

"Cigars," Perkin said.

"Slippers," Simon said. "They were imported from Italy."

"Highly unoriginal. My gifts are just as bad. I bought you a
book of paintings by somebody called Mondrian – I must say I like
the colours – and I bought Perkin an edition of Thackeray. He's
very underrated these days and I hope you'll read him."

"I have," Perkin said. "As a matter of fact I've read *Vanity Fair* six times. But I'll enjoy reading him again. Thank you very much, Tom."

"Thank you for your cigars. I shall buy you something else of course. You may each have something up to the value of twenty pounds."

They seemed to be thinking hard.

"Or you may have cheques, over and above your allowances."

Their faces brightened, but they were silent, trying to conquer pride. They could have delayed the choice of gift until it was too late for Tom to buy it before returning to Ireland, in the hope that he would give them cheques at the last moment, but the uncertainty was unbearable.

"I think I'd like a cheque," they said simultaneously, and immediately felt ridiculous and cursed each other.

"I thought so," Tom said quietly. "I suppose you're both penniless?"

Perkin sighed, and Simon nodded.

"Well, why didn't you say so?" he asked irritably.

Simon pulled a cigarette from the packet. "We're too old to come running to you for pocket-money."

"Old? You're the youngest of the young, Simon, believe me. Trouble is, you've got too many acquired tastes. No-one should ever spend more than five-and-six on a meal until they're thirty."

"We don't eat here all the time," Perkin said. "This place isn't very expensive, anyhow."

"And see your plays from the gallery. What do appearances matter? Good heavens, not one in twenty young people in London has as much money as you. And you have jobs as well."

"Why shouldn't we spend our money?" Simon protested angrily. "Why bother to save it?"

Tom kept silent for a moment, then smiled. "Of course you should spend it, my boy. I only wanted to see if you could lose your temper. I tell you the only thing that's wrong with either of you is that you have no spirit. You're too insipid to make a splash."

They looked exasperated. "That's what everyone says," Perkin muttered wearily. "Are we so dull, Tom?"

"Of course you aren't dull," he said gruffly. "I think you're very interesting, perhaps because of this – debility. But you sit there, with stony faces, which react about twenty seconds after something has begun to pierce your shell. Is it a pose, or indifference, is there simply nothing underneath? Are you interested in *anything*?"

"There's no answer to that," Perkin said quickly. "It's like asking what you believe in. You can't reply in a few words."

"Of course you can. It isn't the same thing at all. When I was your age I was interested in cricket, opera, gambling, and pushing as many women as possible in as short a time as possible. God, I'd love to know the way you copulate. It must be rather like eating hot stew on a cold day."

"That isn't funny," Simon said angrily. "I'm interested in painting, books, films, people."

"Are you?"

"Yes. Do you expect me to babble like an idiot and ask you questions like 'Are you an atheist?' or hit you on the head if you argue that Jean-Paul Sartre still has more to offer than Alain Robbe-Grillet? At least we're too self-conscious to behave like something ghastly just released from a sub-deb party."

"If you did ask those questions there might be some hope for you. There'd be the chance that you might learn some sense. If there were another war, for example, would you care very much?"

"I wish there'd be a war," Perkin said. "I'd like to have something to fight for. I'd like to have an excuse for desperation. It would be exciting to know that in a few hours' time you might be dead. That would be living."

Tom smiled. "So maybe you're human after all. What prevents you from living now? Others seem to manage very well."

"It isn't living, it's making an existence. It's as if your life had been given to you and you didn't really want it. It's always a question of making the best of a situation which is in reality impossible." Damn, he thought. Why couldn't he leave us alone? What's the good of talking like this?

"Do you always feel this way?"

"Yes. It's always in the background. But you can enjoy yourself, nevertheless. It was different when I was younger. I mean when you're a child you live only by yourself, and you can't help seeing things in relation to yourself. Your house has windows, which have nothing to do with light, they're to keep you in or let you out. And the same with doors or fences. You're only aware of the things you touch. Then you realise there's this futility, other people hammer you until you feel mad and dead. You hope that things will get better and you try to make them better and in the end you play yourself out."

Tom pushed aside his coffee cup. "And you think you've played yourself out so soon?"

"Yes. I think most people do, the sort of people I know, anyway. It isn't finished, but nothing is ever as good as it might have been."

"Of course you know that almost everyone has this feeling when they're young? They think they've lost all their illusions and exhausted experience. It doesn't last."

"It isn't a question of disillusionment," Simon said carefully. "Nobody ever runs out of illusions. And this isn't really something we can talk about. I suppose you think we're very innocent. Doesn't it occur to you that it might have nothing to do with age? We know the truth about ourselves. I'm past caring. I know it's ludicrous that Perkin and I should feel the same way. It isn't just us, it's a symptom of the disease of a whole generation. Nobody has a name for us yet, we haven't been turned into a parlour game."

"These generations burn out. I've lived through several, and what's more I belonged to them."

"There's nothing left to care about any more," Perkin said.

"I thought you cared about writing."

"I cared about an abstraction, something glamorous which is not glamorous at all. How could I write about the way I feel? There's so little to say. I have no drama, no tragic or happy endings. Whatever else we do, we go on living in the same way. You can only write interesting books about conflict or reaction."

"One day you should be able to see a pattern, and then you'll be able to write about it, if you're a writer. Wait and see." He sat up to show that he wanted to go home.

Simon paid the bill, and they went into the dark street. Opposite the restaurant there was a hat shop with a huge purple Santa Claus in the window. It seemed incredible that Christmas was here.

"Everyone in Chelsea must be very busy," Tom said. "The streets are always so deserted."

Neither of his sons replied, and they walked towards the main road to find a taxi.

Tom was tired, and went to bed as soon as they got home. Simon and Perkin came to say goodnight to him and each bent down to kiss his forehead. He seemed happy, and looked at them approvingly.

They had tossed a coin to see who would sleep on the couch during Tom's visit, and Perkin lost. He had been lying smoking for about twenty minutes when Simon came and sat on the improvised bed.

"Grisly, wasn't it?"

His brother smiled. "I don't know. He makes me angry, but he likes us. He never patronises or disapproves."

"He's a wonderful man," Simon said.

"Oh, I don't know. The three of us are so alike that maybe we only think he's wonderful. We aren't wonderful. Do you want a cigarette?"

Simon shook his head and stood up. "Wouldn't it be nice if everything wasn't so complicated?"

"Yes," Perkin said contentedly, and fell asleep thinking of Meg.

CHAPTER XII

On Christmas Eve yellow fog lay over London, drifting into shops and restaurants, dampening the cold blank faces of shoppers and hiding the bridges over the river. It was a comfortable substitute for snow. It made people more grateful for warmth and comfort and rest, and hid the faces of the poor.

By a series of lies Perkin managed to avoid extra duty at the shop and met his father for lunch at the Carlton. It amused Tom to annoy his children; when he was feeling expansive he let them choose the restaurant, but when he felt malicious he took them to his club. Perkin chewed his lamb chops cheerfully, and crunched at the fruit salad which consisted of apple and a piece of pear, and hated Tom with all his heart. It was a rather silent meal. Tom had discovered that there was little to say to his sons that was not repetition, and Perkin was preoccupied with murderous thoughts and trying to define the atmosphere of London this Christmas. He dismissed the thought that it was only subjective. It could be seen, it was almost palpable. People breathed the suffocating air and their faces were stronger and more stern. They must be taking stock of their lives as they hurried through a few more hours of the last days of the year. The city flickered in drifting shadow substance that was paler than light. You did something to protect yourself – huddled into your coat and dug your hands into pockets, or bought a dozen cups of coffee. No wonder there has to be an official celebration at each December's end.

Perkin had decided long in advance that there would be no stock-taking for him, but it was unavoidable that he should wonder how his friends were spending the holiday, and inevitably, with each card he stamped and posted, he reviewed their lives, and shook his head, for the year had gone quickly and he had often thought that it would never end. He felt optimistic, for if time passed so quickly there could be no need to worry, and little time for regret.

After lunch they went to the Aldwych, where Tom had to visit his bank, and afterwards walked down Essex Street to Temple Station and the river. They wandered back in the Chelsea direction, agreeing to find a taxi as soon as Tom grew tired of walking. The day was really beautiful, Perkin thought, as he watched the discreetly hidden figures of passers-by, and wished suddenly that he would meet someone whom he recognised, did not know well but would have liked to know better.

"Another year," Tom said, for want of something better to say.

His son pulled a face.

They had made few plans for the next two days. They intended to sit at home and drink or read. Simon was bringing Anne to dinner on Boxing Day. He had not bothered to ask what she was doing the rest of the time.

That afternoon, Perkin arranged the last of the cards on top of the bookcases. There was none from Angel – perhaps she had long since gone to the South of France – and Jonathan had still not sent a card. Henry had sent a plain white sheet of cardboard with a black engraving, and of course there was no card from Meg. Julian's had scrawled on the back: "Switzerland until March. I'll return looking like a ski-ing instructor. Bring you a Swiss pullover. Luv."

So Christmas passed. People turned more gratefully to the source from which they had derived comfort during the rest of the year, for it is an impersonal time, when everyone feels slightly bewildered.

At eight o'clock on New Year's Eve, Jonathan rang. His voice sounded rather flat, but he talked more quickly than usual.

"I've been terribly busy, Perkin. Yes, I had a lovely Christmas and I've got lots of news. I'm sorry I didn't ring before."

"Where are you?" Perkin asked.

"George's place. Look, let's have lunch tomorrow. We can talk then. I'll call for you at the shop."

"All right," Perkin said, puzzled. "How is George?"

There was a slight pause. "Oh, he's very well. He's busy or I'd get him to talk to you. Happy New Year, Perkin."

"Happy New Year, Jonnie."

Jonathan put down the receiver and felt so alone that he was overwhelmingly grateful for the sound of laughter and conversation filtering up from the basement. He sipped the martini which he had poured when he came upstairs, and tightened the girdle of his bathrobe. He wandered into the bathroom, still holding his drink, and turned on the taps. He gazed at himself in the wall-mirror before it clouded. His face was fatter, but he had learned to hold his mouth and head in such a way that it did not show. Besides, he had learned to appreciate the difference between a steak at the Grill and Cheese and certain Soho restaurants. He had learned that the most important thing in life is to eat well and often. He was always hungry, and would have gone on eating if each mouthful had increased his weight by a pound. He would not have stopped eating even for George, and he derived much comfort from the thought.

On the shelf beside the bath were a dozen or so bottles and jars: skin tonic, cleansing lotions, skin creams, lacquers and powders. He now washed his face with lavender-scented soap and applied solvent lotion to his skin to take away the grease and sweat. He still felt self-conscious each time he dabbed at his face with a piece of cottonwool, and if George had been there he'd have laughed: "Honestly, honey, you don't have to be a pansy to care about your appearance. I know a certain very famous playwright who has his face lifted quite regularly."

"Who?" Jonathan would ask immediately, and George would laugh more loudly.

George had taught him to go to a barber once a week, to have a haircut and a manicure. "But always, honey, always wash your own hair. A barber will ruin it."

So Jonathan faithfully washed his hair every five days, once with one shampoo, and twice with another, then brushed it until he was red in the face and his shoulders were aching – it was about the only exercise he ever took.

He carefully wiped the lotion from his face as soon as it had dried, then rubbed his fingers with a pumice stone. He removed the tar stains from his nails with a cream, and carefully examined the result. Not bad. He felt slightly silly, but much better. It occurred to him that the young men whom he now so often admired must take the same precautions, but there was surely no need to *discuss* them, making recommendations and suggestions, as George and his friends so often did. Still, as George said, in twenty years' time he would probably be glad that he had looked after himself.

He only stayed in the bath for five minutes, then wrapped himself in a fresh robe, leaving his body to dry by itself. He dropped into a chair. He felt tired, but so alone that he had to put a record on the gramophone. It was the Ravel minuet from *Le Tombeau de Couperin*. Ingenious was the word for it, but George shook his head disapprovingly if he ever ventured such an opinion.

Jonathan had decided about three weeks ago that his lover was a phoney.

"It's such a pity you don't like good music," George would say, and he would not reply. If he protested it would seem an indication of pride and weakness; if he mentioned what he really believed, George would be hurt. Intellectual respect is a very important aspect of a love affair, if it is not to fall into boredom and irritation. Of course he was the only one who hoped for a lasting relationship. George had told him that it was only a question of time before it ended. But it will not end bitterly, he promised. You will want it to end as much as I. Jonathan could not reply. How could he say that he loved George precisely because he was the kind of person who said these things and applied this belief to the whole of life. He loved his lover because for the first time in his life he wanted to give, and would be quite satisfied if he received a little in return. He would then be able to lie awake at night and feel good because he was really not appreciated; and perhaps there would be ecstatic scenes of reconciliation, with George begging his forgiveness and weeping because he had been cruel. Jonathan would smile bravely, his eyes filled with tears. He wanted emotion, and it looked as if this was the only way he would get it, for George was very unemotional.

When he went into the basement he stood quite still for a moment, smiling at the men who greeted him, and looked for George. He was in the centre of a group in the corner, talking animatedly. Jonathan shrugged as if it hardly mattered, and went to take his place behind the bar.

"Thank heavens you're here," Derek murmured. "I couldn't cope."

Jonathan nodded, and dealt quickly and efficiently with the men who were waiting for drinks.

All George's friends and customers seemed to visit him that night, and he was happier than Jonathan had ever seen him, leaning back and laughing each time someone bent down and whispered in his ear. He came to the bar five or six times to order rounds of free drinks, and his manner was casual. But as soon as he returned to his friends his voice heightened and became ebullient. Jonathan wondered what they were saying: the snatches of conversation he heard were meaningless, trivial, a verbal shorthand which belonged to a closed circle. George had stopped introducing him to his closest friends. Jonathan could never think of anything to say to them, perhaps because he knew it was important that he should be accepted. They greeted him when they came into the bar, and inquired about him on his night off, only because he was George's official boy friend. That was all.

A bell rang. The preceding minutes had been quieter, as everyone waited expectantly. George had hidden an alarm clock under one of the wall seats. There was a moment's silence, then Derek turned on the radio at the bar. Bells were ringing.

"If there were any windows in this place we could open them and hear the bells," Derek muttered to hide his embarrassment. These people, who were not accustomed to embarrassment, were suddenly shy. Then they began to take hold of each other's hands. George began to sing, and everyone joined in, gaining confidence with each word of the song.

Jonathan tried to join in, but the words choked him and he coughed violently. The bar separated him from the rest of the room and the people in it; Derek and Jonathan stood quite alone. George was now standing, looking straight ahead.

Then he stopped singing. His eyes met Jonathan's, flickered. He broke away from the crowd. He came and leaned across the bar and kissed Derek on the forehead. Jonathan waited, still as death. He felt George's presence, then his breath.

"Happy New Year, Jonnie, for all our sins."

He nodded, unable to speak.

Tom Young returned to Ireland on the third of January. It was arranged that Simon and Perkin would go home for a fortnight in July.

CHAPTER XIII

PERKIN thought of Meg constantly during the week after their first meeting, then almost forgot about her, and slipped into his easy abortive routine of life again. As soon as Tom left he began to read the Thackeray edition and worked his way through to the end. The novels made him laugh aloud, something which no novel written in the twentieth century had ever done. Life seemed to languish all through January. There were no parties, or at least he was invited to none; perhaps people had spent too much money at Christmas, and were sleeping their way through the temporary lull. His friends had paired off, also temporarily, he supposed: Simon with Anne, whose speech and appearance had suddenly become sweetly pat and self-confident, and George with Jonathan, whom he saw only once, on New Year's Day. They went to the Jardin des Gourmets in Greek Street, and fought for something to say to each other. Perkin rang Henry during the second week in January and suggested two evenings for a dinner-date, but Henry had other arrangements. He was going away soon, too, for a month, but he would ring when he returned. Julian wrote twice from Switzerland, and his letters were tedious and forced: he was writing this just before lunch with a ski-instructor who knew all about German philosophy; his clothes were wet and he must go and dry them; why didn't Perkin come over for a week; he must go now and change.

It was one of the periods when Perkin could do without people. He was very glad to come home in the early afternoon, watch the trees in the square tossing in the wind – and later bent under snow – then sit down before the fire and read his books, with extraordinary concentration. After Thackeray he returned to Dickens, then Fielding, Richardson and Smollett. It was impossible to say why they fascinated him; at least, they were a huge debauch. He had grown tired of fastidiousness. At the end of February he began to re-read Dostoevsky.

Then suddenly it was no longer enough. He was reading, his mind wandered, and he thought of Meg and began wanting her. He started to walk about the room, restless, edgy, uncertain. He wanted to be on the inside, looking out, that was all. He needed people again, he needed someone, and he chose Meg Santry. The easiest way to contact her would have been to ring Henry, if he had returned, and ask for her address, but the prospect made him more nervous than ever. He wrote to Julian, but was too impatient to resign himself to waiting for a reply. And he only raised the matter casually in his letter. He was ashamed to admit to anyone that he was pursuing her, frightened of a rebuke that would make him seem ridiculous. Once, when he felt desperate, he forced himself to dial Henry's number. He let it ring five times, then tumbled the receiver back on its rest. At night he lay on his stomach, his face buried in the pillow, and wondered when he would see her again. Perhaps at a party, when she was with Henry. He'd pretend not to see her at first, and talk extravagantly to the other guests. He would loudly arrange to dine with someone that evening, and say, "Just let me talk to someone for a moment", and he would go to where Meg was waiting quietly. They'd both pretend to be shy. He would sit beside her on a couch, and gaze at her in silence. He'd be the first to speak.

"How have you been?" he would ask simply.

Meg would shrug. "Well," she'd say, and smile. "How have you been?"

"Well. Henry's just been telling me that you've won a very special scholarship in music."

Meg would nod and spread her hands, to indicate that it meant nothing to her. There would be another long silence. (At this point Perkin's imagination baulked for a moment. Surely Henry would see what was happening and interrupt before they could go any further. There would be no time for long silences at a party. It occurred to him that he was thinking like a writer, but he did not feel grateful for the revelation. He pushed these unwanted thoughts aside, and pressed on.)

Then, looking down, "Meg, I love you." There would be no need for her to reply. They would stand up and leave the party, smiling tremulously. Henry would watch them go, his face ravaged. He would not try to stop them. They were young and in love. They would forget him, for it was useless to worry about his feelings.

In the hall he would tenderly help her into her coat. They would go to a restaurant or a bar, and sit quietly, staring at their hands, their heads almost touching. They would be saddened by the prospect of their love.

That was as much as Perkin cared to imagine as he lay in bed.
He went over the same scene each night, discarding and selecting
variations. He had to force himself back to reality, make himself
believe that he would meet her again, before he could compose
himself to lie still and go to sleep. He recalled everything they had
said together, and remembered her mentioning that she hardly
ever went to see a new film. She preferred those which she had seen
and enjoyed before, and often went to the Hampstead Everyman.

For ten days Perkin travelled through foul weather to the
Everyman, and saw a turgid Italian film so many times that sheer
frustration forced him to like it in the end. In the intervals he
searched the rows of seats and stared at the people around him,
twisting his face ferociously to resist the advances of assorted men
and women. At first he tried to hide his embarrassment and look
as if it was not unusual to visit the same cinema each day and sit
through three programmes, but the usherettes' smiles grew less
amiable, and by the end of the first week he had to stand outside
the cinema for five or ten minutes, screwing up enough courage to
buy a ticket. He learned to sit in the back row, so that he would not
have to turn and look behind him, but there were times when he
felt sure he would be asked to leave. He did not find Meg, although
he could have had for the asking many girls who looked like her.
The Everyman seemed to be their second home. He grew more
and more wretched, and worked through the mornings in a state
of heavy gloom. The journey to the cinema each day after lunch
became a habit, and in the end he forgot why he was going and
spent the intervals staring straight ahead.

Meg, or rather the need which she represented, became an
obsession. Most of the day, and at night, his skin was damp with
sweat. His body writhed in a cold passion. He was ill: the bleak-
ness of the last two years had been bound to have an effect on his
health. His constitution was strong, but no-one can live on himself
alone. One must have ambition, which includes hope and work, or
love. Perkin had none of these things to any great extent. He was
not used to worrying about his health. On many of the evenings he
spent in the cold cinema his clothes were damp and his feet were
soaked. First he had a cold, with blinding headaches and a stiff

body. The cold developed into influenza, and he spent two days in bed. On the third morning his head seemed cleared and he decided to return to work next day. Simon came home to make him some lunch and Perkin collapsed at the table. The doctor arrived just in time to prevent him contracting pleurisy.

He did not remember much about the days that followed. At first he was drugged, and imagined that he was living his everyday life. He called out for cigarettes and a book to read, although he never spoke Meg's name aloud. Anne came to sit with him in the evenings, and talked quietly to Simon over his uncomfortable body. The worst moments came three days after his collapse. Anne had gone into the kitchen to fill a flask with hot lemon juice. Simon was taking a bath.

Perkin awoke and almost cried out in terror. The bedclothes seemed to be slipping from his body. When he sat up he could actually see them moving off the bed, but the edges remained tucked in under the mattress. The walls of the room were also moving, making a dull buzzing sound. His skin tingled. It was the first moment of remembered terror in his life. The terror was nameless. All his dull tangled nerves were rebelling. All the lights were on, and they seemed to be the cause of the nightmare. He believed that he would sleep again if he could switch them off, but he could not move. The night beyond the room was still. He closed his eyes, but opened them immediately, unable to resist the blackness pressing against the walls, moving them towards him, shrinking the room until it was a coffin moulded to his size and shape.

The nightmare ended quite suddenly, and he lay back, too weak and bewildered to be glad that it was over. He thought the flat must be deserted, and it seemed hours before Anne returned. He smiled at her and asked for soup. He felt incredibly hungry.

Next day he was able to sit up and eat a proper meal. He was horrified when he saw the thinness of his hands and body. He must have lost at least half a stone in weight during the last fortnight. Simon had decided not to return to work until his brother was completely cured, and in the afternoon he brought a letter from Tom. He had written to tell him of Perkin's illness as soon as he learned that the worst was over and there was no need to worry. Perkin unfolded the single sheet, sparsely covered with untidy italic handwriting:

"Bloody fool. I suggest you give up your job, which was getting you nowhere, and take a rest. I hope you'll begin some serious work next September or October. Your allowance will be increased, of course, although you don't deserve it. I shall be compelled to do the same for Simon."

Perkin smiled wanly. Next autumn was a long time away. He would accept the increase. Simon whistled when he read the note, and sat down on the end of the bed.

"Aren't we lucky?"

Perkin nodded. "You won't give up your job?"

"No, I like it too much. But I'm glad for your sake. What will we do with the extra money? Buy a car?"

"I don't really want a car any more."

Simon frowned. "Don't worry, you will when you're feeling better."

"Unless Tom gives us a very large increase I won't be any better off. At the moment all I want to do is sleep. Do I look ghastly? Bring me a mirror."

"You look gaunt. I'll shave you, then you can lie down."

"Anne was very kind to me," Perkin said later, his face covered with cream.

Simon dipped the razor into a basin of hot water. "She's naturally kind. I'd have been helpless without her." He hesitated. "I suppose you know she's been living here."

"No. I haven't noticed anything. But I'm glad. Is she going to stay permanently?" he asked blandly.

"Certainly not." Simon laughed. "To begin with, she's too moral even to consider such a thing, and it wouldn't do. She'd make herself indispensable and I'd end up marrying her."

Perkin raised his eyebrows, but remained silent.

"I know what you're thinking, Perkin, but if we do things my way Anne won't get hurt and I'll get a good meal when I want it."

"What about my meals?"

"You'll have to find someone like Anne, or learn to cook."

When the illness was over and he could go out to lunch and for walks, Perkin's skin was transparent and his mind opaque. His eyes and mouth looked larger and his clothes hung loosely on his bones. Convalescence ended and he still did not put on weight, but he felt healthy: completely clean and supple. He could not have said what he did with his time, but he no longer had to worry about escaping boredom. He could sit in Claridge's for an hour over one cup of coffee, and be entertained without knowing it. He no longer cared to wonder if he felt contented or lonely. He looked bright and happy, and fortunately had not yet realised or begun to question it. When he fell asleep his body was moulded to the shape of Meg's body which he pretended lay beside him. During a fortnight's illness which drained him of surplus nervous energy, he learned tranquillity and patience. He waited for Meg as some people wait for a holiday abroad: they know that if they behave themselves and save carefully they will reap their chosen reward in a year's time, and in the meantime they are content to do without any kind of frivolity or impulsiveness. They regard even good meals as a luxury. Perkin saw few people, visited a bookshop almost every day but read few books, and no longer felt it necessary to buy a record which he asked to have played in a shop. He spent a good deal of time in cinemas, but he often set out to see a film and found that he had idled away the time until it was too late to go. He sometimes went out at ten o'clock in the morning and did not return until after six. He would be exhausted, his face and clothes blackened by the smoke of a London winter, and his hair standing on end. He had gone to the Stock Exchange, or somewhere that seemed equally preposterous to his friends, lunched in a Lyons tea-shop at London Wall, then returned to the river and wandered over its bridges. Nothing is more beautiful than winter sunset playing on the dirty water of the Thames, and the dull red light of sunset far down the river, as you watch from London Bridge. He decided that one day he would put it in a book, written for himself alone, and he would not care if everyone else thought it the worst book ever written. But he shook his head almost as soon as he made the decision. He would never be able to satisfy himself. In order to describe this skyline, this evening, you must first know it. You must know the name of each building, you must have sailed down the river beyond the point where the sun now appears to be dying, and with words you must describe colours that a painter can only see and feel. Then you will try to evoke this mood, this feeling of intense thankfulness that you are alive, and capable of seeing joy and sadness, vulgarity and beauty, sometimes separate but more often in each other. You must be able to say why, as you stand on this bridge at sunset with the icy air wetting your face and making your body feverish, you are glad that you are as you are and believe what you believe, although you know that life is a great and insoluble problem that will worry you until the day you die. You must say that you are glad of the suffering and misery in the world, for the game of chance and contrast, hope and despair, is the reason why each of us goes on living. There are people oblivious to the things you see, whose vision is apparently narrower than yours. Beside them you may seem worthless, for they are determined to reach a goal, and after that another goal, and it would not occur to them to see merit or dignity in failure, nor could they see that undeserved failure may be the artistic consummation of a lifetime. You believe that you are unemotional, but everything you enjoy in life is emotional, derived from an emotion you feel in yourself, not one shared with someone else. You will never know if your thinking is shallow. Perhaps the broader vision is easier, and perhaps it is not as broad as you believe. We may love ourselves, other people, money, fame, or any other abstraction or its concomitants, and almost everyone is a little in love with each of them. It may be that this is what everyone believes in, perhaps this is what colours their lives, and not faith or scepticism.

They met again on a tube going to Hampstead. It was a windy day in the middle of March. It rained all morning and afternoon, and after spending most of the day in the National Gallery Perkin decided to go to the Everyman once more, for he liked to repeat each experience he ever had in roughly the same conditions, to conjure with the mood and memory. People were beginning to return home from work, and he had to stand when he got on the tube. He saw Meg without surprise. . . . She was standing at the bottom of his compartment, leaning against an end panel, looking down, her hair dull with rain. He watched her for a moment. She was frowning, and looked like a very serious student. A large cardboard folio was hanging precariously under her arm.

Perkin shook his head and blinked away the tears of joy which suddenly filled his eyes. He walked steadily down the coach until he stood beside her, and took hold of a strap. He leaned forward and softly spoke her name. Her face flickered into life and she turned round. For a moment she stared at him, her eyes widened and dropped, and she turned away, and hid her face in the shoulder of her raincoat. Perkin watched the back of her head and did not speak again. His body had become quite nerveless and he waited, puzzled and wondering what would happen next. He wanted to contact her somehow, tap her shoulder and speak her name again, but he remained motionless. Some passengers got off at Tottenham Court Road, but Meg did not move to take a seat, and the train filled up again. He wanted to put his arm around her body in the raincoat, feel the hard dull warmth of two bodies somehow touching, but he was suspended between the blind urge to touch her and the shyness and inhibitions that he had learned since childhood. He wondered what she was thinking. She must have recognised him, and for some reason she wanted to ignore him. If she wanted to avoid him it meant he was important to her. He wondered why. The train stopped again and again and still she did not move. She might have been asleep. He knew that she would get off at Hampstead: of course he would follow her.

When they came to Hampstead she raised her head and looked through the window, then half turned to him and turned away again, and walked on to the platform. She brushed some water from her coat and straightened the folio under her arm. He caught up and walked beside her.

"Meg."

She turned briefly, and smiled. "Hello, Perkin."

He hesitated until he could talk calmly. "I said hello before. I've been standing beside you all the way from Leicester Square."

She nodded.

"Why didn't you speak?" he asked.

"I don't know." Her cheeks coloured slightly, or perhaps it was a trick of shadow as the train left the station. "I sometimes do with people I don't know well. I suppose I'm shy."

He did not know what to say. They waited for a lift.

"Where are you going?" Meg asked, apparently without interest.

"I'm going to the Everyman. I suppose you're going to see Henry?"

She nodded. In the lift he stood over her, his hand pressed against the wall. She would not look at him. He could not stop smiling foolishly, in ridiculous embarrassment. They came to the entrance, and she recoiled from the rain that was beating solidly outside.

"Why is it always raining in Hampstead?" she asked.

Perkin's face twisted in agonised embarrassment. He thought that he would never again be able to speak two consecutive words to her without losing his voice. He opened his mouth, and it seemed almost paralysed.

"Will you come and have some coffee?" he said at last. His voice was small and he felt that he was being presumptuous and impertinent. At the same time he cursed himself for being so silly. Meg nodded, as if she had never intended to do anything else but have coffee with him. She did not seem to notice his shyness. He felt a great release, and almost gasped with joy and amazement. His impossible request had by a miracle been granted.

He took her arm and dragged her up the hill to the little café called La Bohème. She collapsed breathlessly into a chair, and began laughing, and hid her face behind her hands. Suddenly it was as if a great conspiracy existed between them. He had never felt as near to anyone as he now felt near to Meg. He choked with this idiotic laughter, and shook his head despairingly and motioned to her to get up again. She stood up and he slipped the raincoat from her body.

"We're soaking," he whispered excitedly. It seemed tremendously important that she should not sit in the wet raincoat. He took off his coat and sat opposite her. She was idly stroking water from her hair, watching him all the time. She waved a hand and leaned forward and he put a cigarette between her lips. She gave a little moan of exhausted satisfaction. He went on laughing, and she recognised the laughter but pretended to frown because there was no reason for it. She looked very beautiful, he thought, as he watched her face, which was only a few inches away. Her skin was damp and glowing, and her mouth was as matt and smooth as ever. Her hair hung like satin. He wondered why it was never out of place. She was wearing a plain black dress with a boat neck and wide sleeves that came two inches below her elbows. The backs of her arms were brown, and she wore the same gold watch, turned inwards as it had been the first time he met her. He gazed at the little gold hairs on her forearms, and the paler skin on their underside.

"Just coffee?" he asked with vast amusement.

She pursed her lips. "No," she said decidedly. "I want soup, a mushroom omelet, then fruit salad and cream, then coffee and cheese and a huge chocolate ice-cream." She giggled. "I want to be hideously fat with spots on my chin. I never had them when I was sixteen. That's why I always felt so superior."

Perkin was so pleased that she might have been making love to him. The waitress came and he ordered exactly what Meg had asked for. He remembered it easily because it was his own idea of a delicious meal, although he had never felt confident enough to order it for himself. The waitress was amused despite herself, and made a grimace that was intended to be a smile.

"Shall you order the ice-cream afterwards, sir?"

Perkin nodded, and returned to the delightful position of having his face only a few inches away from Meg's. She turned her head away each time she exhaled smoke, and the gesture made him love her the more. She was a perfect girl: coolly beautiful, with a warm presence that made her seem less extraordinary. Most women who are finely beautiful make a room seem chill as soon as they enter it. There seems to be a shaft of cold air where they are standing.

Meg pulled at the cigarette and turned round again, looking down at the table. He watched her tenderly, and she looked up. They were suddenly quite serious.

"Why wouldn't you speak to me on the train?" Perkin asked softly. Her eyes were examining his face.

"I don't know. Partly, I was annoyed at the injustice of meeting you again just like that. It meant you were real and quite suddenly important to me."

He waited, trying to understand.

She made some vague gesture with her hands. She was hardly ever still while she talked, which seemed to contradict the little silences when she frowned and calculated what she would say, and the aura of calmness she always had.

"You see, there are very few people I think about when I'm not with them. I didn't think about you after that night, and I hardly remembered you when I saw you again. So I had to adjust myself."

"You didn't really want to know me better?"

"No. I'd been working all day and I was tired. I didn't want my life to be one bit more complicated."

"But now you're glad," he said with assurance.

She nodded, and he looked grateful. Neither of them was really hungry, and they only toyed with the food that was brought to them, and made idle conversation, feeling that it would be impolite to probe further into each other's thoughts. They talked about films, Henry Enfield, and the books they had been reading. By the time they were drinking coffee, they had decided that they certainly did not want ice-cream. The waitress left the bill on the table and retired, leaving them to find some fitting conclusion to the meeting. They would either be friends or never meet again. Perkin was almost certain they would be lovers, but it was the kind of sudden attraction which precedes a very tender love affair, or in a moment explodes into irritation or anger. It is impossible to indicate what resolves the situation.

There had been a long silence when Meg said, "I think you look different, or is it because you were drunk that night?"

"I've been ill." He smiled: she would never know that she had indirectly caused his illness. "I didn't look after myself properly and almost had pleurisy. I'm better now."

"You look nicer, more vulnerable."

"I'm extremely vulnerable, subject to all kinds of disorders."

He was not quite sure what he meant, but it seemed obvious to Meg that he was ready to love her. She watched him, trying to decide.

"Are you sure you've had enough to eat?" he asked politely.

She nodded. "I'd be happy to eat like this all my life. I could live on a thousand pounds a year. Henry says he needs four thousand, and he'd be happier if I earned money too."

Perkin disregarded the remark. There was no reason to pretend that Henry seemed important to her at this moment, although she might worry later. He wondered with quiet desperation if he was taking too much for granted.

"I never wonder how much money I'll have ten years from now," he said dully. "It's nice to have a rich father."

"Don't you worry about finding a regular job some day?"

"No." He looked at her body in the black dress. "I suppose I'm a fatalist. I'll be glad to accept whatever comes."

"How lucky you are. I envy you," she said insincerely.

Their conversation tailed away and they felt nervous.

"Do you have to see Henry?" he asked quietly. "Won't you come to this picture with me? I'd like it very much if you could." He felt ashamed of his embarrassment.

Meg nodded. "I'll call Henry and tell him I won't be round tonight."

He paid the bill and helped her into her coat, and they left the café. They felt tired, in the period of nervous exhaustion which results from too much excitement and uncertainty as to what will happen next. The rain had stopped and the air was mild and sweet. The sky was bright. It was almost possible to believe that one day spring would come. They walked slowly to the telephone booths in the station. Meg closed the door and he could not hear what excuse she was giving Henry. She only spoke two or three times, then came out again.

"He says he hopes we enjoy the film, and he wants to see you again soon."

Perkin was convinced that she had told Henry some lie, and he kept silent.

The Everyman was just beginning a series of American films,

and they were showing an enchanting film called *Funny Face*,
but for some reason the cinema was almost empty. Nevertheless
Perkin asked to be shown to one of the pairs of sideseats. Meg did
not protest. They laid their coats on the seats in front.

"I always come to these seats," he whispered, feeling rather
foolish and unable to see her face in the dark. "It's like sitting in
the front or back seats on top of a bus."

"Shush. I hate people who talk in cinemas."

A few moments later he felt her touch his leg, and he took her
hand. She relaxed, and all tension was gone between them. Afterwards he was ashamed to admit that he had enjoyed the film.
There had been other visits to cinemas when he could not have
said what the film was about, but it was easy to feel tranquil with
Meg. He could almost ignore her as long as he was dimly aware
of her body beside him. He could feel her smiling with pleasure
at the lovely colour of the film. Once or twice she laughed aloud,
and then he laughed louder. In the interval he was not sure what
to do with her hand, so he held it in his lap between his hands. It
was long and thin, with short pink nails. The fingers seemed to
continue almost to the wrist, and when he played with the top of
one of them, every muscle and vein in the hand moved. The palm
could not have been more than half an inch thick, and he shivered
when he thought of its fragility. When they left the cinema the
streets were still wet, and the area looked like a very clever stage
without actors.

He turned up the collar of his overcoat.

"More coffee, or do you want to go straight home?"

Meg looked at him oddly. "Home." He took her elbow and they
walked slowly to the bus station, too preoccupied with the thought
of themselves and their relation to each other to talk much. The
night was cold again. He wondered if he should make love to her
that night. Somehow he was frightened for her frailty.

The street where she lived, with its neon lights and coffee bar,
looked like Soho. She opened the front door of her house and went
inside, leaving it open for him to follow her, and did not bother to
ask if he wanted to come up. He closed the door carefully behind
him, and followed her up the dark stairs. They smelt of garlic and

sweat and tinned soup. In one of the rooms someone was playing an old record by the Teddy Wilson trio, and Perkin suddenly felt displaced. He might have been a middle-aged man, remembering the night in 1935 when he followed a lovely girl up the stairs of a dark old house, and wondering sadly what had become of her and her time. Perkin usually did not care to think in general terms, but it occurred to him that despite the efforts of writers to give significance to this decade, it would have a well documented but insignificant place in history. The period between the two wars had been so compressed and without precedent that it had a character of its own, in literature and presumably in fact; but his generation began after the second war, and as there was unlikely to be a third catastrophe which anyone survived, it would continue to live in the shadow, never able to get properly started, and shamelessly borrowing the uncertain talents of previous generations.

The light in Meg's room was weak, and made it seem more sordid than it really was. Perkin gasped when he entered it, horrified by its dismal shabbiness. But Meg did not seem embarrassed, and only smiled carelessly as she told him to sit on the bed because it was more comfortable than either of the chairs. She went to the stove to make coffee, and Perkin sprawled on his elbow, wondering if he should comment on the room.

"It isn't too bad," Meg said, waving a hand behind her. "I'm never here except when I'm working, and it's very cheap."

"Well, isn't this the way young musicians are supposed to live?"

She brought the coffee and sat beside him on the bed.

"It will probably taste horrible."

He shook his head. "I hate coffee and tea anyway. You only drink it because it feels empty to go to bed without eating for three or four hours."

He suddenly realised the implication of the idle remark, and set the cup on the saucer with a jerk, looking pathetically embarrassed, and pleased with himself. He had not behaved so youthfully for years, and was glad to learn that experience had not taught him as much as he believed. He finished the coffee in one gulp, and set the cup on the table. Meg looked flushed, and her forehead was damp with sweat. He could not think of anything original to say to her, so he had to repeat the usual phrases, which are acknowledged to mean something entirely different.

"Do you usually bring men to your room the first night?"

"Oh, thousands."

"And tell them to sit on the bed?"

"Everyone."

He took her hand. "With what result?"

"They try to seduce me, of course. But I don't let them. I laugh in their faces and they run away as if I'd told them I was really eighty-six years old."

Perkin shook his head violently, and buried his face in her hand.

"No, Meg, no. Don't talk like this. This is the way everybody talks. I want us to be different."

She leaned over and kissed his neck, and he shivered at her touch. She nodded silently, and he laid his head in her lap.

"I never thought it would happen," he said with tremendous thankfulness. "I kept wanting it so much and hoping for it, but I'm shy with you."

"Why?" she murmured, her mouth pressed against his neck.

"I don't know," he said. His shoulders began to heave and hot tears rolled down his face on to her dress. "I was very ill, you know, and weak for a long time. A long, long time."

"But you're better now," she sighed, and felt him nodding fiercely.

"I'm better now, Meg."

She gathered him in her arms and kissed his mouth, and he held her face pressed close to his face.

"This is the best thing that's ever happened to me," he whispered. "I thought this would never happen to me again. Do you know what it's like – meeting someone and taking her home and then next morning you find you haven't a thing to say to each other? You're so damned bored with her and indifferent and at the same time you want her to give just one sign that she cares a little and that you matter to her. And you hesitate over breakfast trying to think of something to say, and wondering if you want to see her again and, more important, if she wants to see you again. And more than anything else, you're so ashamed to show that you may have some real feeling, and arrange another meeting, in case she laughs at you and says no. When it was like that, as it's been all these years, I never once made another date for the next night. It was always for the beginning or middle of next week, because I didn't want to show anything more than polite interest. There were some girls who were better than that; but the bloody thing is, when two nice people get together, it doesn't mean that the slightest emotion will be aroused." He lay back exhausted, still holding her against him. "But this is different. I don't know the words to say to you. If I say love you'll laugh at me."

"No, I won't, Perkin." She kissed his mouth and began to draw her fingers across his forehead. "Don't be afraid. Say love to me." She bit her lip. "You make me want to weep. I don't quite know why."

At any other time he might have been offended, but he had completely abandoned himself to her. Once he began to talk he could not stop, and he shamelessly mumbled the truth, or as much of it as he would ever know.

"Say you love me," Meg repeated.

"I—" The word would not come. He lay with his mouth open, trying with his whole being to force the words into existence. He fell away, ashamed. Meg lay down beside him, and pressed the side of her face into his shoulder. This was best, after all. How long since she had lain in utter pleasure with someone young who needed her. One day she would tell him that she could not give him everything he needed, but not yet. She would teach him to go on looking until he found what she had once cherished. She could not forget Tony even for a few hours: as she kissed Perkin she made comparisons, and found differences which it was impossible to put into words. Their clothes, their skin and sweat and smell were not the same. One day she would tell him the truth: he was in no way inferior and a long time ago she might have chosen him. But Tony had come first and she could not forget him. She smiled. She would not have it any other way.

"How can I say I love you, Meg? What about Henry?"

"Henry doesn't matter. You're the strangest boy I've ever met. Forget Henry. It's what we feel now that matters. Isn't that enough?"

"No." He turned to her and lifted her face. "It's almost enough, darling. But it must go on and have some meaning. I can't help worrying, you see."

"It will go on," she said firmly, exasperated. Wasn't this enough for him? Couldn't he stop thinking? Their bodies together formed a microcosm, the walls of the room were space. It was possible to be completely involved in this relationship and forget everything else for a moment. For just a few moments she could forget Tony. Perkin must learn to push aside his apprehension. She saw only his face, felt only his shoulder and neck and head. She could not see beyond these shapes, and almost cried out as she watched his face, an inch away, quivering in uncertainty. She kissed him, but his mouth remained closed. She opened it gently with her fingers and pressed her mouth against his teeth. He lay still and unresponsive. After a moment he pulled away and glanced aside, and when he felt that she was puzzled and unprepared, whispered quickly, "I love you."

She wanted to laugh. He clung to her and said again and again, "I love you, Meg," and he had not believed that any simple words could mean so much more each time he said them.

CHAPTER XIV

ON the evening that Anne returned to her flat, Simon took her to dinner at the Satyr, which is a club in St. James's Street with a dog and a three-piece band. It was Tuesday, and the club was almost deserted, so that two members of the band looked as if they were wondering why they should bother to play. No-one was dancing. The pianist, who was the only player one noticed, was enjoying himself immensely, in a desperate kind of way. Anne and Simon went to an extremely dark corner, lit only by a tiny lamp on the table.

"You look delicious," Simon said politely. "Like a Madonna by candlelight. And your wool dress is delightful. I'm exceedingly lucky to have such a charming companion."

"What a lot of superlatives," Anne said blandly, and was pleased to see his face fall. By this time she had learned to wonder why, rather than glow with pleasure when he paid her a compliment. She had also begun to realise that he was very attached to her, although she supposed he was right when he said that he did not love her. He slept with her almost every night, and because he had taught her to think with a certain detachment, she realised that she had never believed that any man would find her passionately desirable, and knew joyfully that Simon's interest in her bed seemed to increase. She had expected it to wane, because it always did in books and films, and believed that she would hold a man by providing good food and comfort. In truth Simon desired her because after the first awkwardness she was very responsive and still seemed innocent. Once she learned what she wanted she was completely without foolish shame, and never reproached him. She seemed to grow more beautiful each day. Her hair was thicker and smoother, she was always perfectly made-up, and walked with new assurance. But it was all because she loved him. That was the one thing he did not want, and the thing which made her what she was: an impossible situation which he should have ignored until some crisis, but he was too nervous.

"You look lovely too," Anne continued. "I see you've washed your hair. But what happened to your cuff-links?"

The sleeves of his shirt were rolled back to the elbows.

"I lost one," Simon said coldly. "You needn't try to be amusing, you know."

"What do you mean?" Anne asked innocently.

"Well, lately you've begun to make these rather coy little jokes implying that I can't look after myself." Anne's eyes widened. "You notice everything too. But I don't want you to be clever. Just stay the way you are."

"I still don't know what you're talking about."

"Look, sweetie, I am not going to marry you, nor do I depend on you as much as you'd like to believe." He thumped the table. "And I wish you'd stop treating me like an intelligent animal that will do what it's told if it gets what it wants."

Anne sighed and looked sympathetic. "Have you got a headache or something, Simon?" she asked anxiously.

He was about to shout at her, but realised how foolishly he was behaving. He did not reply, and leaned back so that she could not see his face. At once she looked quite miserable and he cursed himself. But he did not apologise, because it would have made him seem childishly bad-tempered.

Anne lit a cigarette and wanted to cry. It often happened that their evenings together would end like this, until later in bed he would mumble some apology and go to sleep. He seemed to want to hurt her. His voice came from the shadows: "That pianist really is terribly neurotic."

Anne glanced over her shoulder at the band. The pianist was a pale thin young man with quick nervous eyes and hands. She thought he looked sweet and wondered if he were poor, then turned round again, unable to think of anyone but Simon. The bitter-sweet tumbling arpeggios made her want to go to sleep.

"Do you want some brandy, Anne?"

She shrugged, and he beckoned to the waiter. "Two double brandies and coffee." He took the cigarette from her lips and pulled at it, leaning his head against the wall. "The music's pretty though, isn't it? But terribly bad." As far as she was concerned the words had no relation to Simon, whom she could not see. They might just as well have been coming from a radio. She nodded dumbly. The pianist played some sweepingly ugly introduction, and then began a song which was popular at that time in the clubs, but was never heard outside them. Perhaps he had written it himself. Simon began to sing to himself, and in the complete stillness of the dark corner the words reached Anne as though they had been sung in an echo-chamber:

> You are there, in the night,
> You are there, at morning light,
> I suppose you're kissing,
> Maybe you are missing
> Someone new,
> But darling,
> Not as much as I miss you.

Simon clapped his hands. "Isn't the end corny, though?"

Anne was looking at the little lamp on the table, and did not reply.

"Drink your brandy," he said harshly. She obeyed, letting the whole glassful trickle down her throat, and went on staring at the lamp.

"Do you like that song, Anne?"

She nodded, and with a great effort managed to talk calmly. "It's very sad."

"Ah. I thought you were terribly bored with me and wanted to go home." He came out of the shadow and kissed her still lips over the table. She came to life again and smiled fleetingly.

"Am I unkind to you, Anne?"

"You are."

He kissed her again. "I don't mean to be. I never think and then I realise afterwards that I've hurt you. I can be miserable too, you know."

"Can you?" she asked, unconvinced. "It's hard to believe."

"Oh yes. Sweetie, you must always believe what I tell you, because it will always be the truth. I'd never tell you a lie. What would be the point when you accept everything I say and do, and somehow manage to forgive me. But why me? Are you one of those people who like to be hurt by their lover?" He shook his head. "Of course not. Then why pick me?"

"There doesn't have to be a reason, Simon."

He watched her for a moment, feeling extraordinarily moved. "You know, I'm learning from you. What would you do if I left you?"

She frowned. "I'd cry my heart out."

He said quickly, "Then go to someone else?"

"No. I don't know what I'd do." She blushed. "I have no modesty, you see. I'd just be lost without you."

Simon said quietly, "In that case you'd soon turn to someone else. You can't live on a memory alone unless you've got something tangible, that was shared, to remember. If I'd given you that, if I'd talked to you more often and given you something real to remember, I'd say you were right. But you can't live on the memory of a few nights in bed. You'd find someone else, all right."

Anne shook her head. "It wouldn't be the same. You forget that you're the first person I've ever been in love with. It makes all the difference."

"Anne, what am I going to do with you? You make me feel old and sentimental and slightly avuncular."

She hesitated. "Just one thing, Simon. I don't care how long it goes on, I won't tie you down. I'll never expect you to marry me. Please believe that."

He brushed the words aside as if he had not been listening. "I can't quite understand it. I was just thinking that it was hard for me to sympathise with you because I'd simply never had that experience of first love. I was a rather quiet little boy until I came to London and then, in about a year, I'd had everything. But I still didn't know what it was like to love someone, completely and innocently. Do you want to hear this?"

"Of course." She knew that he would tell her anyhow.

"Well, there was a girl in Ireland, when I was fifteen or sixteen. Her father kept a shop in the village a few miles from where we lived. And she was the most ordinary girl. You know, she was in three or four church choirs, she went to elocution and music and dancing lessons, she passed all her exams at school but she never did really well in anything. She often looked pretty but never quite right. Her clothes never really suited her, but they were always expensive and clean. She loved Annie S. Swan and horses and dances on Christmas Eve, and she dramatised her life terribly. Anyhow at first I hated her and sent her funny Valentine cards, and then we kept meeting accidentally and laughed insanely when we did. She used to make fun of my red nose and asked me if I'd been drinking beer." Unconsciously he was rubbing his nose and Anne smiled tenderly. "Then one day she came to my house and looked terribly distressed and said that her boy friend didn't love her any more. I'd seen him, and I couldn't help telling her that she should be jumping for joy rather than looking unhappy, but it was merely an excuse for her to come and see me. She'd had this thing about me for years and wouldn't admit it because I always laughed at her. She cried a little that day and told me in a most effectively intense way that she had turned to me because she knew I'd always understand, and so on. And of course I fell for it. I took her to the old draughty village cinema the next night and bought her a half-pound box of Black Magic chocolates and held her hand. I was exceedingly nervous because I'd never kissed a girl and I knew she expected me to kiss her when I took her home. And of course all I did was blush and arrange to see her the next day. It's so funny when I think about it. How can people endure adolescents? I'm embarrassed when I remember what I was like.

"The poor girl (I have a horrible feeling that her name was Alice) wanted me to kiss her and look hot, but she was very patient. We went for walks on Sunday afternoon, and I waited outside until she left Sunday School, where she was a teacher. There was one terrible day when we went for a walk up this road which was almost completely deserted. I wanted to ask her to sit down on the grass by the side but I wasn't brave enough, and when I saw someone coming in the distance I sighed and said, 'Oh, here's somebody else. I thought this road would be deserted.' Of course it was against Alice's principles to take the initiative, and when we got home I wondered why she looked so annoyed. One warm day I was so drowsy that we really did lie down on the grass and Alice lay back with her eyes closed. She was wearing a light cotton dress and nothing underneath and I fidgeted backwards and forwards and tickled her face with a straw. But I couldn't touch her. If I had I'd probably still be in Ireland, painting watercolours with a wife and three children. I think she really loved me."

"What happened to her?" Anne asked.

"I suppose she got tired waiting. One night it was arranged that I should meet her after choir practice but she left by another door and I saw her running down the street with one of her friends. When I saw her again we simply ignored each other. Afterwards it was just one person after another; teachers at school, the head boy one year, and an actress who was playing in rep one summer we spent in Dublin. She was beautiful and terribly poor I suppose, but I'd never have dared to speak to her."

"It was one person after another for me too," Anne said quietly.

"It always is, sweetie. For everyone. Let's go to the Blue Angel. If we get there before eleven they won't charge any admission fee."

"Isn't that a dive?" Anne said anxiously.

"I'll be there to look after you."

The Blue Angel in Berkeley Street is in a basement, but it is not a dive. It is just another club, and the amount of entertainment you get depends on whom you take. Anne would have been content to stay at home and listen to records, but Simon was restless. He liked to say that he had been some place. They went to another dark corner, and this time sat on the same side of the table. Simon ordered another pair of double brandies. He put his arms around Anne, and wished that he could make love to her.

"Beautiful."

"You too."

He bit her ear. "Stop making fun of me. You're not at all beautiful. You're funny. Incidentally I've said the same to a thousand girls. Tell me, what's your name."

Anne put her hand under his jacket and kissed his mouth. "You've been smoking too many cigarettes. Also, remember telling me about the red nose you had when you were sixteen? You still have it." Simon pouted, and she kissed his red nose. "Never mind. Perhaps it will go away when the warm weather comes. Where are you taking me for our summer holidays?"

"You talk too much," Simon whispered. He was holding her as close as possible, and was reflecting that it often felt much more pleasant when they were both dressed. "Do you think anyone would object if we made love under the table? I bet you've never even kissed someone under a table. I have."

A strange expression came into Anne's eyes. "What would you do if I suddenly left, saying that I never wanted to see you again?"

Simon grinned. "Isn't that unlikely? Or don't you like this?" He drew away, and Anne quickly pulled him back. He laughed and kissed her happily.

"You're so certain of me, Simon. One day I'll try to hurt you."

"You need me."

"But do you need me?"

He lay still against her shoulder for a moment. "I'm taking you home to Ireland for a fortnight in July. I was keeping it as a surprise until nearer the time."

"Do you need me, Simon?" Anne's eyes filled with tears, but she was shaking her head. "No, Simon. You don't need me, you don't need anyone."

He held her face between his hands, and kissed her mouth and then her hair and neck, trying to warm her, willing her to believe him. His eyes were closed and her head felt unresisting whichever way he pushed it. "I love you, Anne."

She opened her eyes, and gazed at him, trying to make him deny his words. He did not look away. At last she smiled.

"I can't believe it." She flung herself into his arms.

"It's true. I'll say it to you again and again until I make you believe it. I've been fighting it for so long. At first I almost disliked you for making me care about you. I'm selfish and cruel. I suppose I have such a poor opinion of myself that I could never believe anyone would really fall in love with me. But you've completely reformed me."

Tears were running down her face, and he kissed them away as he talked. "We'll have a wonderful life together, Anne. That's a promise."

"I'm too happy and drunk to think properly," she said. "May I have some coffee to help me sober up?"

Simon beckoned to a waiter, who had been watching and wondering why they were behaving like lunatics.

Anne brushed her hair with her hands. "I won't let you sleep tonight," she whispered shyly. "I'll make you say it over and over until the morning. Simon Young, I'm going to make you suffer for torturing me the way you did."

He bowed his head gracefully. "I shall enjoy suffering for you. I shall be your devoted slave except . . ." He did not finish the sentence. Anne was watching him, and knew what he had intended to say. She bent down and kissed his hand.

"Later. Drink your coffee and get sober and then I'll get you drunk again."

She swallowed the tiny cupful of black coffee. "May I have yours too?"

"Of course." For some reason he lifted the cup and saucer instead of pushing them the few inches across the wooden table.

The cup overbalanced and coffee fell onto his trousers. It was only lukewarm but he could feel it soaking through the cloth and dampening his skin. He was wearing a grey wool suit and the black stain spread down his legs almost to his knees. It was ugly. He suddenly felt shabby and uncomfortable and tired. He felt angry at Anne because she fluttered uselessly and could do nothing to make him feel better.

"Oh, your poor suit!"

"Damn the suit," he hissed savagely. A waiter came with a damp cloth and managed to squeeze most of the coffee away. The suit would have to be cleaned, but meanwhile it would take only a few minutes to dry.

"Let's go home," Anne whispered. "I'll wash the stains away and your trousers will be dry by the morning."

Simon shook his head. "No. I'll go back to my place. I've got a headache anyway."

"Please, Simon," Anne said, smiling. "I promise not to talk. I'll let you go to sleep immediately, if you want to."

"I'm going home," he said. "I'm tired and bored." Her face crumpled. "I'm sorry," he added. "Perkin isn't really well yet, you know. I'd like to make sure that he's all right. I'll take you home in a taxi." He took her arm as they left the club and held her hand in the taxi. He vaguely remembered the words he had whispered an hour or so ago and realised that he must be kind to her: it was tiresome, but his duty. He wanted to go to bed and fall asleep alone, with his arms folded under him and his body stretched in any position he desired.

All the way home, Anne sat quite straight, without speaking or moving her hand in his cold grip. It never occurred to her that a spilled cup of coffee might ruin a whole evening and drain Simon of energy. She would have laughed if anyone had suggested it. All the vitality and light in him had suddenly gone. It was as if he had grown tired of playing a game and, as games are unimportant, had left it without a second thought. He kissed her on the forehead when the taxi stopped at her door.

"I'll ring you tomorrow," he said and yawned. Her mouth began to tremble but she managed to smile.

On arriving home he looked into Perkin's room. His brother was sleeping peacefully and his face was cool. Simon ran a hot bath, undressed and kicked away the soiled trousers with distaste. Twenty minutes later he had forgotten the whole incident, and indeed the whole evening, and was dusting his body with talcum powder. He fell asleep as soon as he got into bed.

Anne stared wildly at the ceiling until three o'clock, and then began crying. She cried her heart out until morning.

CHAPTER XV

THE rain, still slashing the dark street at noon, the black sky and the grotesque sounds of an old piano in the dancing academy opposite, made it seem inadvisable to leave this room, warmed by their presence through the night and forenoon. Perkin lay on the bed, wearing only his trousers, and after washing the breakfast dishes, Meg sat down beside him and played with his toes. There was the inevitable feeling of anticlimax, and they were saved from disappointment only by the knowledge that there would be more nights when the feelings of the morning were forgotten. Meg was happy because she liked Perkin very much; he was less happy because he loved her, and was anxious that nothing should ever take away their intimacy.

Meg bent down and picked up something from the floor. She took his shirt and examined it.

"The collar button's come off." She went over to a wardrobe and took a spool and a packet of needles from the shelf.

He stirred. "Your life. Tell me about your life."

Meg took a pair of horn-rimmed glasses from the pocket of her housecoat and put them on. "You know the facts, and there's little more to tell."

"But how did you feel when the incidents took place?" he insisted.

"I didn't." – *With one great exception* – "I've never been able to understand people who are stricken by love or hate or some calamity. There's always so much to do. I had no time to grieve when my parents died, or to dream when I was told that if I worked hard I might be an excellent pianist. I was caught up immediately these things were said to me. I've always been busy. Each conclusion was a beginning" – *with one great exception, and after all that was a beginning too.*

"I've fallen in love with a fanatic."

"No. Tell me, how can anyone feel bored? There are books to be read and studied and music and pictures and films and plays. When you're tired you can take a bath or go to bed."

Perkin smiled brightly. "Does this house have a bath?"

She answered seriously. "Somewhere. But I don't bath here." He raised his eyebrows, and wondered what a public bath was like. He had never been to one. "But, Meg, everyone has regrets and desires. You can't forget part of your life because it has ended."

She snapped the thread, folded the shirt and put it aside. "All I ever had was work, and work that is completed is of no interest to anyone and best forgotten. I was interested in nothing else. I was bored at college and never thought about it from the day I left."

"Your marriage?" he said uncomfortably.

She put her fingers between the slightly deformed toes of his left foot. They were like little round balls, without nails, except for a thick brown nail on the big toe. "My marriage was very happy. I loved Tony, but it is over. There's nothing more to say."

Perkin smiled. "You mean you still love him and will always remember him and I could never take his place? Well, I don't want to. I understand and I'll never be jealous of him."

"You don't understand," Meg said quickly, "and I shall never explain to you. We won't talk about it, that's all."

He felt certain that he did understand, but he nodded.

"And what about Henry?"

She frowned. "You ask so many questions. I like Henry very much. He's helped me a great deal, you know; he gave me money that I may never be able to repay. I was never in love with him."

"You were prepared to marry him."

"Yes, for security. Does that shock you?"

He shook his head. "But you won't marry him now, of course."

Meg hesitated. "I suppose not. You've been good for me,

Perkin. I thought I could settle down and work and eat good food and go to parties with Henry. Now that kind of existence seems inadequate."

Perkin drew her down beside him and loosened the girdle of her housecoat. At once her eyes dilated with pleasure and he laughed with joy. For a moment he lay watching her body, then he put his hands around her back and drew her down on top of him. He pressed upwards gently and she moaned.

"We're not going to make love," he whispered. "This is delicious. And you're not going to marry Henry. You'll marry me or come and live with me and we'll have a marvellous life. Isn't that right?"

She shook her head fiercely. "I'll have to think about it. I don't know what I'm going to do."

"You'll do what I say. Kiss me."

She opened her mouth and her head fell down to him. He kissed her mouth and teeth and hoped that it would never end. She began to move gently across his body and the pain grew unbearable.

"Damn you, Meg. You're small and perfect and I'd like to make you scream." He pushed her away and pulled off his trousers. "I'll make you pregnant and you'll have to marry me." He fell on her and she cried out. "Why did your husband never give you a baby?"

"He didn't want children. Perkin, please, you won't?"

He could not reply.

"Then do," she shouted fiercely. "Hurt me and make me have children and do anything you wish." The words tailed off and he heard her sigh through the sound of skin against skin and fiery hot motion. Scalding tears fell down her face and he tasted them one by one until he buried his mouth away from the stream that might have drowned him.

When he awakened it was still raining, and the room was flickering in the uncertain light, and cold. The shilling in the meter had been used and the gas fire had gone out. He eased his arm from under her back and she sighed.

"I'm awake, Perkin. It's cold."

He got up and looked for a shilling in the pile of money on the table, then brought the fire nearer so that its heat would reach the bed. He lay beside Meg again and pulled the blanket up to their shoulders. She closed her eyes and came into his arms. He kissed her shoulder, and could think of no words tender enough to say to her.

"Meg, whatever I say, I'll never try to make you do anything you don't want to do."

She smiled.

"I didn't hurt you, Meg?"

She shook her head, and he gently lifted some strands of hair that had fallen across her cheek and let them slip like silk threads through his fingers. His eyes filled with tears.

"I'll make love to you too often. You'll grow tired of me."

He felt her eyes open against his cheek.

"No, I won't grow tired of you," she said quietly, "if you take me as I am."

"Will you come and live with me?"

"No." She turned onto her back. "Keep it the way it is. If we lived together I'd never do any work and I'd be bad-tempered and resent you."

"I'd leave you to work in peace."

"Like you did today? What time is it, Perkin?"

"Four o'clock."

"Four o'clock, and I had lessons at ten this morning. That's the way it would always be."

He grasped her hand eagerly. "Then give up music. You're too lovely to worry about endless study and self-sacrifice. We'd have a wonderful time. Oh, Meg, what good will it ever do you? It's only for people who've got nothing else."

At any other time or place Meg would have been outraged, but she held his face between her hands and said, "Perkin darling, how can anyone be so clever and so foolish at the same time. You've been reading too much lyric poetry. You'll be awfully bored when you're old, Perkin, if you're not wearing corsets and trying to be a beautiful young man. Nothing will interest you and you'll cry your eyes out with self-pity because you're so lonely."

"I'll have a lot to remember," he said unconvincingly.

"It's no good," Meg insisted. "Listen, now you're young and you can meet the people you want to meet and do what you want to do. You're lazy, but you know that you could have these things if you wanted them. One day you'll find that it's too late, and all the wishing in the world won't get you what you want." She kissed his eyes, which were damp with sweat. "Darling, everyone must have a reason for living, and if you lose it you convince yourself that you've found a substitute. What happened to yours?"

"I love people. That's a very moral reason for living. I love you."

Meg said, "You think you know a lot. I do too, but God, we're children struggling along like orphans in a slum. The slightest breeze and we're cold and frightened and clinging to the first person who offers us warmth. I wonder if we'll ever lose our innocence?"

He pulled her very close to him. "Don't bother your pretty head with these solemn thoughts," he whispered tenderly, kissing her. "Do you think I'll ever grow tired of kissing your face?" A few moments later he added, "I never really wanted you to give up your work. It was just a passing thought."

"I know. And you'd never have persuaded me. It's my security."

For a moment he felt quite lonely again, in the cold away from the people who were strange and less uncertain than himself, but he knew that he had only himself to blame.

"I have a fatal lack of organizing ability. I can work, but only spasmodically. There was a period, before I was ill, when I did a lot of reading. I enjoyed it, but it was still work to me."

"It takes years of discipline to accustom oneself to enjoying the best books and paintings and music, but it's worth it in the end; you become a human being, and not just an animal."

"I wish you wouldn't preach to me, Meg. You make me feel inferior."

"That's got nothing to do with my liking you."

A sudden gust of wind blew a sheet of rain against the window, and the room was quite dark for a moment. Perkin sat up and put on his sweater. He felt slightly dizzy. "Do you want a cigarette, Meg?"

She shook her head. He took a cigarette and lit it carefully. "A few days ago I thought it would soon be spring, and now this. I don't know how we survive the winter; it always makes me feel so ill." He realized that he had smoked half the cigarette in four or five long quick drags.

"You're still too thin," Meg said anxiously. "You must have a holiday."

"In July I'm going home." He covered her still naked body with the blanket. "I don't like looking at you when you're cold."

She snuggled against his sweater, and he stroked her hair. "This is better than any old piano," he said, "and don't shout at me. Tomorrow morning I shall beat you if you don't practise." He was silent for a moment, trying in vain to find a solution to their problems, or even to see the position clearly. He realized that anyone not involved would easily find a solution, but he felt tremendously glad that he cared enough to feel bewildered.

"I suppose it's true," he said quietly. "I'm worthless." Meg was hardly listening. She had almost fallen asleep against the warm wool. "And I didn't care. I suppose I do care now, but not enough to make an effort to change. The terrible thing is, I know very well that my worthlessness is the reason why many people would love me. Is that why you love me?"

"Partly," she murmured. "You're not worthless, but you're clever; you could do so much more with yourself. It will all come right in the end."

He finished the cigarette and lit another.

"How much do you love me?"

"I never said I did." She rubbed her eyes and sat up. "Stop asking questions. Accept me as I am or we'll both be miserable." She reached out for her underclothes and he turned his head away.

"I haven't even got a job now, Meg. I've got nothing except you."

She did not reply, knowing that the words were meaningless, even for Perkin. She stepped into her skirt.

"I wish you'd give me your sweater," she said smiling. "It would suit me perfectly."

"I'll bring it to you as soon as I change." He crushed out the cigarette and began to dress. Meg put on a jumper and threw a towel around her shoulders. She went to the mirror over the sink and began to put on make-up. Perkin watched her, fascinated. When he had awakened to see her face on the pillow, he thought that he preferred her face without make-up. Her skin was quite fine, and her mouth pale and smooth without lipstick. He watched her brush out her hair, which seemed always to fall the same way without any trouble. She smoothed cream over her face, patted it with her fingertips, then wiped it away with tissue. She took a long gold pencil from her handbag and carefully ran the lipstick along the edges of her mouth, then began to work inwards. She smoothed away the lines and leaned against the mirror, examining her mouth carefully. Perkin could see little difference in the colour of her mouth, but her skin now seemed paler and less transparent. She took out a mascara-stick, closed one eye, and carefully darkened the upper eyelash until it was thick and jet black. The upper and lower lashes clung together when she tried to open her eye and she separated them tenderly with a fine brush. When she had darkened the other eye she leaned against the mirror and stared into her eyes, to make sure that they were exactly the same shape. She turned to him.

She looked quite beautiful, although her face still seemed to be without make-up. Her face was now very pale, but he doubted if she could ever look unhealthy. Her eyes were very bright and clear.

"I'm disgracefully in love with you," Perkin said helplessly. He shook his head. "Your face looks beautiful whatever you do to it."

Meg smiled. "I like your face too, and you don't have the benefit of make-up."

He felt an odd little pang of tenderness and glanced away shyly. He blew her a kiss and went to the window. The street was swimming with water. Cigarette-packets and litter from the shops had clogged up the drains, and a man in a butcher's apron was poking at one of them with a stick. After a moment he cursed and pulled away the dirt with his hands, his rough face ugly with distaste. The downpour had stopped, but a large raindrop sometimes fell surprisingly. Perkin opened the window, and noticed that even after the rain the glass was filthy.

"Meg, if we can't live together, let me help you to buy a small flat. How can you live in a place like this? It's disgustingly poor."

"I don't live here."

He turned round, startled. Meg gasped and put her hand to her mouth.

"Perkin, surely you realised? Didn't Henry tell you? I've been living with him for over a year."

Perkin's face became quite immobile and he stared at her blankly, wondering why he did not feel empty and angry. Meg waited, her hands thrust forward, for his reaction.

"No," he sighed.

She shrugged apprehensively and passed a hand across her face. "You must have guessed. Everything I said indicated it. I told you he'd given me money. He pays me an allowance so that I can go on studying. It was so obvious."

"I thought you lived here."

"Oh, Perkin! Does this room look like a home? No books or clothes or a proper cooker. I took this room to work in. It's near my teacher and I couldn't practise at home when Henry was writing."

"Home?"

"Henry's house."

Perkin sat down on the bed. He felt cold, but not angry.

"There's this bed – I thought you were so poor that you couldn't afford anything better. I thought you were living on a scholarship or money your husband had left you."

Meg smiled. If there had been any money left when Tony died she would have given it away, rather than spend it on her left-over life.

"Tony?" she said sadly. "We used to spend every penny of his salary as soon as we got it. Sure I have a scholarship, but it's hardly enough to pay for food. I bought this piano myself. Henry pays for everything else." She sighed. "Perkin, you've seen my clothes. Do you think I could afford to buy them on scholarship money?"

"Your clothes look very simple. They can't be expensive."

"They're bloody expensive."

Something snapped inside him. "This bed," he shouted.

Her eyes flashed. "It was included in the price of the room. I sometimes sleep here when I'm too tired to go home, or too tired of Henry, or when he's away. I'm going to have to think of a pretty good excuse to explain last night. I haven't slept with him for nearly a week."

Perkin's eyes widened and in a blind rage he reached out for something to break and destroy. He picked up a record and snapped it across his knee. He heard it crack inside the shiny sleeve. He tossed it aside.

"You coarse vulgar little bitch." He could not look at her. "That old, that little old man. Weren't you disgusted, weren't you sick with disgust? Selling yourself for good meals and a bed." He laughed triumphantly. "God knows, it can't have been a very comfortable bed. Did you choose Henry because he was the first one to make an offer? Was it that you didn't care, that it wasn't important to you? You looked so pure."

Meg walked over to the window and stood facing him, calmly and with distaste.

"Don't confuse purity with cleanliness, darling. As far as I know, I look rather like a high-class whore. And you look pure and innocent. In fact you are, but technically you're not. You've gone mad, Perkin. Are you trying to tell me that you didn't know I slept with Henry?"

"Yes. No! Oh, Meg, yes, I suppose I did know, but I thought it only happened occasionally and you were going to marry him."

"And you consider it more immoral to live with him, in comfort, than to sleep with him when he wants me?"

Perkin felt exhausted and wished that he could forget and lie down and go to sleep.

"All right. I know I'm behaving stupidly." He looked up at her. The dull light from the street was enough to make her pale hair shine, and her face was damp from the air blowing into the room from the street. She was smiling half bitterly, watching him with quiet exasperation. All the anger left him. She was a lovely girl who had been given no choice. She had been forced to accept the worst and she took an easy way not through weakness but because she was tired. God knows, who was he to feel shocked? And there was no use pretending that he was shocked. He shook his head.

"Meg, I'm jealous, that's all. I was trying to pretend that I had you all to myself, now. It didn't matter about your husband, because he couldn't take you away from me physically."

She came and sat beside him on the bed. She reached out and ran her fingertips unsteadily along his thigh. The casual gesture was heartbreakingly intimate.

"I thought I loved Henry as much as I could love anyone. Perhaps I still do. He doesn't need me, but he needs somebody, that is if Henry can really need anyone. I don't know. I love you more than I love him, in my own way. But I don't want to make him unhappy by leaving him. And he has a lot to give me. If I live with you I may regret it, and I'll be angry with you because you forced me to make Henry unhappy. It's all a mess, but only if we think about it. He need never know about us and one day it will all work out, someway. Do you believe that I can love you and love other people as well?" She was thinking of Julian. It was strange to realise that in slightly changed circumstances, he was the one who could love and need her, and never think too much of obstacles or make any reservations.

"I believe you," Perkin said quietly. "It's enough."

"Have I made you very unhappy?" Meg asked gently.

He shook his head. "You make me very happy. When I'm alone I shall want more" – he looked at her – "but I've got a good deal more than I deserve."

She kissed his forehead. "You're very sweet."

They sat with their heads together for a moment, and he wanted nothing more. He sighed wonderingly.

"What makes you like you are?" he asked. "How is it possible that you can know so much and endure so much and still go on smiling, uncomplicated and lovely and gentle? Do you never want to be violent or self-pitying? Do you never feel despair?"

"I don't know, darling. Thinking is bad, I suppose, until you become an old philosopher. It makes you shrill and dissatisfied. We don't become men and women until we learn to be calm."

"Acceptance is the word," he said. He had been thinking that he would never again want to make love to her. Suddenly he remembered how it felt to kiss her open mouth and have his arms around her tender body. He kissed her without passion. They were sitting upright on the bed, and they remained thus, their lips drawing away as they needed breath, and returning to feel this tenderness and gentleness. Meg knew that he was satisfied, and was glad for him.

"I'll see Henry tomorrow and make peace with him."

"Shall I take you to a play or an opera?"

"Something light," she said. "I want to feel young and careless and not very intelligent. I want to be like everyone else and never think of growing old and never have to care for other people, except the one who's with me."

He nodded. "It happens occasionally. We're so unsophisticated at heart."

"Darling," she laughed, "we're so unsophisticated all the time."

CHAPTER XVI

SOMETIME during the evening, if George had not gone out with friends, he would signal to Jonathan across the room, although he was hardly aware of it. The questioning look which lingered for just a little more than a second indicated that he would come to Jonnie's room when everyone had gone home. A frown and blank, irritated eyes meant that he felt tired or bored or was spending the night with friends. Jonnie had not been in George's bedroom since the first fortnight he lived in the house. He had wandered in at two o'clock one morning when he was slightly drunk, and sat on the bed. George was sleeping and cursed wildly when he was awakened. Jonnie did not understand at first and bent down to him. George slapped his face, muttering something under his breath, and turned over to sleep again. At that moment he obviously did not care what happened to his friend. Jonnie rubbed his cheek, thought he was going to cry, then smiled and pretended to be too drunk to care, for the benefit of a non-existent audience. He almost convinced himself that he was drunk and had deserved the slap. He walked unsteadily back to his room, and felt sick as soon as he lay down in the cold empty bed. He reached out for a cigarette and discovered that the packet was empty. He wanted to talk to George, or lie beside his still body, but he would have been glad to talk to anyone. He dialled Perkin's number, but returned the receiver before the number began to be rung. He had no excuse for ringing. Perkin would laugh at him, for he would be ashamed to say that he was lonely. The only other person in the world who might sympathise was Derek, and he would probably offer more than sympathy. Jonnie laid his hot cheek against a corner of the pillow, and decided that he was the most unhappy person in the world.

Next morning George came to his room, looking as if nothing unfortunate had occurred the previous night. He was unwashed and unshaven, and had obviously come straight from his bed. He hated to kiss or be kissed until he was quite clean: his apparent coldness in the mornings often made Jonnie unhappy until he explained to him. Now this was his apology; stale mouth against stale mouth, red-rimmed eyes and uncomfortable skin. At the right moment George whispered that in future he would always come here if he wanted to sleep with him, and Jonnie was too happy to reflect that his own desires were to be ignored. George supposed that he would never be turned away, and he was quite right.

Jonathan was afraid to ask where George went on the nights he spent away from the house, but he sometimes heard snatches of conversation next evening. He gathered that George and his friends gambled and talked until dawn, then tumbled onto each other's beds or couches. George said that one of them must always be in the club. In the daytime he had appointments with his lawyer, his accountant and, although he never mentioned it to his friends, with the men who ran his houses. Jonathan was often quite alone in the morning and afternoon. Perkin seemed to be the only friend remaining from his former life, and when they met for lunch in the new year they both had to strain for something to say. Perkin was eager to hear all about the affair. He mentioned that he had not seen George for many months.

"Isn't it odd?" he said. "Four months ago you were my best friend, and I knew George very well indeed. You hadn't even met. And now this."

Jonathan remained silent.

"I must ring him," Perkin continued, for something to say. "He must be wondering what's happened to me."

"He never mentions you," Jonathan said quietly. "He's like that, you know: kind to everyone, up to a point, but in fact he hardly knows, and certainly doesn't care, that you're living."

They parted soon afterwards, both shouting something about a play or dinner as they walked away from each other.

On the days when he was alone, Jonathan seldom got up before noon. The weather was discouraging and he never had any plans for the day. He often lunched with Derek in his room, and remained there gossiping until it was time to bath and change for work. He would never have believed that he could so easily learn to waste time. There were books to be read and art galleries to visit, but he could always find an excuse for putting them off until some other time. Derek spent all his time in the house, lying on the bed smoking George's or Jonathan's cigarettes and reading Rimbaud, whose poetry he found boring, but whose face he adored. The walls of his room were decorated with unframed drawings of certain French poets, signed photographs of former friends, and a huge coloured pin-up of Sal Mineo, whose face he also adored. He was twenty-two, but in daylight looked a bad thirty.

During that winter Jonathan came to love the basement club. The nights of the heavy snow, the long nights when he could hear the rain beating on the pavements and pouring along the gutter, provided the hours when he lived; he was only happy at night. During the daytime he could see that his face had grown pale and he waited for the evening when he could stand in the shadows and feel his skin glow with sweat. He had no longer any sense of sin, but he felt the atmosphere of sin in this low flickering room. He felt it penetrate his clothes and skin and flesh and he tried to inhale it, for he could not get enough. People came into this room brushing rain from their shoulders, their eyes scanning every face in the first second. They brought with them every feeling and experience and idea that it was possible to have in those streets and houses outside, and lost innocence and illusion were inherent in every word they spoke and every gesture they made, as they watched and waited. Jonathan stood behind the bar, and he might have been an observer in a delightful corner of hell. The red light flickered, shadows moved fleetingly, and the drink sparkled.

One Friday morning at the beginning of May Jonathan wakened in a ray of sunlight. The room was stuffy and the sun felt as hot as any memory he had of summer. He rubbed his eyes and the flashing light cleared. The sky was incredibly blue. He pulled on a bathrobe and went to the dressing-table. He brushed his hair and decided that he did not need a shave. Suddenly he remembered a day at the beginning of October, when he had walked with George on Hampstead Heath, thinking that the spring would never come. It was almost impossible to believe that he now lived with the same person, but George had not changed.

Jonathan realised that he was not looking forward to the summer. He remembered what it was like to be alone on a beautiful day, when everyone else, on a steamer, in restaurants and parks, seemed to be having fun with someone they loved. It was unlikely that George would take him out more frequently just because summer had come.

He bathed and put on his newest pair of trousers and a bright pullover. He was brushing his hair again when there was a knock at the door and George slipped into the room.

"The first sunny day of the year. How shall we celebrate it, Jonnie?" He came and stood behind the other boy, and they looked at each other in the mirror.

Jonathan flushed and looked away. "I don't know. Whatever way you like."

"We'll go for a walk and then to some place fabulously expensive for lunch. Would you like that?"

Jonathan nodded dumbly, and reached out for a cigarette. George quickly took one and bent over the flame of the lighter. Their eyes met.

"Remember how this used to be a habit?" George asked quietly.

"Of course. I was just thinking of the day we went to Hampstead Heath. That night you made love to me for the first time. It was right at the beginning of winter, and I thought I'd never see the sun again. The time has passed so quickly."

George was watching him carefully. He sat down beside him on the stool that was hardly big enough for two people and laid a hand on his knee. He felt slightly guilty.

"We don't have enough time together, but I have so much to do, and it's all the better when we are together. I still like you just as much. I haven't lost interest."

Jonathan buried his face in George's hair.

"Thank God. If I could hear you say that once a week even, I'd always be happy."

"You're not lonely now?" George would have been surprised and pleased if Jonathan had not immediately forgotten his loneliness.

"No, I'm not lonely now."

George closed his eyes and smiled calmly, his Mona Lisa smile. His composure was not ruffled by the fact that he had lately heard some very good suggestions as to why the lady kept her mouth closed. In his limited way he was capable of ignoring all trivialities and achieving contentment. Jonathan's mouth was very pleasant.

"Where shall we go?"

"Anywhere." He searched frantically for the name of some place in order not to burden George with the making of a decision. "Trafalgar Square."

"How clever of you," George said, still smiling mysteriously. "We can lunch in Soho . . ."

When he had gone, Jonathan quickly changed into a suit. As he was knotting a new tie in front of the mirror, he noticed that his face looked rather ugly. His eyes protruded and his mouth was an odd shape. He had looked better an hour earlier. He tried desperately to compose his face but could not manage it. He wished that George had not made him feel so happy, for his face was distorted because he was smiling grotesquely. He hoped that George would not mind too much.

There was a broad strip of sunlight along the street, and the houses seemed to be melting with steam as they dried on this first hot day.

When George arrived they walked to the end of the street, to find a taxi.

"When do you want a holiday?" George asked.

Jonathan hesitated. "When are you taking yours?"

"July. I'm going to Greece for a month."

"Alone?"

He nodded.

"Can't I come with you, for a fortnight anyway?"

George frowned and was glad that he had raised the matter, for now it would soon be resolved and he would be able to forget it. "I'd love to spend some time with you, honey, but I would like you to stay behind and take care of the club."

"Derek could do that, couldn't he?"

George hailed a taxi, and did not reply until they were sitting in the back. Jonathan's face was ridiculously pathetic with sudden misery. "I'd be less worried if you were there," he said carefully. "Derek would give free drinks to all the little boys in London."

"I'd pay for my own holiday," Jonathan said desperately.

"That's got nothing to do with it. In fact, I'll give you the money to go to Greece in June or August, if you like."

"It wouldn't be the same," he said plaintively.

George brushed aside his rising irritation and looked out of the window. A good lunch and Jonathan would be reconciled to going alone, but he wondered if he had been right in giving him the job. It would have been better to choose another Derek, the sort of boy who knew what to expect from this kind of relationship. The streets they passed were crowded with people enjoying the sunshine and wearing hastily prepared summer clothing. Jonathan was staring straight in front of him, his face quivering under the calm mask which he had forced on it. He certainly looked much better through the sun-glasses. They relieved the sallowness of his skin, and made brown the shadows under his eyes and around his mouth. George took off the glasses in order to disillusion himself. Jonathan had a large spot on his chin. George turned back to the window and lit a cigarette without offering one to his companion. He coughed. He had been smoking too much, or perhaps he was getting tuberculosis. It was one way to die.

They left the taxi at Leicester Square and walked down past the Garrick; George talked lightly, and was certain that if Jonathan still felt miserable it was because he wanted to be.

"They've turned off the fountains," Jonathan said sadly.

"Well, honey, we can sit on the side without getting drenched." They walked down the steps.

"Do you want to feed the pigeons?" George asked.

"No. They'd probably mess my clothes."

They sat down and George dipped his fingers in the half-inch of water on the blue and green bottom. He wet his forehead.

"Delicious. Would you like some peanuts or a Coke?"

"No." Jonathan frowned, then laughed. "George, you are ridiculous." George acknowledged the compliment by bowing his head. Jonathan moved closer to him.

"Do you remember the first time we met, at Perkin's party?"

George sighed imperceptibly. "Yes."

"You said then that you wanted to die. Was that true, or were you very drunk or trying to impress me?"

"Oh, I don't know. I don't want to die any more than most people, and they manage to live for a long time. It isn't natural for me to want to die at thirty." He considered. "Sometimes I feel very tired, though. I was never young and all my life I've been trying to go back and discover what it's like to be normal. I've been missing something I never had. I was dead before I was born, I felt empty as soon as I was old enough to compare my life with other people's. It's impossible ever to go back. I am what I am, and I won't change." He smiled to himself and decided that he might as well use the occasion to satisfy Jonathan with a half-lie. "I like to make fantasies, you know. It's possible to delude yourself in the most unsatisfactory circumstances. That's why I want to spend a month by myself. I shall sit somewhere with a drink and pretend that I'm in another place, ten years ago. I'll be able to pretend that I'm like other people. It works for a while. It's almost as good as the real thing."

"And I can't help you?"

"Of course you can, a little. But not quite enough."

In a moment of unselfishness he wondered if he should warn Jonathan not to care too much for him, but then he laughed at himself.

Jonathan did not know what to say so he said, "It's all very sad."

"Unfortunate is the word," and George smiled his enigmatic smile again, feeling rather uncomfortable. He felt like an easy actor ad libbing furiously, and wished that he could forget his appearance and talk sincerely.

"Why did it have to be you?" Jonathan said. "Why couldn't I have met someone uncomplicated who loved me and could make me happy? It isn't too much to ask. There must be people like that in the world."

"I'm willing to believe that there are, and I may have met them without recognising them. Do you know any?"

"No. Oh, I'm all wrong. It's just that we can't see those sort of people. We automatically disbelieve what they say because we don't understand them. Why are we different?"

"Heaven knows." George laughed. "No, I meant who the hell knows. I really believe in fate, honey. We fail because we don't try hard enough or aren't well enough equipped. Luck hardly comes into it." He hesitated. "That's why I don't worry too much about hurting people. Do you understand?"

"Yes, but . . ." Jonathan shrugged and did not bother to continue. George relaxed comfortably and turned to watch the lunch-hour crowds who were beginning to come down to the Square. A young man had come to sit beside him at the fountain. George turned to him lazily, then looked away and seemed to be staring at the trees. His face was completely blank. After a few moments he turned again to the young man, and gazed at him frankly.

The young man took a packet of Gauloises from his pocket and put a cigarette in his mouth. He seemed fascinated by his surroundings.

"Do you want a light?" George hunted in his pocket and produced his lighter. The young man nodded and bent down. He looked up as he drew away and blinked slowly, two or three times. He moved nearer to George, obviously willing to talk to him.

Jonathan stared at them for a moment, feeling jealous, then turned away.

George touched the packet of Gauloises.

"It's a long time since I've smoked one of those."

The young man shrugged. He was a very beautiful young man,

very proud of his packet of Gauloises because it was blue and new and full. He liked almost everything that was new and shiny. He was wearing black trousers and a very clean pullover which he had bought at Harrods. He decided that there was no need to give one of his cigarettes to George.

"Do you speak English?" George asked.

"Of course," the young man said. "I speak English and French. I am French-Canadian. I was born in Quebec. My name is Charles."

George giggled. "Of course your name is Charles. What else would it be?"

Charles did not smile, or rather his smile did not broaden. He never stopped smiling and showing his perfect teeth. He went on smiling in the most unfunny situations. He had discovered the secret of happiness.

"Are you on holiday in London?" George asked politely. He knew this type of young man very well, but he had never met such a beautiful example.

"No," Charles said slowly, as if he found it very hard indeed to disengage himself from the contemplation of his serenity and answer a silly question. "I live in London. I want to be a pilot."

"Really?" George asked wonderingly.

"I am going to a school for pilots," Charles said happily. His happiness was almost painful to anyone who watched him for too long.

"How long will it take you to become a pilot?"

"A year." He said a year because it was the easiest thing to say. He had no idea of time. The sun shone for him in winter. He would always be twenty-two years old. He would always be sitting by the fountain in Trafalgar Square, smoking Gauloise cigarettes on the first hot day of the year.

"It must be a very pleasant life," George said, "going to school and learning to fly. Do you know many people in London?"

"Enough," Charles said contentedly.

"My name is George," George said, feeling ridiculous. "I own a club in Chelsea." Charles opened his eyes a little wider to indicate that running a club might be almost as pleasant an occupation as learning to fly aeroplanes.

"You must come and see me one evening," George said.

Charles opened his eyes again. "That is very kind of you."

"I'll give you my card. You must come soon. I'll be away for part of the summer."

Charles looked carefully at the card and put it in his pocket. He had almost forgotten to look at George to see what he was like. He never bothered about the details of people's faces. In the first moment after meeting them he received a pleasant or an unpleasant impression, and that was enough. He had never tried to discover what constituted a pleasant or unpleasant impression. He had hardly ever tried to discover anything. He was very stupid, but even the cleverest people did not care, because they would have given a great deal to discover the secret of happiness which he had found.

Jonathan had almost fallen asleep in the sun.

"Who was that?" he asked dismally.

"A French boy. I may be able to use him." He put his arm round Jonathan's shoulders. "Let's go and have some lunch. The sun has made me feel hungry."

As they walked away George turned to wave to Charles. He was sitting quite still, his eyes closed, while he guarded his happiness.

CHAPTER XVII

THE hot spell lasted for three days, and was followed by weeks of warm rain. Julian returned to London at the end of the first week in May, and rang Perkin the evening after his arrival.

"How was the weather in Switzerland?" Perkin asked automatically as soon as he heard Julian's voice.

"Lately not much snow and very little sun. I stayed because of the ski instructor I told you about. He was the most remarkable man, Perkin. Out of season all he did was read philosophy." His voice sounded stronger and happier.

"You haven't become some kind of fanatic?" Perkin said anxiously.

Julian laughed. "Go on talking. Perkin, I feel so wonderfully happy, and I don't know why. God knows, surely it isn't because I'm back in London."

"I feel so happy too. Can it be spring? I'm in love, Julian."

"No! I'm not in love."

"Well, I heartily recommend it. I'm even beginning to believe in things like having children."

"I don't believe it." Julian hesitated, then added in shocked tones, "You're not thinking of getting married?"

Perkin smiled bitterly. "I'm afraid it's impossible with this woman. No, all this madness will soon pass."

"I have to admit that I'm glad." Julian's voice hardened. "My worst dream is that all my friends will get married or die or become respectable in some other way and leave me to drink alone for the rest of my days."

"You haven't changed," Perkin said.

"No. Look, I'm giving a party on Thursday. Will you come?"

"I'd love to," Perkin said eagerly. "I haven't been to a real party for such a long time. May I bring Meg?"

There was a short and awkward silence. "Why Meg?"

"She's the one I love."

Julian sighed imperceptibly and closed his eyes. When he opened them his eyes hurt and he realised that he had a headache. He reached out and poured more gin into the tumbler beside him.

Perkin spoke again. "Surprised?"

"Yes, I am. Of course it was inevitable. Everybody's in love with Meg. I'm terribly sorry, Perkin. I've just been talking to her on the phone and she's coming with Henry."

"I forgot that you'd be asking them," Perkin said quickly and calmly. "It's all very complicated. I'll explain when I see you."

"There's no need to explain, Perkin."

"Well, I'll find someone to bring."

"And bring Simon and his Anne. She sounds very sweet."

When he had rung off Perkin wandered about the room for a few moments, then went back to the telephone. He began to dial a number then changed his mind and replaced the receiver. He no longer felt happy.

He picked up the receiver again and dialled Angel's number.

CHAPTER XVIII

JULIAN's front door was open, and Perkin and Angela went straight in to the party. Simon followed, leading Anne by the hand. For a moment she held back, listening to the music and laughter. Then she remembered that she was no longer shy and afraid of parties, and smiled at the back of Simon's smooth neck. She had not unlearned the habit of being alone, and had constantly to remind herself that there was no reason to be frightened.

Julian was wearing a very colourful pullover which he had brought from Switzerland. His face was very brown and shining with the glow of his guests and conversation and gaiety. He looked surprised, then leaned down and kissed Angela's lips.

"Angel! I didn't know that you were a friend of Perkin."

She smiled. "We're old friends, but I didn't tell him I'd already met you."

Perkin raised his eyebrows. "In what circumstances?"

"At a club," they said simultaneously.

"Isn't it strange, though," Perkin said. "The same people. We move in such a narrow little world."

Angel glanced at him affectionately. "You made that remark four or five hours too early. Dance with me?"

He nodded, and patted Julian's arm.

The room was already full, and there were four or five couples dancing. He held Angel very close to him, almost in an embrace. His eyes searched the room for a moment. Meg had not arrived.

"Well, sweetie, darling, love, or what you will? Where have you been?" He leaned back to look into her eyes, which had always seemed to recoil when he looked into them, although they were brave eyes. She looked much older. It was impossible to tell in what way.

She looked at him for a moment, then rested her head on his shoulder.

"It was kind of you to think of me and bring me," she said at last.

He hesitated. "It makes me very happy to see you again. It's been six months. You know, it's been a long and a short time."

He felt her nod, then she raised her head and kissed his mouth. He returned the kiss as she moved away. Her lipstick had the same smell and taste.

"Well now," he said softly, "let's admit that we still like each other very much. I feel very close to you, Angel. How about you?"

She nodded. "Please, please don't ask me if I got to the South of France. I never did."

"What about your painter?"

"He's gone away. I don't know where he is. Don't be polite to me. Say whatever you want to say and tell me what you're thinking."

"Of course. I'm thinking . . . I'm thinking that the last time I danced with a girl at a party was the night I danced with you. And I'm feeling very sentimental, because we're so alike. We should have seen each other often. Why didn't we?"

"I was waiting for you to ring me." She shook her head and he touched her face for a moment. "The last time I danced with anyone like you was when I danced with you." She laughed inwardly at the foolishness of her words, which were an exact expression of what she was thinking.

They were dancing clumsily, fitting their movements to the rhythm of their mood.

"How many have there been?" he asked quickly. Her rather coarse hair brushed against his face and he tried to catch it between his lips.

"Oh, Perkin, I don't know. I've stopped playing that shocking game. I mean, when I realised that I shocked some people I began to play up to them, but it became so tiresome. I was rather cruel to you that morning. Remember?"

He had never thought about it.

"I was so angry with you," she went on. "You didn't care very much and on that account you felt sorry for me. I wanted to tell you that I didn't need you."

"You needed someone?"

"Of course. You, if you'd needed me."

He felt an odd pang of nostalgia. "You're a wonderful girl, Angel. You'd give a man understanding and as much love as he needed. I used to think that you were selfish."

"People had been telling me that for so long that I came to believe them. But I want to give someone everything I've got. Time after time they betray me and tell me they don't want me. I wish I knew why."

"Some people don't need anybody, but we only say we don't, and we wait for the right person. Unfortunately, when we do our love isn't necessarily returned." He patted her shoulder. Her green dress was not very pretty or very new. "I might have loved you if circumstances had been a little different. Perhaps I do love you, but there is someone else."

"There always is. Every time. I have this man, a picture dealer. I'm working as his secretary. He's very rich. I'm not very interested in art but I'd picked up a little knowledge from various people. He has Sutherlands, Max Ernsts, Picasso drawings from his ballet-boy period. There's even a Klee in the lavatory – moisture-sealed."

"There's a joke there."

"It had already occurred to me. But I don't really care about him. I like his company, that's all. At first I thought I was in love with him. It happens again and again. Perhaps you're fooling yourself too."

"No. This is it, for my sins. She'll be here tonight. You'll see her. She is very beautiful."

"You don't sound very happy."

"Well, in some ways I feel very happy but the position is rather complicated."

"It would have to be, otherwise you wouldn't have fallen in love."

He frowned. "That's very cynical and completely untrue. I'd have loved her if she were willing to come to me with no reservations. I could have fallen in love with no one else in the world."

"You have changed, darling. I almost believe you."

He smiled. "You see? Already we're biting at each other. Why couldn't you pretend that you really believed me and felt very glad for me?"

"I couldn't have convinced you. You'd have wondered immediately why I accepted it so easily."

Perkin laughed. "All right. You know me too well."

Neither of them had anything more to say.

"I'm extremely jealous," Angel said at last. "You've made me feel very discontented and emotional and I haven't had a drink all evening."

"Come and get one."

They drew apart and walked to a tray of drinks.

"Here's to your love."

He looked so pleased that she burst out laughing. He flushed, and drank deeply.

"Have you seen *My Fair Lady*?" he asked, inanely.

"My friend's taking me next week," she said seriously, to relieve his embarrassment.

Perkin did not hear. He had become quite still. Meg had just arrived with Henry. He watched as she closed her eyes and raised her face to accept Julian's kiss. Then she smiled, made some remark that made him laugh. She seemed to be giving him all her attention. Henry beamed and glanced quickly round the room. He did not seem to notice Perkin. He went to Simon, who was standing in a corner, alone with Anne, and at once began to talk animatedly. Perkin felt oddly jealous, but not on Meg's account. Henry looked so assured. When, he wondered, would he be able to move and talk like that, drawing vitality from the experience of a lifetime of work and talent properly used? Meanwhile he felt like drawing a chart of his friends' movements since they arrived at the party. He would do it so accurately, and guess quite cleverly the motive of each action. How petty it seemed. Meg was still talking to Julian. She had not once looked round the room. She was wearing a very simple red dress.

"What's her name?" Angel asked coldly.

"Meg. How did you guess she was the one?"

"You wouldn't ask if you could see your face. Her name would be Meg. That kind of girl always has a name like Meg."

"What kind of girl?" he asked irritably.

"The kind of girl who should have a name like Foresta or Juno or something equally silly. But a name like Meg makes you feel cosy and protective. Is she as frigid as she looks?"

His mouth curled with distaste. "Try not to be a bitch, darling. No one could be less frigid, although it's none of your business."

"Oh, I'm sure you don't recognise it as such. Tell me, did she have a baby brother or somebody who died, who was the only person she ever really loved?"

"She was married." He glared at her. "What exactly are you trying to say, Angel?"

"Without giving away any feminine secrets, that your beloved is the kind of girl who was born to have a long-lost love. I'm sure she always bears up bravely under the too-apparent strain, though. Who's the man?"

"You've already met him. Henry Enfield, the writer."

"She lives with him?"

"Yes."

Angel laughed harshly and triumphantly. "I knew it. I know all about your Meg."

He watched Meg's calm face for a moment. Julian was talking quickly, his expression oddly tense. Occasionally Meg laughed, and covered her mouth with her hand. It seemed to be hurting her to laugh.

"Please explain," Perkin said quietly, turning to face Angel.

"There's nothing more to say." She smiled sympathetically. "Meg is a type of girl I've met before, that's all. I've shared rooms with them."

"Is that any reason why I shouldn't love her?"

"No."

"Go on."

Angel smiled wearily. "Look, I envy her because I never had a big love that would last me the rest of my life. I'll bet she makes a big thing of it."

"You have two red marks at the corners of your eyes," Perkin said quietly. "How did you get them, Angel?"

She looked surprised, and her face quivered. Then she laughed and turned away. She put her arm round the neck of a young man standing behind her. He was very surprised.

Julian left Meg to greet some new arrivals. She brushed her hair back with a quick movement and turned to survey the room. Her gaze wandered over the faces of the guests, occasionally dropping to examine their clothes. Her eyes met Perkin's.

He felt himself blushing.

They watched each other for a moment, across the room. Meg smiled slightly and continued to gaze at him calmly. She might have been looking at a painting. He crossed to her side, and no longer dared to look at her face. He stared down at the red dress. They had slept together the previous night, and he was worried that she might be tired of him.

"Are you all right?" he asked at last, with heartbreaking awkwardness.

She smiled reassuringly and reached out to straighten his tie. She uncreased it deftly and tucked it inside his jacket. As he felt her fingers pressing for a moment against his chest, he wanted to kneel before her in thankfulness.

"Am I standing too close to you?"

She shook her head. "Henry has his back to us."

"When do I see you again?"

"In about a week. I think I could manage Tuesday." They had been spending at least two nights together each week, but Henry wanted her to go to the country with him for a few days.

"We have only another five or six weeks, then I'm going to Ireland for at least a fortnight."

"It will soon pass."

He shrugged nervously. "Is Henry taking you away?"

"I want to go to Munich in September. I suppose Henry will come with me."

"He's looking very well and happy. He suspects nothing?"

"No. His new book has just come out in America, you know. It's having a great success." She pretended to look reproving. "When are you going to write a book that will have a great success?"

"Oh, when I'm fifty. I want all my earlier books to flop dreadfully. It would be so frustrating to have success at the beginning.

I'd never be able to convince myself that I deserved it."

"When are you going to write your first flop?"

"Are you ashamed of me, Meg?" he asked quickly.

"No," she explained patiently. "I'd enjoy being proud of you, but success wouldn't be a reason for liking you more than I do. I was thinking of your self-esteem."

Perkin did not seem to have heard. "I'm just beginning to realise your position," he said quietly. "I mean, Henry Enfield is a very famous and celebrated man. I used to regard him as my equal, but in future I shall treat him with more respect. What's he doing here anyhow? How does Henry Enfield come to know people like Julian and me? We haven't started. We don't even show signs of beginning."

Meg sighed. "He enjoys the company of younger people."

"And you live with him," Perkin went on. "You actually live with a famous man like Henry Enfield. No wonder you want me to be successful. I must seem very unimportant to you."

"Don't be such a fool," Meg snapped angrily. "If you're in a mood for self-pity, go home. You've got yourself to blame for what you are, so for heaven's sake stop complaining." Her anger died as soon as she saw the hurt way in which he recoiled from her, and she laid a hand on his arm. He steadied himself, took her glass quite casually, and went to find a refill. As he handed it back to her she noticed that he was holding a large tumbler, apparently filled with gin. Julian had given the larger glasses to his more intimate friends.

"It's Martini straight from the bottle," Perkin said defensively. He grinned lopsidedly. "What a pretty dress you're wearing. I should have mentioned it sooner."

"I'd rather you were silent, Perkin, if you can only talk easily to me when you're drunk."

He blinked. His eyes looked pale and naked.

"Can't I do anything right, Meg? Earlier today I felt so happy. We were happy last night and this morning. What happened to us?"

"I don't know."

"I'm so moody lately." He lowered his voice. "We wouldn't fight if we were in bed." She recalled the previous night with difficulty, and nodded.

"I'm doing this to you, Perkin," she said stiffly. "I'm bad for you."

He closed his eyes and leaned nearer until his sleeve brushed her arm. He would be pleased if he could always have some physical contact with her.

"No," he murmured. "How could you be bad for me? You're all I want." He was like a lonely child, constantly in need of some tangible evidence of affection. "I only wish I could see you more often. Do you think of me every day when we don't meet?"

"Naturally," she said, because it was less trouble than explaining why she rarely thought of him except when they were together. Her imagination had dulled lately, with regard to almost everything. She arranged a meeting with Perkin for a week later, and forgot about it until an hour before she was due to get ready.

"I can't stop thinking of you," Perkin said. "Do you know that I can hardly bear to sleep alone. If I thought I was never going to sleep with you again life would be intolerable."

Meg awoke as if from a bad dream, and quite suddenly wanted to screech and shout and tear him to pieces. She thought she was going mad. She still looked calm: her body was a lifeless shell enclosing a sizzling mechanism which was jumping and curling before a seemingly inevitable explosion. Her eyes shrank and her stomach shuddered.

"Tony," she screamed inwardly, and for a split second lost all awareness, so that she might have shouted the name aloud for all she knew or cared.

She took a deep breath and the last agony of grief ebbed. It could never happen again, or she would lose all sanity. She straightened her shoulders. The air around her felt cold, and Perkin's face looked pale in the heavy light. She heard Henry laughing at the other end of the room, and hated him.

So this was the power of a memory. She had once tried to imagine Tony's body as it must be in the grave: decayed, hideous, the colour of dirt if it had not already rotted away. She had imagined his face distorted in every possible manner, but could not bring herself to loathe it, for it retained his essence and his spirit which she loved. She had seen him when they had straightened his body in the coffin and covered the scars and holes with cotton and make-up, but despite their grotesque trickery she found it impossible not to believe that he was only sleeping. Tony could not be defeated so easily. She felt no need to look down and make certain that his chest was rising and falling gently as he breathed. She had seen that look on his face many times in the past, as he slept beside her. He always slept with his mouth slightly open, for his upper lip jutted out slightly: his teeth had been straightened when he was a child. Now his lip was curiously straight, but she was sure that when she bent down she would feel his warm breath against her ear. She moved nearer to the coffin, then fainted.

Tony was alive as long as she lived. Meg and Tony lived together until she died. The fact was inescapable, like loving someone whom it is absurd to love and leaving him again and again but always returning because he is the only reason for continuing to live as a sensate being.

"So you see, my life is in your hands," Perkin said shyly. "You're not bad for me, unless it's bad to make someone come alive and start caring. I'd do anything for you. Write a book, leave you alone and promise never to trouble you again, get you anything you wanted."

Meg fumbled for a moment, adjusting herself to his presence, searching for the attitude which he demanded of her. It was like struggling to be born, over and over each day.

"I command you to write a book," she said lightly.

He laughed. "If you really cared and wanted me to write, I'd begin at once. But I know you don't."

She shrugged. "There you are. I called your bluff."

"One day I'll write a book for and about you," he said quietly, "and it will be the most painful thing I'll ever do, for I will only write it when you are gone and I have nothing else to do."

She gazed at him bleakly. "What a pessimist you are. I'd better leave you as soon as possible. I know you won't be content until I do."

"Let's dance," he said. "We've never danced together."

She smiled and took his hand, half-enchanted again by his youth and charm.

"Weren't you jealous when you saw me talking to Angel?" he asked hopefully. She was so light that he could hardly feel her body moving in his arms.

Meg puzzled for a moment. "Who is Angel?"

He shook his head ruefully. "Never mind, darling. Oh God, you've made me happy again."

"You're mad. And don't hold me too close or Henry will come and take me away from you."

Perkin frowned. "Now you've made me unhappy again. But only for a moment. Listen, what you said about my wanting to be unhappy – I've done with all that. I've grown up."

Julian was watching them from his position by the door. Since his return he had been feeling splendidly healthy and disengaged: even large quantities of gin and the shock when he realised that Perkin was in love with Meg had not been enough to make him feel depressed. His ski-instructor had told him to go beyond hope to acceptance and he had obeyed delightedly. So it was as easy as that! As soon as Meg and Perkin began to dance together he felt as if something had been taken away from him and knew there was no reason to suppose that he had changed.

It occurred to him that this was the last party he was likely to give or visit until the autumn. Somehow he would have to live through the summer, if there was a summer. But he knew from experience that July, August and September were the most boring months of the year. Everyone was away from London and the people one met in bars very much wanted to be away. He spent the mornings in some park trying to read a book, the afternoons at the pictures and the evenings at a play which he had probably seen before: there were not enough good plays to go round. At night he would crawl from one club to another, his clothes sticking to his back. And then he would remember nothing until ten o'clock next morning. If it was a dull day he would feel more depressed; if the sun were shining he would feel even lonelier. The only alternative to staying in London was Cannes or Venice, but life would be no different there and he could not endure hot sun on his face for more than five minutes or he was sick.

He decided that he would kill himself if something did not happen soon. It would be a fittingly artistic end to his short life and he would arrange it to look like an accident, so that his acquaintances would have no excuse for moral speculations. He was the only person in the world who could bring his life to an end, except by a trick of chance, which seemed curiously unwilling to become involved with him. At one time he thought that life would resolve itself, maybe happily. But he had long been disillusioned. The choice had been given to him: go on and on although every part of you says that it is hopeless and nothing will get better; or destroy yourself, and perhaps forever be committed to regretting the happiness that was waiting for you next day or the day after.

He was vaguely aware that everyone had stopped dancing.

"I'm afraid poor Julian's out of this world already," somebody shouted, and laughed.

He cursed himself. He had forgotten the gramophone, and the last record had played itself out. He shook his head and waved to his guests and went to the gramophone. They would dance in the same rhythm whatever music he played.

He drew back the curtains and opened the window to let in some air. It was not yet dark and the evening was warm, but he felt the damp seeping through his jacket as he leaned on the sill. Far below the streets were wet. A man and a woman in evening dress came out of a flat in the mews and drove off in their car. The sky was red somewhere far behind the rooftops. He could make an end to this, but suddenly he was not quite certain if he wanted it to end. That was the *impasse*: he stood paralysed before the innumerable pleasant or tiresome complications of life. He would never come to any decision without a stimulus. It was improbable that life would ever offer him one.

He felt a hand on his back and someone wriggled out beside him.

"What have you done with Perkin?" he asked quietly.

"Turned him over to Henry," Meg said, staring across the city. "What a beautiful view, Julian."

"Yes." He reached out and slowly brushed her hair away from her face. "Why do you never cut your hair? You always look exactly the same."

"I can hide behind it when it's long. Where's the river, Julian?"

He pointed. "Over there, but you can't see it behind the buildings. I'll take you for a drive later, if you wish."

She shook her head. "Henry will want me to go straight home with him. Say what you want to say."

Julian smiled. "You got yourself into quite a muddle while I was away, didn't you?"

"Yes. No, it wasn't my fault."

"What are you going to do about it?"

"Nothing. Just wait. It will sort itself out."

"I wish I had such faith, but it would be a pity if you lost Henry. He'll always be there to look after you."

"Then I'll try not to lose him," she said calmly.

The sky seemed to have grown dark in a moment.

"I'll always try to help you if I can," Julian said, "if you need money."

"Are you really rich, darling?" she asked without interest.

"I don't know, but I always seem to have more money than I need. Now go back to Henry. You haven't spoken to him all evening."

Meg shrugged. "He likes me to mix well at parties. It gives us something to talk about when we get home."

"Is it as bad as that, Meg?"

She shuddered. "Please, Julian, I thought we understood each other. Don't be like the rest. They're vultures, probing to find what makes me work, how I think, what I think every moment of the day, asking me to explain precisely what emotion I feel for them. I wish everybody would leave me alone."

She sighed furiously, ashamed of her outburst.

"You don't want me to leave you alone," Julian said flatly.

"No. Unless you're like the others."

He laid his hand on her arm. "I don't have to ask how you're feeling. I know, or I understand you enough not to ask. I didn't intend you to answer my question about your life with Henry."

She was silent for a moment. Then, "Are you as fastidious in your relationships with other people, Julian?"

"I don't have relationships with other people," he said. "I don't know what I have."

Henry passed a hand over his short untidy hair, which was prematurely brittle and grey. He felt nervous, and when in company he allowed himself to be nervous for only one reason: he felt distinctly out-of-place. It was something which had not occurred since his first success as a writer. He was, of course, famous for the genial ease with which he handled almost anyone of whatever status. This evening he felt uneasy because he found it impossible to convince himself that he wanted to talk to anyone except the young people he had already met. Julian was tiresome but attractive; Perkin always curiously ephemeral, and he would have liked to know why, and Simon and Anne seemed to be charmingly selfish, each wanting something that the other could not give. Henry liked them, while disapproving of the attitudes they struck with such facility, but he had no desire to meet any more of their kind. He was the oldest guest at the party, but everyone knew how much he liked young people. He had treated them as equals, but lately had not bothered to hide his irritation when they contradicted him and he knew that he was right. Perhaps he was growing old. He had a strong sense of the ridiculous and pathetic, and decided that he must soon give up going to this kind of party. Too many people had met him already; he rather wished that he had been a little more aloof.

But to Perkin and Simon he still seemed completely assured. Anne had clung desperately to Simon's arm all evening and had spoken hardly a word: she felt awed. Her confidence had collapsed as soon as Henry smiled at her. Perkin was talking extravagantly. It was the only way in which he could hope to match Henry's apparent self-possession.

"Yes, but, but – what does it matter? I knew everyone else was laughing insanely but I cried my eyes out."

"It was all so second-rate," Henry murmured.

"And sentimental," Simon added.

"It doesn't *matter*. Why criticise sentimentality? None of us would want to live without it and why expect more of art? I know it wasn't a very good play, but if you cry, for heaven's sake admit that you enjoyed the play, instead of laying down certain precepts which must not be broken."

"And sordid," Henry said. "We were intended to sympathise with those people but they were so worthless. And in reality they wouldn't be at all attractive. They'd be shabby and unwashed and vulgar."

Anne swallowed. "I loved it," she said, and blushed.

Henry tittered. "Yes, my dear, but I'm sure you'll admit that it was all pure escapism."

She smiled vaguely. She had not prepared herself to speak again. Simon took hold of her arm, smiled briefly at Henry, and led her away. She cried out as his fingers dug into her flesh.

"What's wrong?"

"Let's go and make love. It's about all you're good at," he said, with an odd mixture of tenderness and brutality.

She was entirely satisfied by the remark. He was the only one with whom she was ever completely at ease, in fact she had little desire to meet other people.

He led her down the hall and opened a door.

"But this is Julian's bedroom!"

"He won't mind." Simon locked the door on the inside and roughly took hold of Anne. "I've been waiting for this all night."

She responded with complete confidence and after a moment he pulled her onto the bed. Five minutes later he drew away and sat on the edge of the bed. She raised herself on an elbow and took hold of his neck, pulling him backwards to her breast with all her weight. She cradled his head and began to kiss him passionately.

He had not seen her for three weeks after the evening he spilled coffee on his trousers at the Blue Angel. He had forgotten her. Then one night he had come to her flat soaked with sweat and rain. He had been walking around the West End for two hours, staring at streetwalkers and turning away in disgust. Anne was knitting a sweater. Her hair was unwashed and untidy and she was wearing an old dressing-gown. Her face looked almost ugly. She was pale and her eyes were raw and red. Simon took her in his arms and kissed her again and again, and told her many times how much he loved her. He was shivering and his clothes were sticking to his skin. He kneeled on the floor beside her chair and buried his face in her lap. She sat quite straight in the chair, and tears rolled down her face. She did not understand what was happening. He had said that he loved her, and then he had left her alone. She was hardly surprised. She could think of no reason why he should love her, and she supposed he had suddenly realised that he was making a fool of himself over someone who had nothing to give him. She had never met his girl friends. Presumably they were incredibly sophisticated and efficient and would never bother him by asking for more than he could give. She laid her hand on his back and it was at once soaked in water. Her dressing-gown was wringing where he had held her against him. She wondered how she had become involved in this ugliness, then realised that she was seeing the relationship as it would appear to other people. She did not think it at all ugly. She got up. He buried his face in the seat of the chair. He was trembling with exhaustion. She brought the fire nearer, and took off his shoes and socks. There was a puddle on the floor beneath his feet. She put her arms around him, and unbuttoned and pulled off his jacket, then his tie and shirt and vest. When she saw his body she felt cold with longing to have it beside her in the bed. Tomorrow she would have her hair cut and she would try to make herself as pretty as possible. She felt quite ashamed that she had not taken proper care of her appearance while he was away from her.

After that they spent almost every night together.

Simon let her kiss his face for a moment and closed his eyes. He realised with a shock that he was falling asleep and pulled away abruptly. Anne was smiling eagerly.

"Come home," he said roughly. She nodded and got up. When they were at the door she put her hand to her mouth, turned and ran back to the bed. Simon burst out laughing as he watched her carefully straightening the covers. She stood back to make certain that she had done the job properly, and gave a satisfied little nod.

He put his arm around her and they left the flat without going into the party again.

Julian lay down on the bed, and sighed thankfully. His bedroom was plainly and sparsely furnished, a deliberate and restful contrast to his living-room. He waved aside the glass which Perkin held out to him and closed his eyes. For a moment tiredness drove away all thought.

"It was a very successful party," Perkin said, and sat on the end of the bed. "I don't want to go out for supper unless you're hungry."

"Good. If you want it there's some chicken in the refrigerator." He opened his eyes and turned his head to look at Perkin. "I'll get my woman to clear up in the morning. I expect you're as tired as I am."

Perkin nodded. "Then I'll go home and let you get to bed."

"Stay for a little while. I want to talk to someone."

"You always do. So do I. Lately I've been seeing hardly anyone but Meg."

" . . . whom you love?"

"Whom I love."

There was a moment's silence.

"Me too," Julian said quietly, and was glad that the room was fairly dark and his face was in shadow. "I love her very much – but not in that way."

Perkin laughed cheerfully, because he felt safe. "Thank goodness for that. But aren't we a vicious little circle! None of us must ever have children. They'd turn out to be freaks." His voice sounded oddly desolate in the cold room.

"What does that mean?"

He shrugged. "God knows. Perhaps after all our children would be healthy and wise. Anyhow, it won't happen. I hate the little buggers. They smell and bring unnecessary complications. I'd be a very bad father."

"We must all die out," Julian said, pretending to joke. "Our children would be unhappy. The sins of their fathers would be visited upon them, or something like that. I've seen it happen so often.

A nymphomaniac mother invariably produces a nymphomaniac daughter, the only difference being that the child does it more deliberately."

"Julian," Perkin said, "does Meg love me?"

"I don't know," he said quickly. "It's hardly my business."

Perkin shrugged. "I don't suppose I really care. I'm beginning to know the meaning of resignation."

"Ah. You're getting older."

"Yes. And learning a new kind of detachment. From myself, not from other people. That means I'm really growing up. I know it's about time."

"Of course you'll continue to live in the old way, because it's become a habit and there's nothing else to do?"

He nodded. "No, there won't be any conspicuous changes. I'd feel terribly silly, as if I'd been converted or something." He got up and went to the window. He looked up at the sky, which was high and clear, and rather wished that he could have thought of something more original to do.

"Have you been to the Planetarium? Of course not, you weren't here when it opened. But there's a wonderful moment when the lights go out and you wait for a split second, wondering what's going to happen. It's rather disappointing when you first go in, the roof seems so low. Then quite suddenly the sky appears, and you catch your breath in wonder. It's terribly high and vast and beautiful and you feel as if something wonderful is happening to you for the first time for many years. You feel so happy, and five minutes later you've grown accustomed to it and you're only vaguely interested and slightly bored."

"Go on," Julian said quietly.

"There's nothing else. I'd go back just for that first moment but I know I'd be disappointed. I'd have outgrown it, like a film you saw five years ago, and when you see it at the Classic the women have padded shoulders and the music is too loud."

Julian yawned. "Never mind. Let's go to the Planetarium one day. I'll enjoy seeing the look of misery on your face when you're disappointed."

Perkin nodded. "I'll see you often. We can hold up the bars at night and lunch at Hammersmith and on the river and go to concerts at the Festival Hall."

"And drive like hell out of London when it's too hot and crowded . . ."

"Hot? Some hope."

" . . . and eat Wimpies at Lyons' and go to Kew and Westminster Cathedral and Brighton . . ."

Perkin laughed excitedly. "And Sundays at the Royal Court. But do they have them in summer?"

"It doesn't matter. What else? Quick, tell me."

He searched his memory frantically. "Well, absolutely everything. You'll come to Ireland with Simon and Anne at the beginning of July and meet Tom and see our home which is beautiful."

"And we could always go to the Tate. If Meg won't come alone we'll even bring Henry and I'll take him to the restaurant while you make love."

"There must be hundreds of places we've never been to, odd little corners." He clapped his hands. "Julian, we could fill every hour of every day with fun and always have something to do. If we're bored it will be our own fault."

"The solution is so simple," Julian said eagerly. "It was under our noses all the time. Why didn't we think of it?"

"Tower Bridge, Madame Tussaud's – just like tourists, and Sadler's Wells and the Old Vic . . ."

"And Covent Garden. We'll all go to every night club in the hope of seeing Princess Margaret."

"Rowing on the Serpentine, the Soho Fair, every jazz club, every play, the prostitutes of Stepney."

"Life will be wonderful," Julian said enthusiastically.

"The Zoo!"

CHAPTER XIX

'A *Worried Man*—by Henry Enfield.'

Henry stared at the words he had written on the foolscap pad the previous night, just before he went to bed. It was an old trick: just before you go to sleep try to concentrate as hard as possible on the raw material for the next day's writing, and it may come a little easier when you actually start work on it. Or the energy you save can be used to enhance the felicitous little touches for which you are famous. Henry was a slow writer, but his output was steady and fairly large: he worked from nine in the morning until three or four in the afternoon.

The short story *A Worried Man* was to be about a man's obsession for the smell and colour and feel of lavender. He was worried because something was missing. He felt that he was not using lavender in every possible way, and at the end he would regain his peace of mind by discovering his oversight: perhaps his mouth-wash smelt of cologne. Henry said the first sentence aloud, but could not force himself to write it on the page. He leaned back in his chair, untroubled. One of the things which made it easier to sit at his desk each day was that he knew from experience that sometimes he changed his mind and decided not to do any work at all until tomorrow.

He took out an emery board and began to tidy his nails. It was twenty-past nine and Meg had gone to practice. The house was deserted, and the room flickered as the sycamore in the garden swept backwards and forwards in the wind. It was the beginning of June and the weather had been miserable, but Henry did not care very much. He had no great liking for the open air. He carefully reshaped a lopsided nail, then put down the emery board and took up his pen. He wrote the word "sycamore" in his careful hand-writing on a slip of paper, and smiled with satisfaction. Then he returned to shaping his nails.

Meg was having an affair with someone, presumably Julian De-la-Noy or Perkin Young. He had reasons to suppose that it could not be Julian, and besides, he was more like a brother to her. Henry wondered how long it would last. He was accompanying her to Munich in September, and he hoped that it would all be over by then, otherwise the holiday might not be very enjoyable. Apart from that the business affected him very little. They had never had much to say to each other in the mornings, for he was usually too busy opening letters, but at least he had drawn comfort from her presence. He had always known that they had little in common, and helped to remedy the situation by introducing her to most of his friends as quickly as possible, to give more common ground for a relationship. Meg hardly ever talked about his books, but he knew a little about music and tried to mention it every day. He felt panic when he first recognised the signs that she was meeting someone else: the unfinished sentences, the way she hesitated and then decided not to contradict him when he expressed some view with which she used not to agree. It was obvious that each time she was remembering someone else's point of view. He felt almost glad when he decided that Perkin must be the man. It was certainly a physical attraction then, and Meg needed someone more substantial. She was always a little tired and she would become annoyed as he sapped her energy. Only an older man could be content to give more than he received; and it is nearly always the woman who contributes most to a lasting relationship.

Henry hoped that he was right. He supposed that he loved Meg, and if he did not, she was decorative, intelligent and calm. He had grown used to her and she would not be easy to replace. He was never too involved not to analyse a situation clearly, and he was clever enough not to lean towards self-abnegation, and also to realise that his summing-up might be entirely wrong, or subtly in error, which frightened him more. He was old; Meg was young. He was rich; she was poor. He looked pleasant, but no one would ever find him obviously attractive sexually; Meg was beautiful, he desired her more than she would ever desire him, but he was considerate.

He smiled. At least he was a good deal more attractive than he used to be. He had been poor and nervous and frail and lonely. He had written his first book at night, choking over the gas-fire of a bed-sitting-room in the Edgware Road. When he was too exhausted to write he would go to the pictures, all the time knowing that he could not afford the price of a ticket and would have to take bread and jam for lunch at work next day. He was not very tall, and sometimes he was glad of it, for it enabled him to hide down in the seat when the lights went up. When war came he was at once turned down for the army and he was so hideously disappointed that he knew he must appear laughable. He was not sure if he preferred to be laughable or pathetic, but he always felt that he was one or the other. His first novel sold surprisingly well and it was a measure of his imaginative talent that it was at all convincing. It was about young people. He had never felt young or known any young people. It gave him confidence to realise that his readers supposed the book to be autobiographical. His second novel was good and it was truthful, and some people who had come to know him well began to reassess his character. By that time he had enough confidence to rebuke them.

Now he rarely thought about his past, but he sometimes wondered about the faith in ultimate success which had seldom left him, although never in his life had he been given reason to suppose that you usually got what you wanted, even if you wanted it enough and were prepared to make sacrifices. Henry Enfield's accent had long ceased to be merely careful, and he knew how to look arrogant, but at times he lapsed into genteel Cockney to amuse his friends and give himself an opportunity to philosophise. He was an illegitimate child; his mother worked as a tracer in a large engineering firm, and for fifteen years he had shared a tiny room in West Kensington with her. When he was very young he liked to indulge in fantasies. His father would appear one day and beg his forgiveness and take him away to a wonderful life, after disposing of his mother by giving her a large lump sum of money. These fairy-tales came true for other people. Henry had read about them, but he knew that nothing of the kind would ever happen to him.

He believed that he had been born to be a writer, a belief that could be analysed out of existence, and could not be argued convincingly or defended. He supposed that his dreams were no stranger than those of thousands of adolescents, except that he had more reason than most for wishing to escape from his environment. It could be said that he did not lose his dream because there was nothing to replace it. Everything he experienced would be sifted and filtered, and discarded or put away until he could use it. Every letter he ever wrote would be a literary composition. Every attitude he ever struck would be an exercise in gauging effects.

He got up and poured himself some Scotch. He had a lot to be thankful for, and most of all for these small consolations. He rarely drank in the mornings, but it was good to know that he could enjoy almost anything he wanted when he was not writing. He knew that he looked more pleasant each year. He was always clean and expensively, although not elegantly, dressed. He had another twenty years before he began to deteriorate. He found himself becoming more and more susceptible to atmosphere: the faintest recollection of smell, sound, colour and the aura which someone had lent a place in the past combined to give him a deeply moving sensation which lasted for a moment, and was followed by tranquillity. He no longer needed people to cancel years of loneliness, although it was almost impossible to escape from the social life which he had carefully built. He was content to be alone, or with someone who understood him.

Meg was a strange girl and he knew that he deluded himself in thinking that she would ever try very hard to understand him. But he understood her, and was touched to watch her wilfully destroy her youth and life. He would have liked to tell her that she was the fool of thought. She had principles, although she would have laughed if he had ever been able to tell her. She believed in faithfulness and unselfishness, but he would have tried to tell her that as she was faithful to her dead husband she must be unfaithful to himself, who lived. If she was truly unselfish she would forget Tony and stop hurting himself. Perhaps it was just as well that he could not talk to her. He would never be able to convince her that he was right, and she would probably hate him for trying to destroy the memory to which she clung.

He sighed, and wondered if he did not envy her. It occurred to him that she might never have come to him if she had not believed that she had finished with loving. She might have wanted someone young who would share her feelings rather than understand them.

He supposed that she believed herself to be always unhappy, but when she despaired she would not talk to him about it. He first met her at a party where she knew no one but did not seem to care that she was out of place. He had watched her as he talked to his friends, and expected her to slip away at any moment. The literary editor of a weekly came up to him and suggested that he review fiction for a period. It was a wonderful opportunity and he grasped it eagerly, but all the time he was watching Meg. He quickly arranged a luncheon date and went over to her.

They talked animatedly and without hesitation, as people sometimes do who later discover that they have nothing in common. She had been in London for six weeks, and was staying in a boarding-house in Kilburn and using her teacher's piano at odd hours when it was not needed. Henry took her to dinner at his favourite restaurant, and afterwards asked her to come home for a nightcap. She scarcely believed him when he told her that he was a successful writer. She had never heard of him. He told her that he had been to New York and he wondered foolishly why he had not met her there. At midnight she began to glance at her watch.

"I think I've missed my last train on your underground." He nodded. "I have the car outside. But I hope you won't go home just yet." He smiled. "I hope you won't bother to go home at all." But he had seldom been able to make her react dynamically. She always fell in with his wishes, accepted most of the things he said, showed how grateful she was for the help he had given her. She was warm, and yet their relationship was unreal as if it might end tomorrow and there would be no indication that it had ever existed. For that reason, if she left him he might only regret the intimacy there might have been if she had ever come to life. She was so beautiful.

Perhaps she was attracted to Perkin Young because he reminded her of Tony. Henry did not know. He had never been able to get a clear idea of Perkin, and he had no idea how much the affair would mean to him. If they were really in love he might give them his blessing and let Meg go, but he was certain that it would not last three months.

Henry drained his glass and set it on the table. He got up and went to his desk. On the top he had arranged first edition copies and reprints of all his books, with the translated editions. There were about seventy volumes in all. He sat down, stared at the paper for a moment, and began to write. It would not matter if all the love and happiness in the world passed him by. This was his only reality.

There was nothing like that wonderful fortnight when the notices came in.

CHAPTER XX

Aɴɴᴇ's hand trembled a little as she opened the door with the key that Simon had given her. It was the first time she had ever had a key to someone's flat. She felt very mature. He had known that she would be pleased and he felt oddly happy as he made the gesture. He was certain that she would never visit him without an invitation.

The flat was empty. She shook the rain from her coat and switched on the fire. Perhaps Simon was working late. She combed her hair and studied her face in the mirror, turning one profile and then the other, and squinting to see what she looked like. Her mouth was too full, and she looked babyish. She wished she had a mouth like Meg, the girl Perkin had been talking to at Julian's party. She wondered idly if they had been having some kind of affair, but wasn't Meg Henry's fiancée? She did not wonder for very long. Simon was the only one whose relationships she cared about. The flat was just as untidy as it had been before she put it in order during Perkin's illness. She sighed lovingly and began to empty ashtrays and pick newspapers from the floor. She heard the door open, and smiled. She would pretend not to hear him until he put his arms around her and kissed the back of her neck. He could not just say hello when she had her back to him.

"Hello, Anne?" Perkin said, surprised.

She started, and felt like kicking him. He laughed when he saw the ashtray in her hand.

"No, darling, you mustn't," he said gently. "It's sweet of you but by tomorrow the place will be in a mess again."

Anne shrugged and sat down. He stared at her for a moment, then tossed her the evening paper.

"Would you like a drink?"

"Yes please. Gin-and-lime."

He prepared her drink and poured some gin and lemonade into a tumbler for himself.

"Cigarette?"

"Yes please." She blushed. "I said that be – I mean, isn't the weather terrible?"

"Yes, isn't it?" he said seriously, and sat down by the fire.

"I'm so looking forward to Ireland in July," she said excitedly. "I've never been there."

He stared at her, then cursed his brother: so Simon had not told her that she would not be going. He hesitated.

"Simon has been rather worried about that, Anne. If he's very busy at work, he won't be able to go. Apparently there's a big Arts Council exhibition about that time, and his shop is doing some work for it." She stared at him uncomprehendingly. "I was wondering if you'd come with me even if Simon can't make it. You could bring a friend if you wished."

She shook her head. "It's terribly kind of you, but if Simon can't come I'd rather stay with him in London." Her voice trembled slightly. "It doesn't matter very much."

He saw how disappointed she was, and could have killed Simon. She passed a hand over her forehead, and said brightly: "Do you know if we're going out to dinner, or are we having it here?"

He raised his eyebrows. "I was going to grill a steak. You're welcome to join me. I was feeling lonely."

Anne frowned. "But where's Simon?"

"Simon's in Venice," he said automatically, then stared at her in horror, as he realised what must have happened.

"*Venice!*" Anne stood up. "Don't be silly, Perkin. I'm having dinner with him."

He smothered the laughter which suddenly rose in him. He went over to her and took her hand in sympathy. "Good God, Anne, didn't he tell you?"

She gazed at him for a moment, shuddered, and collapsed into the couch. He sat beside her and held her hand tightly. "He must at least have phoned."

She shook her head, and her face crumpled. She buried her head in her knees and cried wildly.

"Well, he'll certainly write to you from Venice." Perkin bit his lip when he realised how ridiculous the words sounded. "Oh Anne, darling, I don't know why he did it. I took it for granted that he'd told you."

She shook her head violently. "Was it to do with his work?" she cried.

Perkin did not reply at once. "No," he said hopelessly.

She screamed with rage. "Oh, Perkin, how could he? He knew how much our holiday meant to me. He said he was looking forward to it as well. When did he go?"

"Friday. It was quite sudden. He came home early on Thursday night – he said he'd been to the pictures with you – "

She nodded.

" – looking very strained and restless."

She sat up, forgetting her tears as she tried to find the reason for Simon's sudden departure.

"That's right. He complained that he was very tired, and told me that I was to come here tonight. He said he'd rest over the weekend."

"Well, I was here alone, and he wouldn't sit down but wandered up and down the room until he nearly drove me mad. Then he suddenly told me that he'd decided to go to Venice next day if he could get a plane ticket. God knows where he is now. He said he'd write when he found a hotel. He didn't know where he was going to stay, he's never been in Venice before."

"But why?" she cried.

Perkin smiled a little foolishly. "I suppose it was just a whim. I don't know what he told his employer. There is this exhibition in July, but Simon could have got away then if he'd really wanted to. I just thought he was using that as an excuse for . . . I'm terribly sorry."

Anne wiped her eyes roughly. Her face was grim. "I'm dreadfully tired of it all, Perkin. I don't understand him. I don't know why he acts this way. I'll never be sure of him again."

"I think Simon loves you," Perkin said quietly.

"Loves me? He doesn't care what happens to me, he doesn't care if he makes me unhappy. If he really loved me he'd be so anxious to keep me that he wouldn't dare do a thing like this. Why, Perkin? You must know."

"It's possible that he quite suddenly wanted to get away, and he didn't stop to think about anyone."

"He'd think about me if he loved me."

For a moment her simplicity irritated him. "Oh, we aren't all as uncomplicated and pleasant as you, Anne. I knew Simon was in love with you, but he wouldn't admit it. Perhaps he loves you too much and he doesn't want to love anyone."

"Why?" she asked in amazement.

He made some vague gesture. "It's hard to say."

Her eyes filled with tears again. "I don't understand you. How can I be expected to bear all this when I don't know what it's all about?"

He swallowed a mouthful of his drink, and he was annoyed when it tasted as frivolous as candy floss.

"Can you understand him not wanting to love anyone? He loves Tom, our father, and he loves me, but that's different. We don't tie him down, in many ways we're all alike. But you demand faithfulness and tenderness and sometimes you aren't prepared to accept him as he is but want him to be more unselfish. He can be unselfish, but perhaps not just at the times you want him to be. Do you love him, even now?"

"Yes," she said miserably. "At the moment I hate him."

"You must understand, Anne. For one thing he's a painter. I don't know if he's good, he doesn't know himself, but domestic worries and entanglements, the least little thing, might make him uncontrollably angry and drive away all the creative energy he's got, however much it may be."

"I'll leave him alone when he asks me. I swear I will."

"That isn't it." He wandered over to the window, then back again to the fireplace, which was boarded up. "I don't know how to explain this to you. I can't explain it to myself. It never occurred to Simon or to me that we would ever care for someone as much as we cared for ourselves. I do now, and so does he. But he'll go on resenting you a little, probably through some mistaken idea that his selfishness is a sign of an artistic temperament, or maybe because he simply likes to be unhappy."

She frowned, but signalled for him to go on.

"Anne darling, you're the best thing that's ever happened to him, and I mean that quite sincerely. You're the only girl – woman" – (she flushed a little) – "in the world who can make him grow up. If you love him you'll understand, and what you can't understand you'll take on trust."

"I have to take him," she cried desperately. "I've nothing else."

He smiled rather cynically. "I'll make a bargain," he told himself. "If Simon will be happy, I don't matter. It doesn't matter what happens to me." He turned to Anne. "Then what have we been talking about?" he asked harshly.

She looked away. "He made me so miserable."

"You must accept that."

She got up to leave, shy again. "I'm sorry I ruined your evening."

"You didn't. You've made me happy. Come and wash the lettuce while I grill the steak. Come on."

At ten o'clock they were sitting by the fire, listening contentedly to records and talking about Simon. The phone rang. It sounded like a warm reminder of friendship. Perkin lifted the receiver and smiled gaily. Perhaps it was Simon ringing from Venice.

"Hello?"

Tom had died in Ireland an hour ago, quite suddenly.

CHAPTER XXI

JONATHAN followed the red umbrella, which looked beautiful in the rain. The body gliding gracefully beneath it was wearing a very clean and new raincoat, drainpipes with a black-and-white check, and pale green suède shoes. The effect was devastating, and Jonathan followed the young man along the King's Road, hoping to catch a glimpse of his face. They were going in the same direction. Twice the young man turned at the corners where Jonathan was going to turn. He felt certain that he was going to the club, and was glad that they might have a chance to talk. The soles of his very new suède shoes sucked at the pavement. He crossed the road, was approaching the door of George's house, had stopped.

Jonathan sighed with relief. He had a glimpse of very yellow hair as the young man carefully let down his umbrella. He lifted his face to the sky, carelessly daring it to make him unhappy with its silly rain. He was the young man whom George had talked to in Trafalgar Square. Jonathan uttered a little moan of dismay.

He waited for a few moments until he was certain that Charles was in the club, then went into the house and straight up to his flat. He changed quickly, brushed his hair and washed his hands. He was late for work.

The young man was not in the bar. There were no customers, and Derek was proudly reading *By Love Possessed*. He grinned when Jonathan came in.

"This is smashing," he said, rolling his eyes and reverting to his Kilburn accent for a moment. "The bit in the back of the car makes me sorry I missed all that."

Jonathan ignored the remark. "Where's George?" he asked sharply.

"In his room," Derek said, puzzled by the look of desperation on his face. "Wait a minute," he called, as Jonathan rushed from the bar, "you know he doesn't like to be disturbed."

Jonathan held on to the banister to prevent himself from rushing up the stairs and bursting into George's room. He was certain that Charles would be there. There was a sickening dull pain in his stomach and his eyes were swimming in tears ready to fall as soon as he discovered that his suspicions were justified. He crept gently up the stairs, one at a time, pressing himself against the wall. He listened outside the door, but could hear no sound. He gently turned the handle. The room was dim, lit only by the reading lamp. Still he could hear nothing. He opened the door wider, and stood watching for at least a minute.

They did not hear him.

He closed the door as carefully as he had opened it, as if he were leaving a sickroom. Then he leaned against it and cried soundlessly. It was the first time he had ever been betrayed in a love affair. The tears rolled into his mouth and he tasted them greedily. He told himself over and over again that he had never loved anyone the way he loved George and that he would never love anyone else, as if it were a magic spell that would bring George back to him. He realised that he had been expecting an incident of this kind.

He suddenly realised that he was beating his fist against the door, and, terrified that George would hear it, ran quickly down the stairs. He wiped his eyes as he went into the bar.

Derek was immediately sympathetic. "Oh, was he angry, Jonathan?"

He shook his head, and sat down beside him on a stool.

"No. He has someone with him."

Derek stared at him. "You've been crying."

"Yes. He has a boy he picked up in Trafalgar Square one day."

Situations like this made Derek feel most maternal. He put his arm around Jonathan's waist, and his large eyes grew even wetter than usual.

"I'm so terribly sorry, Jonnie," he said with the utmost sincerity. He also felt rather triumphant, for he had told himself that if George remained faithful for more than three months, he must be impotent or utterly tired of the world.

"It's all over, Derek. It's finished; it couldn't succeed because I'm one of those people who just go on and on taking it on the chin without ever having any luck. I wasn't born to be happy. I loved him without any reservations and I didn't feel guilty or sinful and the only thing I was afraid of was that he didn't love me. I only wanted someone to love me. Is that too much to expect, just to have *someone* to love you?" He wished that his body and his brain would suddenly disintegrate, that he could simply cease to exist.

Derek shuddered, and gazed straight in front of him.

"Didn't I warn you that it would end this way? I knew that George would never care enough to be unselfish."

"He's so nice," Jonathan said. "He was so nice to me when we first met. He didn't try to seduce me or take advantage of me in any way. He waited until I was ready."

"He's nice to everyone. Why not, when he doesn't care enough to be unpleasant? And he's conceited and vain. I suppose you were a challenge to him."

Jonathan shook his head. "It's my fault. I wasn't good enough for him. He's had such a hard life. He was so poor, he had to sell his body because it was all he had."

Derek stared at him. "You fool! Do you think that prostituting yourself makes you unable to love? You don't know a thing about it. It makes you tired and weary and more able to love someone if he comes soon enough. George is thirty. He's been rich for five or six years. Does he look as if he ever suffered from malnutrition? He uses that as an excuse, because he's incapable of loving."

"You don't know it all," Jonathan cried. "When he was a little boy his father tried to – his father attacked him. That was enough to ruin his life."

Derek gaped at him, then began to laugh hysterically.

"You fool," he shrieked, "you bloody little fool." His face, which he always held at just the angle at which it looked smooth, began to wriggle into lines. He doubled up with laughter. "You believed it, you believed it."

Jonathan backed away in terror. "Why are you laughing? It isn't funny, oh God, it isn't funny!"

Derek suddenly stopped laughing, and watched him for a moment. His face became anxious and he looked away, sickened with pity. "George tells that story about his father to everyone he thinks foolish enough to believe it. It's a standing joke among his friends. They understand him, though. Do you?"

"I don't believe you."

"Oh, be sensible. George's parents were richer than yours and millionaires compared to mine. They're still alive, although he never sees them. They were ordinary upper middle-class people, and George could have been a barrister or a company director or whatever else the children of such families can be. I wouldn't know, you see. But that wasn't what George wanted. When he was twenty-one or so he borrowed money from his father to open this club."

Jonathan's eyes were closed; his body was resting limply on the stool, supported by the bar.

Derek shrugged. "Did he tell you that he wanted to die the very first time he met you? That was true, all right. I'll bet he does. He loves-loathes himself so much that he's more mixed up than anyone I've ever met."

Jonathan opened his eyes, and blinked again and again. Derek was obviously telling the truth.

"How do you know this?" he asked inevitably.

"It's common knowledge, but I think one of his rich friends told me one night when George had refused him. Do you think they'd be on such good terms with a little guttersnipe who'd managed to make good, even though he did own a queer club? If I owned a club like this, with boys laid-on, I still wouldn't get the same kind of customers."

Jonathan got up, and put a hand on the counter to steady himself. Derek's face softened.

"I still love him, although he's meaningless and worthless." He added proudly, "I don't think you could forgive as much as I've forgiven him."

"Yes, I could," Jonathan said calmly. "But, Derek, it's all over. I'm so tired."

"I'll look after the bar tonight."

He took it as a matter of course. "I'm going to my room. When George comes down, when that boy has gone home, will you tell him that I'm ill and I want to see him?"

Derek nodded. "The boy's name is Charles. I knew all about it."

He was not surprised. "How long?" His cheeks were flushed and the inside of his head seemed to be sinking lower and lower to blackness. The red light of the club was getting darker and darker. He remembered nightmares he had when he was a child. His mother would leave the light on when he went to bed, because he was terrified of the darkness. But the light was even more terrifying, and he would grow hotter and hotter until he screamed for his mother. When she switched off the light and leaned down to him the room grew cool again and he fell asleep.

"A month or so."

He nodded, and made a vague friendly little gesture and went upstairs.

He was awakened by the sound of the front door slamming. It meant that the club was closed for the night. It must be after eleven. His body was drenched in sweat.

He threw back the sheets and turned over the pillow, rubbing his face against it. Then he lay back, his face towards the window. He had turned off the lights before he sank down, exhausted on the bed, and now the vague light from the little window played a fantastic chiaroscuro with the darkness of the room. He heard voices on the stairs. Light footsteps came to his door, stopped. He waited breathlessly, ready to shout "Come in" as soon as he heard a knock. There was a moment of complete silence, then the footsteps passed on. His body curled frantically into a ball, and he pressed his face against the damp, hot sheets. It must have been Derek, it must have been Derek.

The door opened quietly, and when he looked up he knew that George had been watching him. He was incredibly good looking, with the light from the stairway behind him.

"Come in," Jonathan said, and lay back.

George closed the door, and still in darkness came to the bed. He sat beside Jonathan, and leaned down and kissed his forehead. Jonathan immediately began to cry.

"You've been drinking a lot," Jonathan murmured, and wondered if George could see his tears. He felt a strong and smooth hand settling on his own hand, which was dry and hot. He looked up at George's face, which was calm, although his eyes looked faintly troubled.

"I can see your face quite well," Jonathan said softly. "Can you see mine?"

George nodded, smiling, but did not speak. Jonathan would speak soon enough.

"Derek told you that I saw – Charles?"

He nodded again, and his hold on Jonathan's hand tightened. "But you've already forgiven me. Charles is a very charming boy. That's all. He's impenetrable. I'll never understand him."

Jonathan tossed his head nervously. "But you wanted him more than me. I suppose you wanted him more than you ever wanted me."

George sighed. "Look, honey, don't be hurt. This happens to everyone. You don't know enough about our world to understand, but it means nothing. Two people living together get bored. Actually these little affairs are a good thing. They mean nothing."

Jonathan stared at him. "You don't love me."

"I never pretended to love you," George said wearily. "I like you very much and I hope that you'll stay here and work for me and be friends with me. You'll meet someone. He'll come in one night and you'll realise that you never loved me."

"I'd be just like Derek. Seeing you would drive me crazy, if I knew that I was just like Derek to you. What happened to us?"

George sighed. "That was friendship. Had anyone ever been kind to you before? Perhaps we should have remained just friends. But it wasn't my fault."

Jonathan was silent for a moment. If George went now, he was lost for ever. He searched for the right words. "George, I don't expect you to love me. There's no reason why you should. But if I love you, won't my devotion mean anything to you?"

George fidgeted and yawned. He hoped that Jonathan had not seen it. He was making an effort to keep his eyes open. "One of the terrible things you'll have to learn," he said quietly, "is that you can't make yourself love someone just because he loves you. I'm so indifferent, honey, and there's nothing I can do about it."

Jonathan relaxed, and slowly pulled the sheets over him.

"Could you spend just one more night with me?"

"No. I've heard that one before. You'd feel no better, and afterwards you'd ask for another night, then another. It's hopeless."

"Then go away. Leave me."

George got up. "Don't be sad, Jonnie."

"I'll be all right," Jonathan said cheerfully, but his voice cracked. He swallowed. "I promise never to trouble you again. I understand and I'm sorry I troubled you." *Now you must see that I love you.*

George could think of nothing to say. He felt embarrassed. "I'm glad, then," but the words sounded so unconvincing. He walked to the door and all his movements were awkward.

Jonathan could not cry. He desperately wanted to cry and willed himself to cry, but the tears would not come. For the first time he had come up against something irrevocable. He lit a cigarette which sickened him, but he must do something to fill the emptiness. The tip of the cigarette caught on the sheet and shreds of burning tobacco fell on to his shoulder. The pain had died by the time he summoned enough energy to react. He was alone. There was no conceivable way of filling the endless days, and no means of forgetting. If only he could cry.

But this could not be happening to him. There must be at least a thousand people in London whom he could learn to love as much as George. But what could he possibly do tomorrow? He would try to sleep until ten, then go out for breakfast after spending at least an hour bathing. Breakfast would take half an hour. If he bought papers and magazines and drank a great deal of coffee he might make it stretch to an hour. Perhaps some West End cinema would be open at noon. He could walk to Leicester Square. No. He would not have the energy to walk. He would take a bus, and on the journey he would smoke and finish the magazines if he had not already finished them, or watch the people in the streets. Then the film, then lunch, then another film, then work in the evening and he might see George. But he must never see George again or return to this house. What would he do? Why bother with vain attempts to fill the emptiness, when futility would make him sadder and more lonely.

When at last he began to cry he regretted it. He would gladly have stopped loving George if he could escape the weary pain and misery and heartbreak, but it was inescapable. He had once believed that he was inadequate, unable to despair or go beyond tiredness. Now tears blinded him and ran from his nose and an inferno was inside his skin.

He shuddered convulsively, staring at the window. Beyond, in the London night, dancing-clubs and restaurants would still be open, and people would be having a gay and wonderful time.

The bar opened at lunchtime on Saturdays. He felt vaguely surprised when he felt the warm air in the street. He had expected rain. He walked quickly to the King's Road, then down towards Sloane Square, looking for a chemist's shop. At the first one he came to he bought a bottle of aspirins, and examined the change. One shilling. He had two at home. He went further down the road, to the next chemist's, and bought another bottle of aspirins. As he turned to go out he noticed a stand of shampoos on the counter and remembered that he had not washed his hair for a week. He reached out, then checked himself. He smiled. What was he thinking about? He left the shop.

The air was uncomfortable, and he would have liked to lie down on the pavement and go to sleep.

He entered the house as quietly as he had left it, and balked for a moment at the thought of climbing the stairs. He took hold of the banister and pulled himself upwards, one stair at a time. Once he stumbled and almost tripped on the hem of his loose coat. He locked the door on the inside, took off his coat, and let it drop on the floor. Then he heard the rattle of the bottles in one of the pockets, and bent down to take them out. He swayed, and remained still until the dizziness left him. Holding the aspirin bottles, he went into the kitchen. Afraid of fainting, he got down on his knees to put the shillings in the meter, and turned on the gas in the oven, to make sure it worked. He had never used it. When he heard the hiss of escaping gas he turned off the tap.

The oven was low and small, but he had to use it because there were no gas fires in the flat. He took out two racks. They were greasy and left black lines on his hands. For a moment he was not sure what to do. If he lay on the floor the oven would be too high for him to put his head in; but even if he got down on his knees it would be too low and when he collapsed he would probably fall out on to the floor.

He went into the bedroom, and pulled a large trunk from under the bed. He dragged it into the kitchen and placed it so that one end was level with the oven door. He lay on it, stomach downwards, and now the bottom of the oven was on a level with his head. His feet dangled in air. Experimentally, to make certain that nothing would go wrong, he eased his head into the oven. He shouted with disgust and quickly pulled it out again. His face and hair were covered with black grease.

He stood up and went to the mirror, almost crying with rage. When he saw his face he sobbed, half-laughing. He looked pathetically comic. He scrubbed his face with a bar of washing soap, then held his head under the water tap. He wandered into the bedroom again, looking for a towel. He stood in the middle of the room, suddenly too tired to make any decision.

Oh God, why bother?

He fell on to the bed, and went to sleep.

CHAPTER XXII

T HE house was almost empty; the housekeeper was leaving at the end of the week, and then it would be closed. It was for Simon to decide what would finally happen to it. He had sent postcards from Venice to the London flat, but with no forwarding address. He did not know that his father was dead. Two days after the funeral a card arrived for Tom: "Venice is enchanting, but I'll be home for a few days in July – Love. S." The father had died as he lived: to a distant and faintly ironic accompaniment from his children.

The days in Ireland that June were clouded and stormy with heat. The sea was tepid, and although the summer had hardly begun the trees near the beach were dry and brown with salt. The house had turned yellow, for Tom had never bothered to have it painted after his sons left. Perkin never gave a better performance than when greeting his father's friends and a few relations. He was calm and pale and brave, and he made not a single error in judging what to say and how much to say and when to say – that he was very sad and quite unable to comprehend his loss. Most people thought him surprisingly elegant and intelligent for someone so young, but at any sign of ease or insincerity in the mourners he hardly tried to conceal his contemptuous dislike. He wanted to be alone, and then be sorry. He had quite returned to his former detachment, and when he was left alone watched himself grieve in this perfect setting for an elegy. It was an opportunity he must not miss, to regret his youth and the death of the only person who could have interpreted it for him, if he had ever wished, or thought it proper to give any advice at all.

But the thoughts and memories which Perkin had rehearsed with such facility died in his mind when he was faced with reality. He wandered in the garden, but kept to the rough and tiny lawn: it was inconceivable that he should scratch his hands and pull his careful clothes to search for overgrown passages in the bracken. When he was a child it had reached above his head; now it seemed flattened and came only to his waist. And then he turned and stared at the house above, and loyally recited, "What does this house think of me now that I have grown up? Does it approve of me, or does it sadly shake its head?" – and the words fell from his lips, meaningless and futile.

He put on drainpipes and a sweater and went down to the beach, and it was no smaller and just as beautiful as he remembered it. He walked along the sands, and had to smile with pleasure as he remembered things he had forgotten to remember. Somewhere here Tom had buried his dog. Then digging with his toe he found rock an inch beneath the sand, so the grave must be further on. He discovered that he had forgotten measurements, and perspectives had been distorted by time. Climbing some rocks at the end of the beach, he saw a longer stretch of sand beyond. Perhaps he had never before visited this part of the coast. Then he saw at the top of a promontory a lighthouse which he had seen before and missed as he re-explored the place where he lived when he was young.

The massed grey clouds, the paleness of the sea, and the dark browns of the sand and rotten seaweed made the view look like a snow scene. From a distance steam rising looked like mist. He knew he was home again when he smelt the charred bitter smell of salt and decaying weeds and fresh new grass. He and the housekeeper were leaving on Friday, and he was certain that he would never return to the old house, unless some crisis drove him back. He had enough energy in him to resent the air of time having come to a stop. The place was already dead, and made him feel that he had died in infancy. The realisation that he would like to go on living here rather frightened him, and he thought how terrible it would be if he could not force himself to go away.

He wandered on the beach, dressed like an actor playing a beachcomber, and wandered in the house. The old nursery, which had been in an attic room, was larger than any garret you would find in London. Tom's library was magnificent, beginning with Chaucer and ending with Thomas Hardy and in between hundreds of books that Perkin had never read. He realised that he had probably read as many twentieth-century novels as there were books in this room, which covered six centuries of literature. Again Perkin was tempted to stay and read for at least another month, but the atmosphere was stifling and almost sinister. He might return here when he was old.

And then there was Meg.

On the last day, sitting in the library, he had a strange sense of rebirth, as if with Tom's death part of his own life had come to an end and he had to find a new beginning. It was no fallacy. Simon and Perkin were on their own now, and had to account only to themselves. Perkin was too wary to suppose that it would make any apparent difference, but there would be a subtle change in attitude. They must find new roots, or move uneasily.

Nothing had changed. In London it would be almost possible to believe that Tom was still alive, or rather they would probably make themselves believe it. They must find something that would fill the suddenly empty space.

The plane to London left in the evening. Perkin packed his case, emptied it, then repacked it, and still had an hour before the car arrived to take him to the airport. He went down to the library again, and searched the shelves for a book to take with him. He picked Darwin, of all things:

> "When on board H.M.S. *Beagle*, as naturalist, I was much struck with certain facts in the distribution of the organic beings inhabiting South America, and in the geological relations of the present to the past inhabitants of that continent. These facts, as will be seen in the latter chapters of this volume, seemed to throw some light on the origin of species – that mystery of mysteries, as it has been called by one of our greatest philosophers."

He looked at the bookplate: *Thomas E. Young*.

Oh damn, oh damn, oh damn.

He went into the garden, and down the slippery steps to the beach.

CHAPTER XXIII

"I don't blame myself," Simon said quietly. "Perhaps I should, but what would be the use?"

"Of course not," Perkin said. "Your being away at the time was just a very unfortunate coincidence."

He did not like to remember the terrible day when Simon came home from Venice: since he heard the news of his father's death he had been prowling nervously round the flat, looking desperately for something to do. The fact that it had all happened when he was away, and had ended before he returned, made it seem unreal to him, and he questioned Perkin about obscure little points, half hoping that they had not been attended to.

Simon jumped up from his chair and went to the window. "God, this flat, this place, gets on my nerves. Rain, rain, rain, and claustrophobia. Shall we get a bigger flat now?"

Perkin shrugged. "Shall we go on living together? I suppose you know we're rich?"

His brother nodded.

"So we could afford to have separate flats. What do you think?"

"I don't know."

"Will you go on painting, Simon?"

He frowned. "What else is there to do? Look, I had nothing else to do in Venice but eat and stare and think. Can I paint, or did I never get beyond art school? Technique, yes, and I could teach art history, but have I got anything more to give the world than the others who were attracted by the colour and the glamour and ended up working in shops and agencies?"

"I wouldn't know. You just have to go on working and one day, if you're lucky, you'll find out. Of course there's no reason why you should work, there doesn't have to be a reason. I'm very romantic and I think you should." He hesitated. "I was attracted by the glamour of writing, and I thought I had a talent, but it isn't the same as *wanting* to write. I don't suppose I ever will, now. One great artist in a family is enough."

Simon gazed at him for a moment. "So you give up, just like that."

Perkin smiled and stretched lazily. "I thought I'd be honest with myself. What have writers got that I can't afford?"

"You know very well what they've got. It seems a pity. What on earth will you do?"

"I don't know."

Simon said, "I thought we'd go to Ireland next month, just as we'd planned."

"You go. Take Anne. At the moment I feel that I never want to see that house again. Sell it, Simon."

Simon came and sat beside him. "All these sudden decisions. Why?"

His brother looked at him calmly. "I want my life to be neatly organised now. And then, when there's nothing to distract me, I'll wake up each morning with an empty day before me, and I'll have to find something to do. And that way I'll find out what I want to do, even if it's – nothing."

"Are you going to look for a flat right away?"

"I think so. I'm tired of Chelsea. I thought Richmond, or I've always wanted to live by the canal at Warwick Avenue."

"What about Meg?"

"I'm going to see her in the morning."

Simon gave a perplexed sigh. "I suppose there's nothing more to say. Everything is changing so fast."

"I thought it was about time something changed. We were becoming grotesques, behaving for the last five years as if we'd left Cambridge six months ago. I must be something – a drunkard, a lecher, a simple young man, but I must be *something*. I was thinking, and it's a terrible thing to say, that if Tom's death made you feel lonelier and feel the need to work harder to forget the loneliness, then it was – a salutary thing."

Simon pointed to his brother's heart. "In there, you have something harder than I've ever come across before. Underneath your smooth skin you have a steel plate and a core of something harder than steel, and a nice streak of vulgarity that could amaze anybody." He could not help laughing. "It's just as well you never really had many ambitions, for God help anyone who stood in your way."

"I'm the kindest little person you're ever likely to meet."

Simon went to the cabinet and filled two glasses. He handed one to his brother.

"Here's a toast, to the future."

"Oh no," Perkin said quickly. "Toast it and it's sure to be a disappointment. The past, that's over."

He put down his glass and frowned. "The thing is, I hate these climaxes, because tomorrow we're likely to find that not a thing has changed. And after all, how can I change? I've done almost everything there is to do, I mean, everything I'm likely to want to do."

It was the end of June, yet the rain beat down unceasingly. The waterfront was looking most fabulous. They arrived at the Festival Hall early, and walked beside the river until they found a sheltered seat.

"I realised that you loved me, and I thought I loved you, and suddenly it all seemed like a trap, and more than anything else I wanted to get away. I'll admit, at that moment I simply didn't care about your feelings, but it was you I was running away from, and as soon as I got to Venice I realised how much you'd be hurt. But I was quite incapable of doing anything about it. I didn't want to commit myself to anything." He added soberly, "In about a fortnight's time I'll take you to my house in Ireland. If you still want to come."

"Oh yes," Anne said.

"What did you do while I was away?"

"I read, learned a lot of new words. Simon, wherever you go, you'll be taking Simon, it will always be Simon and Simon. I'll be there, because you'll need me when you get bored with each other."

"No," he said, through clenched teeth. "I'll make you understand, someday."

He put his arm around her shoulders, and looked at her, wondering if she wanted to be kissed. Her eyes clouded, and he leaned down and put his mouth on her mouth.

"We'll go into the hall now," he said gently.

It was a very popular programme: Beethoven's fifth piano concerto, and Schubert's ninth symphony. Anne watched, enchanted, her eyes darting backwards and forwards through the orchestra, her body softening with pleasure as the full theme of the concerto burst forth. Simon almost went to sleep, hearing nearly every note before it was played. But it was impossible not to be moved, although one wanted to do more than feel the music. He suddenly wished that he were painting. If he could keep this elation, disciplined by his knowledge of technique, he would be happy to paint for the rest of his life, and need nothing else. That was the unattainable ideal.

Anne flopped back in her chair as the music ended, too exhausted even to clap.

"Come and get a drink," he said.

She nodded, her eyes shining. The evening was perfect. The ice in the gin was the most delicious, the coldest, her lips had ever touched.

"You liked it, darling?" he asked, laughing at her enthusiasm.

"Oh yes!"

"We'll go to hundreds of concerts."

"I'll learn all about music, and how to criticise it."

He took her hand, and kissed the fingertips, then hastily put it back on the table.

"Well now," he said unsteadily, "I'm getting very sentimental." He glanced at her, and quickly looked away. Her eyes had filled with tears. "How can you forgive me so easily?"

"It wasn't so easy. But what else could I do?"

He shook his head.

"Then, Anne, will you marry me?"

She stared at him.

"Yes, but, Simon . . ."

"It's sudden, I know, for you anyhow. I've been thinking; and no matter how rebellious I am, I'm not sure that I can do without you. You'd better not answer right away."

She was speechless. He buried his face in his hands. "It would be the strangest match ever."

"In a church?"

"A registry office – no, a church. I don't know."

"A church." She blushed. "I'll marry you, but I can't believe that this is real."

"You're crazy to take me." He burst out laughing. "I feel very foolish. I'd intended to be very tender, and tell you all the reasons why you shouldn't marry me, but I'm so grateful to you."

Anne sobbed, and quickly brushed her eyes.

"I love you, Simon, and this time I trust you, but – I know I shouldn't say this – I'll really believe it when I see the licence."

He roared. "I wouldn't have you any other way." He was almost afraid to look at her, but took her hand.

"Perkin planned this," she said.

"Yes. My darned brother is too clever. Come on, let's go somewhere to celebrate."

Her face fell.

"Oh, can't we stay for the rest of the programme?"

"Why, of course."

"And then celebrate?"

He nodded.

"Everyone else has gone back to the hall. We'd better hurry."

They got up and ran to the stairs. He put his arm around her waist and almost carried her to the top. It was the first concert she had ever been to.

CHAPTER XXIV

PERKIN waited on the dark stairs for a moment, listening. It was only the second time he had heard Meg play. He did not recognise the music. It was clear and bright and sad, and like a popular song it would lose something each time you heard it, so that in the end you would be bored. The music stopped abruptly, and Meg's voice called, "Come in, Perkin."

He opened the door, surprised.

She had drawn her feet on to the stool, and she was sitting with her chin resting on her knees; her hair had fallen over her eyes.

"I saw you coming in the street. I was standing at the window."

He closed the door and went to her. He brushed away her hair with his mouth and kissed her brow. He did not touch her with his hands. They slowly drew away, from each other and themselves.

"You look wonderful," Meg said, with great sincerity.

He was wearing a loose, heavily striped shirt, and a pair of cheap linen trousers. He put the light raincoat he had bought that morning on a chair.

"I was so very sorry to hear about your father," Meg said vaguely.

Perkin shrugged. "I have some news. Simon and Anne are going to be married."

She smiled.

"We must make it a double wedding," Perkin said.

She frowned.

"How is Henry? And Julian?"

"Well."

He went over to the window, and stared down at the street, as he had stared too many times before.

"You know, I suddenly feel quite lost in London. I can't remember what I used to do before I went to Ireland."

"You were away for only a week or so."

"I know," he said, making a joke of it. "Oh, Meg."

She was silent.

"Come to the window, will you? I want to look at you."

She came quietly, and stood beside him. He turned round. "My calm, clear darling. It can't be possible to fall out of love as easily."

At once her face cleared. She gave a sigh of relief that no-one but Perkin would have perceived.

"Have we nothing to say to each other now?" he asked.

She was embarrassed.

"I mean, there must be a reason for it. I hardly thought of you in Ireland. I quite suddenly stopped wanting you."

"Of course there is," she said, most awkwardly. "As much reason as there was for loving me."

"Don't you think we should discuss it a little, or justify it? I shall never understand what happened between us."

"It doesn't matter," she said helplessly.

"What will you do? Whatever will become of you?"

"What became of all the women like me, and all the men like you? They aren't missed, perhaps they aren't missing."

He sat down on the bed, and tried to feel lighthearted.

"It's so *unsatisfactory*."

"Oh well," Meg said, "if we'd had a fight and sworn that we'd never speak to each other again, it would mean that we were probably still in love."

"I do still love you, in a way, but not that way. There are times when I wish I was eighty years old. I'm tired of being young." He stared straight ahead. "I have this feeling of release, though, as if I had nothing more to worry about. There's nothing more to trouble me."

"I'll make some coffee," Meg said. "I know exactly what you mean. You feel dead; and when there's nothing to care about, you can be almost happy. I've been like that for so long. I'd have been so frightened if you'd gone on loving me. I'm tired of pain. I couldn't endure any more of it."

"Yes."

CHAPTER XXV

"I'LL BUY you a plane when you learn to fly," George said extravagantly.

Charles did not reply. He frowned, concentrated, and shook the dice. Nine.

"Ha!"

He carefully fingered the money lying beside him on the bed, wondering if he should invest some of it.

George shook his head. "I bet you know just how much of that stuff you have, down to the last pound, you little mercenary."

"I buy Bond Street," Charles said, and handed over the toy money with great carelessness.

They were playing Monopoly.

"I am banker next time."

"All right, honey." George yawned. "Don't you ever get tired of this game? If you're good, one day I'll take you with me when I see my lawyers about real real-estate."

"Now?"

"No." He smiled despite himself. Charles lived only in the present, and soon forgot any promises made to him.

"You want a drink?"

Charles nodded.

"Here then."

Charles frowned. "It is very small."

"But if I made it larger you wouldn't drink it. You know you hardly ever finish a drink."

"It does not matter." He pushed his car over the board for a moment, then shut it with a snap. The car fell on the floor, and Charles's eyes filled with tears.

"You are very unkind, George." He gave the name the French pronunciation.

George took the glass, emptied the contents into a tumbler, added a large lump of ice, a very little more gin, a lot of tonic, and a blue straw.

Charles's tears disappeared, and he sucked happily and noisily.

"I wish I knew what made you tick," George said, "you selfish incomprehensible little bugger. Charles, what is the French word for bugger?"

"I do not know. You teach me all the dirty French words I know."

"You are stupid."

"I am not, I am not," Charles shouted. "You are not kind. I will go away. I will leave London. I will fly away. I will never see you again."

George shrugged. "I don't care. Go."

Charles quickly finished the drink, licked the straw and got up. "I go now." He walked to the door. George did not look round, confidently expecting to feel a hand on his shoulder and hear a voice say, "You are not kind." He heard the door close, and was seized with panic. Without stopping to think he rushed to the door, calling "Charles." The boy was already half-way down the stairs.

"Charles," he shouted desperately. "Come back, honey. I was playing a joke."

Charles turned, closed his eyes for a moment, and said, "I do not like your jokes." He looked like a cat.

George giggled hysterically. "Well, honey, at least you never say anything surprising. Come back."

They returned to the room, and sat down on the bed. He put his hand on Charles's neck, and stroked it.

"Never do that again."

Charles smiled. "You did not want me to go."

"You'd really have gone, too." His eyes hardened. "You don't care, little boy, do you?"

He went on smiling blissfully.

George put a hand on his knee.

He smiled reproachfully, and yielded with a sigh.

CHAPTER XXVI

"WELL, then-there-now," said Julian, who had recently seen a television programme on the Method. "It's the seventh of July, summer has come at last and you're a very lovely girl, so stop frowning and I'll buy you a delicious lunch."

Meg nodded, and combed her hair before the mirror.

"You are a lovely girl," Julian said softly.

"Oh well, go on telling me and I'll love you as a brother for the rest of my days. Julian, you don't have to try to make me happy. I'm quite happy."

"And no regrets about Perkin? He ditched you just like that, did he?"

"No!" Meg insisted. "You don't understand." She washed her hands. "Come here."

She put her fingertips to his cheeks, and stared into his eyes. "Not bad. You'll do. But how much . . ."

"Shush. No recriminations."

"All right, but . . ."

He put a finger to her lips and shook his head. Meg sighed. "Let's go then."

They walked down the stairs and opened the heavy door. Julian put on his sunglasses.

"You know, I'm sure everyone thinks this house is a brothel," Meg said.

He smiled. "Isn't it a beautiful day," he said inadequately, as they walked down the street. "Let's take a taxi to the Green Park, or do something equally silly."

They hailed a taxi at the end of the street.

"An exceedingly delicious lunch," Julian said with satisfaction.

"I wish I had a large straw hat," she said. "Too much sun always makes me feel ill."

"I'll buy you a large straw hat with a vulgar motto and a streamer."

Meg giggled.

As they approached the park they passed a fruit barrow. "Stop here," Julian commanded. When he had paid the driver he led Meg back to the barrow. Green apples, red strawberries, purple cherries, brown nuts and some very tough-looking pineapples.

"A pound of cherries," Julian said.

As they walked in the park, eating cherries and dropping the stones on the path, Meg said, "I bet we look the sort of people who wouldn't be seen dead eating cherries in the park."

"My dear Meg," he said, "you always look so wonderful that anyone would be surprised to see you doing anything at all."

They walked on.

"I feel eighteen again," Julian said cheerfully. "I mean, I feel the way most people must feel when they're eighteen."

CHAPTER XXVII

Perkin sat by the window, brushing his hair dry in the sunshine. Flecks of dandruff turned to gold dust as they fell to the floor. He leaned back when his arm grew tired, and watched the square, the green trees and the people. There was the smell of rain drying in the new warmth. How long would it last?

In August I go away to a warmer country, to toast in the sun and lose the chill of London.

The telephone rang and he did not move, although he had to resist the quick automatic action of reaching out for it. It rang sixteen times, then stopped, and he relaxed again.

I will return in September, brown and well-fed, warm and alone, and I will build a white tower, where I can live alone and be happy. One day I may meet somebody, and if I never do I shall have myself.

He laughed when he realised that he could count his friends on the fingers of one hand. In fact, he had none at all. They had all gone somewhere, they had died. But there were all these years that must be lived through.

I will not die.

He began to brush his hair again. His face was clean and he was almost smiling. Occasionally his eyes twitched nervously and he frowned. It was a new shyness, a retreat until he realised that there was no reason to be afraid.

In August I go away to a warmer country.

THE END

ALSO AVAILABLE FROM VALANCOURT BOOKS

MICHAEL ARLEN	Hell! said the Duchess
R. C. ASHBY (RUBY FERGUSON)	He Arrived at Dusk
FRANK BAKER	The Birds
WALTER BAXTER	Look Down in Mercy
CHARLES BEAUMONT	The Hunger and Other Stories
DAVID BENEDICTUS	The Fourth of June
PAUL BINDING	Harmonica's Bridegroom
CHARLES BIRKIN	The Smell of Evil
JOHN BLACKBURN	A Scent of New-Mown Hay
	Broken Boy
	Blue Octavo
	The Flame and the Wind
	Nothing but the Night
	Bury Him Darkly
	Our Lady of Pain
	The Household Traitors
	The Face of the Lion
	The Cyclops Goblet
	A Beastly Business
	The Bad Penny
THOMAS BLACKBURN	A Clip of Steel
	The Feast of the Wolf
JOHN BRAINE	Room at the Top
	The Vodi
JACK CADY	The Well
MICHAEL CAMPBELL	Lord Dismiss Us
R. CHETWYND-HAYES	The Monster Club
BASIL COPPER	The Great White Space
	Necropolis
HUNTER DAVIES	Body Charge
JENNIFER DAWSON	The Ha-Ha
FRANK DE FELITTA	The Entity
BARRY ENGLAND	Figures in a Landscape
RONALD FRASER	Flower Phantoms
GILLIAN FREEMAN	The Liberty Man
	The Leather Boys
	The Leader
STEPHEN GILBERT	The Landslide